CITY OF STEEL...
HEARTS OF GOLD
My Lackawanna

By Ralph J. Galanti, Jr.
With Joanna B. Nervo

NFB
<<<>>>
Buffalo, NY

NFB
119 Dorchester Road
Buffalo, NY 14213

For more information visit
Nofrillsbuffalo.com

This book is dedicated to the

Galanti Athletic Association
Charter Members

Baker, Phillip
Biellak, Alexander
Bracci, Alphonse
Bracci, Amerigo
Bracci, Harry
Camilloni, Leo
Carestio, Ralph
Carestio, Rosario
Cipriano, Daniel
Cipriano, Humbert
Clarone, Angelo
Collareno, Earl
Conti, James
Conti, Lawrence
Core, John
Covino, Carl
Cswaykus, Frank
Cswaykus, John
DiCenzo, Edwin
DiCenzo, Frank
D'Allesandro, Arnold
D'Amico, John
D'Amore, Ralph

Fistola, Louis
Galanti, Eugenio
Galanti, Ralph
Giancaterino, Adolph
Giancaterino, Victor
Ginnetti, Alfred
Ginnetti, Armondo
Giovenettio, Leo
Grasso, John
Hacic, George
Jennetti, Dominic
Jennetti, Vince
Juran, Evie
Juran, Joseph
Kollander, John
Kujawa, Leo
Manzetti, Ed
Marinelli, Frank
Marinelli, Ralph
Marrano, Carmen
McCann, Thomas
Moretti, Anthony
Moretti, Carmen
Morgan, Ed

Muruska, Andrew
Palumbo, Michael
Pepper, Thomas
Petti, Paul
Petti, William
Pietrocarlo, Armondo
Pietrocarlo, Fermino
Popich, Stephen
Preciak, Stephen
Ranalli, Anthony
Ranalli, Jim
Ranalli, Pat
Renzi, Frank
Renzi, William
Rogers, Joseph
Rushnov, Adam
Rushnov, Stanley
Snyder, Louis
Sobaszek, Stanley
Staniszewski, Eugene
Staniszewski, Walter
Tobias, Michael
Topinko, Joseph

Honorary Members

Diane, John
Giovenettio, John
McCann, Joseph (Judge)

Ruether, Joseph
Russell, John

Valenti, Virgillio
Venturi, Louis

Author's Notes

I was always intrigued with people who grew up during the Depression years. My father and mother, along with their families and friends, were part of it; the era that Tom Brokaw called, "The Greatest Generation." I spent most of my childhood with these people listening to their stories, their dreams and everyday life encounters, some funny and some very sad.

I always had a passion for writing even though my profession was in athletics. I was a college athletic director and men's hockey coach at Erie Community College in Buffalo, New York. But I did not want to write about sports. I wanted to write about this wonderful generation of men and women who grew up under very adverse conditions.

I decided that when I retired, I would write a book about this era. I coerced my dear friend and colleague Joanna Nervo to help me accomplish my dream. She is the only person I know who could type faster than I could talk and could also add a different perspective to the story. My wife, Diane, was very supportive in this venture and helped with much of the research. This book is about nine years of research, writing, editing and in some cases, arguing. During these nine years, I took a hiatus of two-and-a-half years to become the Chairman of the Empire State Games that were held in Buffalo, New York in 2010.

After the Empire State Games, I lost the drive to write the book. I was exhausted. Then one day Joanna hinted, "Are we ever going to finish your dream?" I looked at her and told her I would read what we have written and go from there. Once I read it, the fire was once again ignited! I wanted to finish it.

Although this story is primarily fictional, there are some historical facts based on research that are woven into the story. Many of the characters are true to life although some are fictional characters that are a figment of my imagination.

I apologize if any of the language I have used in this book is offensive to some readers but I felt it was necessary to make the story realistic. I hope the readers will truly sense how unique and wonderful these people were during that difficult era.

Last but not least, I hope that everyone will recognize what a holy and great man Father Nelson Baker was and that he was truly a saint among men.

Now that I have finished the book I think to myself would I do this again…. You betcha!

I hope you enjoy your journey through this book as much as I enjoyed writing it.

Be Happy,

Ralph J. "Chico" Galanti, Jr.

Chapter 1

The three of them sat in the bushes waiting for Virgilio to appear. "When do you think he's going to be coming?" said Ziggy. "I don't know for sure but it should be soon," Ralph responded. "I hope he hurries because I got a goddamn thorn from these bushes sticking in my ass," said Ziggy. Coco, whose real name was Isaac, asked him if he wanted him to pull out the thorn. Ziggy said, "If you touch any part of my ass, I'll break your goddamn hand!" Coco, in his fake trembling voice, said, "I'sss so scared. You got my little brown ass turning white." Ziggy turned to Coco and gave him the finger. The three of them were getting a little anxious on this hot August evening in 1932.

"Shhh," said Ralph. "I think I hear him coming." Strolling down Elm Street in the Bethlehem Park section of Lackawanna, New York, was Virgilio, looking dapper in his new suit and fedora. He had bought the suit two weeks ago in the basement bargain shop at Kleinhan's Department Store. He paid $23, which included extra pants, a shirt and tie. It was a real bargain, especially during the middle of the Great Depression. He was also carrying two bottles of scotch which he paid top price for from a local bootlegger. He was going to make sure that they would be put to good use tonight.

Coco whispered, "Raffs, do you think he suspects what's going to happen?" He had always called Ralph "Raffs," ever since they were toddlers growing up in the First Ward in Lackawanna. He could never pronounce Ralph. The closest sound that came out of his mouth was "Raffs."

Isaac's mom, Crystal Freeman, was one of the prettiest black women in Lackawanna. She was tall and very light skinned with high cheekbones that made her look like a model. Her son, Isaac, definitely took after her with his looks and light skin. She nicknamed him Coco because of his light features, but also because, as she told everyone, "he is the sweetness of my life." She always tried to correct her son's pronunciation of Ralph, but it was to no avail. Even today, at the age of 17, he still called him Raffs. It was just more fun to say.

Did Virgilio know what he was in for? Ralph said, "I don't think so. He wouldn't have gotten so dressed up and be so freaking happy whistling that dumb Italian love song if he didn't think he was going to get laid tonight."

Ralph, Ziggy and Coco were not the only ones waiting to see what happened to Virgilio that night. There were approximately 100 people hiding behind trees, in the bushes and in the alleys of Bethlehem Park. All were waiting to see Virgilio's reaction. This was one grand setup!

Chapter 2

Two days earlier, Ralph, Coco and Ziggy were sitting in front of Ralph's father's delicatessen. His father was Eugenio Galanti but sometimes he was called "Jimmy." He was one of the many young Italian immigrants who came to the United States from Italy in the early 1900s. He settled in Lackawanna, hoping to find a new and better way of life. The city was brand new and boasted one of the largest steel plants in the United States...the Lackawanna Steel Company. There were many jobs available for anyone who was willing to work, and he was more than willing.

Eugenio worked in the steel plant and saved enough money to buy a small delicatessen in the heart of the Italian immigrant community. It was called Galanti's Confectionary and was the focal point where many of the youth in the First Ward would congregate. Although many of the young people were of Italian descent, it was also a melting pot of all the different races and ethnic backgrounds that were part of the First Ward.

The three youngsters saw that Virgilio was walking up the street toward them. Ziggy said to Ralph, "Are you all set to begin?"

"Yeah," Ralph said, "but make sure we look serious and for Christ sakes, don't anybody start laughing."

When Virgilio was within 20 yards of the boys, he saw them talking very animatedly but could not make out what they were saying.

The first words he heard distinctly were, "she has such big boobs, I wouldn't know what to do with them."

Then Ziggy said, "But Ralph, it's an opportunity of a lifetime. You might get lucky and it might be the ride of your life!"

Coco chimed in, "Raffs, the only reason you would say no is because you're too chicken or not adequate."

Ralph answered, "Screw you, Coco."

Two words got Virgilio's immediate attention: "she" and "boobs."

"Boysa," Virgilio said in his broken English, "whatsa up?"

Now the boys knew they had him baited.

"Oh, nothing, Virgilio," said Ralph. "It's something that you would not be interested in."

"Wella try me boys," said Virgilio.

"Well," Ziggy said, "Ralph has a chance on Saturday night of getting a little from Mrs. Gawronski. But he's chickening out."

"Wadda you mean?" said Virgilio, whose interest had piqued even more when he heard the words "getting a little."

Virgilio had been in the United States for only a year, coming from his small hometown of Maddaloni, near Naples, Italy. He said he came to Lackawanna to find work. Rumor had it that the reason he had to leave his hometown quickly was because the mayor of Maddaloni was going to cut off his testicles for "bopping" his wife. Virgilio was a good looking man with a pencil thin mustache and wavy black hair. He was a handsome, short and stocky 42-year-old "Don Juan."

Ziggy stated that Mrs. Gawronski was a lonely woman since her husband was always on the road, driving truck for the steel plant. Married for just a year, she was a nice Italian girl who fell in love with a big, strapping Polish stud from the Second Ward. The only consolation for her family was that they decided after they were married they would live in Bethlehem Park, which was only two blocks away from her family.

Ziggy told Virgilio, "You know these interracial marriages to Polacks don't work out. The poor girl needs a little company so she invited Ralph over Saturday night to spend a few hours talking. But I think she wants to do more than talk."

Ralph looked at Ziggy and said, "You're a dumb ass. It is not an interracial marriage and I do think she just wants to talk. But if my mother found out I was going over to a married woman's house and she told Pa, he would kill me."

Virgilio sympathetically said, "Raphael, you-a right. Your mama and papa woulda be embarrassed. Leta me handle it. I'll take you place tomorrow and givea the young girl gooda conversation."

The boys knew they hooked him. Poor Virgilio did not know that the setup had begun. The young wife, Connie Gawronski, her husband, Walter, and probably half of Bethlehem Park would be in on the caper. It was planned weeks ago when things were becoming boring in the neighborhood and they needed some excitement. What better way than to set up some poor, gullible, DP (a derogatory name for immigrants) who was always looking for some excitement involving the opposite sex. Virgilio just happened to fit the bill.

Coco said, "Raffs, I think Virgilio is right. Your Pop would be embarrassed and would kill you if he found out."

"Youa see, Raphael, even you chocolata friend knows I'ma right," Virgilio said.

This burned Coco and he thought...*I might be chocolate, but I'm sure a lot smarter than you, you dumb son of a bitch.*

Ralph, said to himself...*gotcha!* "All right, Virgilio, you can take my place Saturday night. You have to be there no later than 9:30 at night, when it's dark out. Walk to the front door, knock three times, wait and then knock two more times. Her husband will be on the road until next week so I think she's going to be very, very lonely."

Virgilo said, "Alla right, boys, I'll be there on time. I'll do you a favor so you won'ta get in trouble. That poor young wife needsa some grownupa talk."

He left the boys in front of the store, walking away like a "banty rooster," thinking that Saturday would be the night where his charm, good looks and intelligence would win over the distraught and lonely maiden. He had to go home now, he thought, and prepare for his evening of bliss.

The boys, meanwhile, had their own preparation to do. The setup has worked. Now they had to get everyone ready for Saturday's evening of fun and excitement.

Chapter 3

It was one hour before Virgilio had to leave his little apartment to go to Bethlehem Park and he was thinking how lucky he was that he decided to go to Galanti's Confectionary the day before to pick up some stogies. Instead of just having a good smoke, he was now preparing for the pleasures of the night. He thought… *How dumb could those young boys be and how lucky I am. It is too bad that the chocolate one is smarter than those two dumb Dago boys. Imagine, giving up a night of pleasure because you're scared of your mama and papa.* He said out loud to no one in particular, "Virgilio, you a handsome man. After I geta finished witha her, she gonna say come back some more, you love making machine!"

After putting the final touches on his mustache and adding a few more dabs of "a little dab'll do ya" Brylcreme to his wavy black hair, he looked in the mirror, gave himself a confident wink and he was ready to go. He gathered up the two bottles of scotch he had bought from the bootlegger down the street, put on his fedora and out the door he went to Bethlehem Park.

Virgilio lived about a half mile from the park, in a single apartment on Ingham Avenue, a popular street where many Italians lived. The walk was enjoyable as the evening was warm and the stars were bright in the sky. As he made his way down Ingham Avenue toward Bethlehem Park, the streets were lit with gaslights and many of the people were sitting on their porches enjoying the evening. All Virgilio could think about was Connie. He never saw her but if she had big boobs like the boys said, that's all that mattered. It had been several months since he got laid, and it cost him two bucks for a woman who had a smaller chest than he had. Now, he's going to get it for free and with big boobs to boot. He was walking on air!

Virgilio was a block away from Bethlehem Park. He was passing through the Old Village, which was between Dona Street and Smoke's Creek. The Old Village was built by the steel company in 1903 for its employees, who were charged a nominal fee for rent as long as they worked for the company. It was a wonderful little community in and of itself with rows of houses, some of them single-family dwellings and others with apartments. There were a few trees that lined the dirt roads but every street had its wooden sidewalks. Many of the residents, who were mostly of Italian descent, tried to grow rose bushes or shrubbery in front of their homes and had small vegetable gardens in their backyards to give them a sense of the "old country."

In late 1920s and early '30s, the buildings were becoming dilapidated and many were unsafe to live in. Bethlehem Steel, which bought out the Lackawanna Steel Plant, started to build new housing for its workers that was called Bethlehem Park. These were single homes that had modern conveniences, such as running water and bathrooms. They offered to sell them to the steel workers at a reasonable price as long as they worked at Bethlehem Steel. Many of the Old Village residents took advantage of this offer and moved across Smoke's Creek into this beautiful community.

Virgilio entered Elm Street and started walking to the end of the street, where Connie's house was located. The Gawronskis were one of the families who could afford to purchase a home. It was an unusually quiet night, thought Virgilio, but it was a perfect evening for love-making. He stopped whistling an Italian song when he was twenty yards away from the house and had unknowingly just walked past Ralph, Coco and Ziggy, who were hiding behind the big rose bush three houses away. When Virgilio was ten feet from the door, he hesitated. The boys thought that he changed his mind or that some of the people who were hiding behind the trees and in the alleys made noise that alerted him. This was not the case. Virgilio stopped and looked around. Seeing no one, he reached down his pants and scratched his balls. Already, he was getting a hard-on. He proceeded to the door and gave the three knocks, waited, and then gave two more.

All of a sudden, the window opened above the door on the second floor and Connie screamed out the window, "Run, run, my husband's home!" With that, her irate husband, Walter Gawronski, yelled out, "You son of a bitch. I'm going to kill you!"

He shot a shotgun high into the air. The blast sounded like a bomb to Virgilio, who quickly dropped the two bottles of scotch, peed in his pants and turned around and ran like hell.

Of course, everyone was in on this setup, including Walter, but he got carried away and yelled one more time, "I'm going to kill you," and shot the gun again. This time, Virgilio turned around to look and he ran right into the gas lamppost. The sound of Virgilio's head hitting the lamppost could be heard all throughout Bethlehem Park as people were laughing and running to where he was lying. The instigators, Ralph, Ziggy and Coco, were the first to approach poor Virgilio, who was flat on his back, not moving at all.

"Geez, geez," said Ralph, "I think he might be dead." Ziggy said frantically, "What are we gonna do?" Coco chimed in, "I saw this in football practice, I think we grab his belt and lift him in the air so he can get his breath." Ralph said, "Jesus, Coco, he didn't get hit in the nuts, he got hit in the head. I think we better call an ambulance."

By then, there was a large group of people around poor Virgilio. Many were laughing until they saw him lying limp on the ground. Someone said, "Is he dead?" But no one wanted to touch him until they heard a faint groan from him and they knew that at least he was alive.

Ralph went close to him and said, "Virgilio, are you OK?"

"I thinka so," Virgilio said. "Whata happened?"

Ralph said, "Don't you remember what happened?"

"No," and with that Virgilio's eyes rolled back and he passed out.

Fifteen minutes later, an ambulance pulled up and started to give Virgilio first aid and placed him on a stretcher. He was put into the ambulance and taken to Our Lady of Victory Hospital. Two police cars also arrived because they received a call from a neighbor who heard gunshots fired on Elm Street. After the police questioned Ralph, Ziggy and Coco, they were brought back to Galanti's Confectionary to talk to Pop Galanti.

The next day, after finding out that Virgilio would be okay, everyone was talking about how exciting and funny the events of that evening were... everyone but poor Ralph. That night the police explained to Pop Galanti what had happened. They told him there was a prank devised by his son and his friends and although there were no serious injuries, it could have been a tragic situation. After the police left, Pop Galanti sent Ziggy and Coco home with a tongue lashing, but had something different in mind for his son.

The next day, inside the store where the chimneystack went up to the roof from the furnace below, was poor Ralph. He was tied to the chimneystack with rope and on top of his head was a sign stating "Stupido," for everyone to see. He was going to stay there for the better part of Sunday morning. There was Ralph, daring not to smile but thinking… *Boy, that was one great night of funzies!*

Chapter 4

Pop Galanti was sitting near the kitchen door in his usual chair. He sat there because he could view the whole store in comfort. He was looking at his older son, Ralph, who he had tied around the chimney in the middle of the store, and was thinking … *what am I going to do with this boy? I tied him to the chimney to try to embarrass him for the crazy thing he did last night. All he wants to do is to have fun and joke around. He's a good boy, but I got to teach him a lesson if he's going to be somebody in this world. These are tough times and what he calls "funzies" can get him into trouble, if not jail. I'll keep him tied up for another hour but I'll warn him if he does something like this again, I'll tie him up for a week!*

Eugenio's mind started to wander as he reflected back on his own youth. He was born in Baselice, Benevento, Italy, in 1889 to poor but loving parents. A boy grew up quickly during this time, becoming a man around the young age of twelve. The boys worked wherever they could find jobs to help feed their families. School was not an option; it was a privilege only for those who could afford it. Eugenio was fortunate because his mother was a believer in education and taught him at home in the evening, after he returned from a full day of work on the farms. At fifteen, he was taller and stronger than most of the boys his age. His size and his enormous, powerful hands got him many jobs that other boys his age were unable to get.

Giovanni, his older cousin, left for America in 1908. He would write to Eugenio and tell him what a great country America was, with lots of work available. He told him that if he could save enough money for the trip to America, he would let him live with him until he could support himself. Eugenio always dreamed of going to America and he would talk to his mother during the evening while she was teaching him. He told her how much he would love to go visit Giovanni and maybe earn enough money to send back home to help the family. She would pat him on the head and say in Italian, "My son, I will talk to Papa and maybe he will let you go in a year or two. In the meantime, work hard, learn and keep your dream."

After a couple more years, Eugenio convinced his father that he should go to America. His father finally but sadly agreed, thinking this would be best for his son because he saw no future for him in their little town. He told Eugenio, "Figlio, it is now time you leave the nest and try to make a better life for yourself in America. Always remember your mama and I love you very much and hopefully you will make us very proud." So in 1910, at the age of twenty-one, with very little clothing or money, he embarked on his long journey to his new life in America. He would never see his parents again.

After a long and arduous journey across the ocean, he arrived at Ellis Island ten pounds lighter. He had never been on a boat in a large body of water, let alone the Atlantic Ocean, and had no idea what to expect. He spent most of the time either in his bunk or on the rail and rarely made it to meals. When he did, it only took a half hour before the food would quickly exit his body. It was one trip that he would not soon forget.

After going through immigration at Ellis Island, waiting hours and hours in the long lines, he finally showed the inspector the letter he received from his cousin giving him directions to his upstate home in Olean, New York. Although Eugenio spoke and understood limited English it was enough for him to pass through the immigration process. He followed the Inspector's instructions to the train station and along with a group of other immigrants, he boarded the train and traveled to what would be his new home. Olean was a small community in Cattaraugus County in Western New York that was 63 miles southeast of Buffalo and only a few miles from the Pennsylvania state line. After a couple of train transfers, the trip took over a day, but to Eugenio it was heaven sent compared to his trip across the ocean.

When he arrived in Olean, Giovanni was there to welcome him with open arms, saying, "Eugenio, come stai?" an Italian greeting asking how you are doing. Eugenio hugged his cousin and gave him kisses on both cheeks, responding in Italian, "Wonderful, just wonderful."

Giovanni gathered the few pieces of luggage that Eugenio had brought with him and they traveled up Green Street, where he lived in a boarding house. He turned to Eugenio and said, "I hope you liked the train you rode on because tomorrow you'll be working for the Pittsburg Shawmut & Northern Railroad Company. I spoke to the foreman and he said he could always use another good worker at the station. But let me warn you, Eugenio, it is hard work and long hours, but decent pay." Eugenio responded, "Thank you so much for helping me get a job and I promise you no matter how hard the work is, I will never disappoint or embarrass you." So, they both went to the boarding house and celebrated with a glass of wine, cheese and bread.

Eugenio started the next day after he filled out a few papers. His first job was to help unload the box cars that were filled with coal. He worked there a solid twelve hours, only taking a half hour lunch break to eat his cheese, prosciutto and bread that his cousin had prepared for him the night before. He soon got the reputation of being a hard-working young man and was asked to work six days a week, between ten and twelve hour shifts. He didn't mind because he wanted to make as much money as possible so he could send some home to his family and also give some to his cousin for his generosity. He was also very frugal and wanted to save for the future.

Eugenio was very lucky because there was a wonderful college located in Olean called St. Bonaventure. The Franciscans offered night classes, free of charge to all the immigrants who wished to learn the English language and American customs. The classes were held two times a week in the evening and he was one of the first to sign up. Immediately after work, Eugenio would go home, clean up, get a quick bite to eat and rush off to St. Bonaventure. Within six months, he was conversing in his new language.

After Eugenio had been working for one year, Giovanni said to his cousin, "Let's go celebrate our one-year anniversary. Eugenio, you have worked hard all these months and you need some fun. Especially since it's Saturday night and we both don't have to work tomorrow." So, the two walked down Green Street to a local tavern. Eugenio looked at his cousin and said in Italian, "You know, I love this town and I hope to make this my permanent home." Eugenio didn't know that the events of that evening would change his destiny forever.

Eugenio's daydream about the past came to an abrupt end when he was startled by a ringing bell. Someone came into the store and the little bell above the door came alive with jingles. He got up to see Coco and his mother entering the store. He said, "Hello Crystal, how are you?"...while ignoring her son. Coco went to Ralph, who was still tied to the chimney and said, "Hi, Raffs." He then went to see Pop

Galanti and said, "Mr. Galanti, I came to apologize to you and Mrs. Galanti. What happened last night was entirely my idea and not Raff's. I take the full responsibility and I hope you let him go."

Ralph yelled out, "No way, Pa. I did it! I talked Coco and Ziggy into it." "Wella boys, no matter who-a did it, you both and Ziggy are all to blame. But I appreciate youa trying to help you friend. Youa good boy, Coco."

Without the boys noticing, he gave Crystal a quick wink, went to where Ralph was tied and released him. He told them both to get the hell out of the store and gave his son a quick but soft swift kick in the ass.

He then turned to Crystal, who was smiling at him, and said, "They really are gooda boys, although Raphael is going to be the death of me." Crystal chuckled and said, "The both of them will be the death of us! Jimmy, I was coming here to talk to Philomena. Is she home?" "Yes, I willa get her from upstairs. Please watch the store."

Eugenio went upstairs to get Philomena, who was cleaning. He told her that Crystal was waiting for her downstairs. Every Sunday morning after church, Crystal would come to the store and she and Philomena would sit and talk for hours about everything. Ever since Crystal's husband was killed in a steel plant accident ten years ago, this had become a ritual between the two women. Eugenio loved it, because they would sit in the store for hours talking, behind the candy counter where there were two rockers and a chair. They were on an elevated platform from where they could see everything in the store. That meant Eugenio was free for at least a couple of hours.

He went back into the kitchen and instead of sitting in his usual lookout spot, he sat in his favorite cushioned chair. He leaned back and continued to reminisce about how his life had changed that fateful autumn evening in Olean.

Chapter 5

Giovanni and Eugenio walked into the Reinhaus Tavern, a popular gin mill that was frequented by many of the railroad workers. Most of the workers were of German or Dutch descent and came to Olean from Pennsylvania when the Pittsburg, Shawmut and Northern Railroad had a depot in the town.

The tavern was usually crowded on Saturday night and this night was no exception. Some of the patrons had been in the tavern since they quit working at four o'clock in the afternoon and it was now nine in the evening. Giovanni and Eugenio found some space at the bar and sat down to have a beer. At a table near the bar, there were four boisterous and drunk rail workers who were arm wrestling. Every time the barmaid would pass by the table, the biggest one would give her a slap on the rear end with a hearty laugh. He ordered another round of drinks because he had just beaten one of his buddies in arm wrestling. The loser would have to pay for the drinks.

Eugenio was watching and said quietly in Italian to his cousin, "Who are the loudmouths?" Giovanni told him that they worked for the railroad. The biggest guy was called "Hans" and he was known to be a bully. His uncle was the general foreman for the railroad so he had some influence. Eugenio shrugged his shoulders and they continued to drink their beer, talking about the old country.

The bully started looking around the room to find someone that he could sucker into arm wrestling for drinks. He had not lost all night and he didn't intend to pay for any drinks. He yelled to the next table, where a small Irishman sat with his friends. He challenged him to arm wrestle for drinks. The little Irishman sheepishly shook his head no, knowing that he definitely would lose, that it would cost him money and probably a broken arm. The big man, Hans, kept on pressuring him until he glanced up at the bar and saw Giovanni looking at him.

"What are you looking at, you fuckin Dago?" Giovanni turned and ignored the big German and started sipping his beer. This irritated the German even more. He said again, "Hey, you asshole Dago. Do you have enough guts to arm wrestle for drinks or are you and your buddy faggots?" Eugenio understood most of the words that the German said except he didn't understand what "faggot" meant. Apparently, it was not part of the vocabulary that the Franciscans taught him. He quietly said in Italian to his cousin, "What is faggot?" His cousin replied under his breath, "Frocio." (in Italian, it meant homosexual).

When Eugenio heard this, his anger started to build. Giovanni, who knew his cousin was usually mild mannered, never saw him look this way at anyone. The glare he gave the big bully would have stopped a bull in his tracks. Eugenio got up and walked quietly toward the big man and said, "I lika to try you game." Hans, who was three inches taller and forty pounds heavier, thought this was going to be easy pickings and said, "Sit down Dago and get ready to pay."

They sat across from each other at the table and a crowd started to gather around. The small Irishman went over to Giovanni and said, "Friend, you should get him out of here before that son of a bitch hurts him." To say the least, Giovanni was a little worried about his cousin.

Hans' companions told the two of them to place their elbows on the table and to grasp hands in an arm wrestling position. They told them that when they said "go" both were to start arm wrestling and may the better man win. They all smiled and winked at Hans. The two men gripped each other's hands and the bully was astounded that even though he was taller and heavier, his hand was engulfed by the smaller man. Eugenio stared into the other man's eyes and when they said "go," he squeezed Hans's hand so hard that you could hear bones break. Eugenio forced his arm down to the table so quickly that he broke the bully's forearm. The big man cried out and his companions were stunned as they watched him rolling on the floor, writhing in pain. Eugenio got up, smiled at the big man and said, "Frocio, you pay!"

He then walked to his cousin and said, "It's time to go home." As they left the tavern, the big bully was screaming expletives at them while the small Irishman and a group of others patted them on the back. Eugenio winked at Giovanni and said, "Not too bad for a couple, of how you say it, faggots?"

The next day was a beautiful Sunday. Giovanni was getting cleaned up to go on a picnic with a young Italian lady he had been dating for two months. He asked Eugenio if he wanted to go but he politely declined, knowing that three would be an inconvenience when two are in love. Eugenio decided to stay home and write a letter to his parents. As usual, he also included some money from his earnings in the envelope. The rest of the day he spent just lying around knowing that a week full of hard work awaited him.

Monday morning, they both got up at six o'clock to prepare to go to work. As they left and started to walk down Green Street to the train depot, Eugenio felt uneasy but didn't know why. As the two men reached the gate, one of the team leaders on the work gang asked

Giovanni to go to the general foreman's office. Eugenio started to go with him but was told only Giovanni was summoned. He watched his cousin go through the gate and into the office.

After fifteen minutes, Giovanni left the office and started walking toward Eugenio. He looked pale and irritated. Eugenio asked if there was anything wrong. Giovanni shook his head and did not say anything but made a motion to follow him. They went outside the gate, around one of the sheds and Giovanni started to curse and talk very quickly in Italian. Eugenio told him to hold on and not talk so fast and asked him what was the problem. Giovanni calmed himself, took a deep breath and said, "Eugenio, I am so sorry. The foreman told me that you cannot work here anymore. He said that he did not want someone working here who took advantage of a man who had too much to drink, punching and kicking him while he was on the ground and breaking his arm." "Whata do ya mean?" Eugenio replied with a puzzled look on his face.

"It seems that the big bully is also a big baby. He told his uncle who is the general foreman that you took advantage of him while he was drunk. He said that you punched him, knocked him on the ground, called him a 'Kraut' and stomped on his arm, breaking it. I told him that is not how it happened, but he did not want to hear it. He said if I was part of what happened or even if I condoned it, I could also be looking for a new job. I'm so sorry, Eugenio." And with this, he started to cry.

"Don't a worry. It is because of you that I am able to be here and I always will remember what a good cousin and friend you are." And with that, Eugenio turned around and went back to the boarding house.

That evening after Giovanni came home, Eugenio started to tell him what he was planning to do. He told Giovanni that several days ago he overheard some railroad workers talking about a new city near Buffalo. It was a city with a large steel plant and they were looking for workers.

The next afternoon Eugenio went into town to see if anybody knew more about this city. Mr. Johnson from the market told him that the new city is called Lackawanna and it was named after the steel plant. He said that they were definitely looking for workers and the pay is good.

"So, Giovanni, I have decided to go there and hopefully, get a job."

"Eugenio, I can't believe how lucky we are. You won't believe this but we have a paesano who lives in Lackawanna. Do you remember the Paolozza family from our village?"

"Yes, they had the good looking girls, Philomena, Maria and Luisa. They moved to South America for a few years and were coming back to Baselice when I was leaving for America."

"That's them," said Giovanni. "Their aunt, Maria Grazia Giovenitti, lives in Lackawanna and I found out that she brought over her two nieces, Philomena and Maria. I will write them a letter about you and tell them that we will come to visit them next month. Also, I will ask them to see about work in the steel plant."

"But, Giovanni, I can't stay here without a job and the little money I have saved, I will need for the trip to Lackawanna. I'll leave in a couple of days. Just give me their address and I'll find them."

"No way, I brought you here and I'm the only one who can kick you out! You stay here with me and keep me company for a month. You can pay me back by doing the cooking, cleaning, running errands, shopping and being my personal Italian slave," said Giovanni with a laugh.

Eugenio smiled, said thank you and gave him a giant bear hug that almost broke Giovanni's ribs. In one month, he would leave Olean, returning only one more time in his life, to attend Giovanni's funeral.

Chapter 6

As the boys left the store, Ralph was rubbing his back end where his father had just branded him with his foot. He was happy that it was his foot and not his hand, for he would have felt it for a couple of weeks.

He turned to Coco and said, "Don't ever do that again. Don't ever take the blame for something that I did. Do you hear me?"

"Yessum, Mister Raffs. I's won't do that anymore. You is on your own." Coco said giving his best imitation of Jack Benny's sidekick, Eddie "Rochester" Anderson.

"Very funny. I thought I was the comedian."

The two went to lie on the grass under the large oak tree on the grounds of Lincoln Annex School, which was located next to the store. Although it was only 10:30 in the morning, it was already 78 degrees out and would probably be in the 90s by mid-afternoon. They began to talk about the upcoming school year, graduation and what they would be doing next year. Walking toward them were the Carestio brothers, Ralph and Rosario, Armondo Pietrocarlo, Gene Staniszewski, Stanley Sobaszek and Gunther Dochester. Soon there would be many other young men congregating in front of the store, for this was their favorite hangout.

Most of them had nicknames, which were given to them by Ralph for no rhyme or reason. The nicknames stayed with them for the rest of their lives. Armondo was Ziggy; Gunther was Doc; Stan was Sobey; Ralph was Waddie and his brother Rosario, Brad. The only one who escaped unscathed was Gene. Ralph figured the poor guy had enough problems with people remembering and pronouncing his last name.

"Man, I knew you would be tied to the chimney again, but this time, I thought you'd be tied to it on the roof," said Ziggy. "I never saw your father so mad."

"Last night was great," chimed in Waddie. "I nearly pissed in my pants laughing when I saw Virgilio hit that lamp post. You could have heard the bong two blocks away."

Sobey added, "I thought the poor bastard was dead. I thought today we would be visiting the three of you at the jailhouse. By the way, did anybody find out how Virgilio's doing?"

Coco said that his mom and Mrs. Galanti went to the hospital the night before to check on him. He has a big bump on his noggin but he's all right, except maybe for his ego. The group was wondering what he would do when he found out the whole truth. Coco stated that he would probably be in the hospital for few more days. Brad added, "You three assholes probably have a couple of more days before he gets out of the hospital and comes looking for you. I heard he has a blade that he carries and he will cut off your balls for souvenirs."

They were all lying on the grass, leisurely talking when Waddie asked what they thought about the Lindbergh kidnapping.

That March, the famous hero Charles Lindbergh, who was the first person to fly solo across the Atlantic, had a tragedy befall him and his family. His twenty-month-old son, Charles Lindbergh Jr., was kidnapped from his home and two months later was found dead only four-and-a-half miles from his residence. The nation was in mourning and people were out for vengeance.

Ziggy said, "If they find the bastard, they should castrate him first." Doc added, "And they should cut off his fucking balls, too!"

Everyone looked at each other for a couple of seconds and then started to roar with laughter. Doc said, "What's the matter?" "You're a dumb bastard," said Ziggy. "Castrate means cutting off the nuts. I think maybe that happened to you, you eunuch."

Doc replied, "I might be a eunuch but I'm not a dumb guinea like you. By the way, what the hell is a eunuch?"

This time, the guys were rolling in the grass laughing like hell. Only Doc, they said, only Doc.

They were debating what to do for the rest of the day. Some suggested playing a little softball when the rest of the guys came; some said maybe play cards in the store. Coco said, "Why don't we go to the Park Theatre? I heard the two movies playing are *Tarzan-The Ape Man* and *Horse Feathers with the Marx Brothers*." Doc wanted to go to the movies because he wanted to see the Marx Brothers, especially Groucho who was his idol. Doc loved Groucho because he was the smartest of the brothers and was always surrounded by dummies. He thought the both of them had a lot in common.

"Where the hell are we going to get the five cents each to go to the movies?" said Gene. "I don't have a penny to my name."

"Who said anything about paying," Doc snickered. "I have a secret way to get into the theater without paying." Everyone wanted to know... how?

"What we'll do is combine our money to get me and Ralph in. When the show starts, one of us will go to the emergency exit door located in back of the screen, the other will go to the usher and say he is violently sick and he has to go to the bathroom quickly or else he's going to throw up in the aisle. While the usher takes him to the crapper, the other will quickly go open the door and let everyone in. It works every time."

"What happens if it doesn't work?" said Brad. "Then the rest of you guys are screwed and me and Ralph will tell you about the movies so you don't have to see it yourself." Ralph thought it was a great idea. Unfortunately, the rest of them thought it sucked.

They all emptied their pockets and between the seven of them, they were able to muster seventeen cents. This would allow two of them to go into the theater and once they got everyone else in, they would have some money for popcorn, candy and soda pop to share. After much debate, they decided Doc and Ralph would be the ones to buy the tickets and let the rest in. Doc was picked because it was his idea; Ralph was the other one because they reasoned that if he got caught that he could "bullshit" his way out.

The group walked to Bethlehem Park, where the Park Movie Theater was located. At that point, Ralph and Doc went to the ticket booth and the rest went to the back of the building where the emergency door was located. Ralph and Doc bought their tickets and went into the theater, which was nearly filled with kids. The lights were still on because the movie had not started. Doc motioned to Ralph for them to sit in the front seats so they would be close to the screen and the back door. The show would start in five minutes and Doc looked around to make sure he knew where the usher was standing. He recognized the usher. He whispered to Ralph, "Sal Lenti is the usher today. That's the son of a bitch that caught me the last time I did this and he threw me out of the show. Not only is he an ugly bastard, but he's strong and mean. What the hell are we going to do?"

"Oh, that's great," Ralph said. "Here we are in the show on the guys' money and they're waiting out in back and now you're chickening out."

"I am not," Doc said. "It's just that I know that it's not going to work. This guy might look stupid but he's not. Besides, I don't want to get my ass kicked again."

Ralph started looking around and he saw three young girls sitting four rows behind them. He knew who they were, the three Marrano sisters, Josephine, Carmela and their kid sister, Gracie. He turned and whispered to Doc that he had an idea. Doc told him to go for it because it was their last resort.

Ralph got up, went to where the Marrano sisters were sitting, smiled and said, "How ya doing Josephine, Carmela and little Gracie?" Josephine smiled back and said, "We're doing okay, Ralph. How about you?" Then Gracie blurted out, "Listen, jerk, I'm not little Gracie, I'm Grace or Gracie, but not little Gracie." Carmela gave Gracie a little nudge with the elbow and told her to be quiet. Ralph thought that of all the Marrano sisters, which were a total of five, Gracie was the prettiest but also the most feisty. But Ralph also was thinking... *the poor bastard that ends up marrying her will have his hands full.*

Ralph explained what they were going to do to help their friends get in the theater because they had no money. He wanted to know if one of them would act sick and go to the usher for help. In the meantime, they would quickly go behind the screen and let their friends in. While they were talking, the theater became dark and the movie Tarzan began. Josephine and Carmela told Ralph they were too scared of getting caught and being thrown out of the show. Ralph pleaded to no avail. Suddenly, Gracie got up and said, "I'll do it. As soon as I get him in the lobby, you hurry and let them in." Before her sisters could stop her, she was heading up the aisle toward the usher.

They saw Gracie's silhouette talking to the usher for a few moments. All of a sudden the usher quickly followed Gracie into the lobby. Ralph and Doc got up and ran to the back of the screen. Doc was the lookout while Ralph opened the back emergency door very quickly and in came their friends. Waddie asked, "What the hell took you so long?" Ralph told them he would explain later; they had to hurry before the usher came back.

There was no need to rush because Sal, the usher, did not come back. After they settled in their seats, Ralph looked around and saw that there was an empty seat next to the two Marrano sisters. He got up and sat next to them and whispered, "Where's your sister, Gracie?" Josephine said she didn't know where she was and she was getting nervous. Now, all three of them were getting a little worried and they all got up to go to the lobby to find her.

There, they saw Gracie eating candy and drinking pop with Sal the usher. As they approached, she pointed at her sister Carmela and Sal gave a big smile. Josephine was angry with her and asked her what she was doing. She said they were waiting for her and when she didn't come back, they were very worried. She grabbed Gracie's arm and led her back into the show with Carmela and Ralph tagging along.

Ralph whispered to Gracie, "What did you do to get him to stay in the lobby for so long and for him to give you pop and candy?" Gracie, in a very low whisper, said, "I told the usher that I had a secret to tell him but I couldn't tell him in front of my sisters. He would have to come into the lobby. When we got there, I told him my sister, Carmela, had a great big crush on him but was too shy to tell him. So after the show, I told him I would introduce him to her. He was so happy that he bought me candy and pop."

Ralph whispered back, "Does Carmela know?" Gracie said, "Hell, no, but you owe me, you big jerk!" Ralph thought to himself… *I take it back. This little gal is not only feisty but fearless and clever. She's going to make someone a terrific wife, unless she kills him first.*

Thanks to Gracie, the guys were able to enjoy the movies but poor Carmela was becoming annoyed as the usher kept coming to her during the movies and asking if everything was all right. Gracie dared not tell her what was in store for her after the show.

Chapter 7

It had been over a month that Eugenio was Giovanni's "Italian slave." The time had come for them to make the trip to Lackawanna, New York, to meet with their paesanos, the Giovanetti family. Giovanni wrote to them and explained the situation and asked if they could help Eugenio get a job in the steel mill and find him a place to live. They wrote back saying that there were many jobs available in the steel plant and he could live with them until he was able to pay for his own apartment.

Maria Giovanetti also hinted in her letter to Giovanni that she had her two beautiful nieces living with her, Philomena and Maria, both from Basilice, Italy. Perhaps an arrangement of marriage could be made if Eugenio and one of the sisters were compatible.

Before they left Olean, Giovanni mentioned this to Eugenio. "You know," he said, "it may be the time that you should think about settling down, getting married and raising a family." Eugenio just smiled, nodded and said, "Perhaps."

Giovanni was able to purchase two train tickets to Buffalo for him and Eugenio. One ticket would be round-trip, the other a one-way fare. They boarded the train and headed to Lackawanna for what would be a new life for Eugenio. When they arrived at the train station in Buffalo, they were greeted by Dominic and Maria Giovanetti. After hugs and kisses, they boarded the horse-drawn carriage and headed to Lackawanna.

As they were traveling down the road, Dominic pointed to the large billows of smoke that were coming out of the steel plant's chimney stacks. He turned and said to Eugenio in Italian, "That is your new place of employment. Starting two days from now, you will be working at the Lackawanna Steel Plant." Eugenio could not believe the size of this mammoth steel plant and sat in awe of it. He never saw this type of large industry in Italy where he lived or in Olean. He was amazed and he thanked Dominic for helping him get a job there.

They eventually arrived at the Giovanetti's house on Ingham Avenue. Eugenio thought it was a nice house but what made it even nicer were the two beautiful women who were standing on the porch. Eugenio was thunderstruck when he saw Philomena and made up his mind that she would be his wife.

Philomena and Maria Paolozza were standing on the porch and saw the buggy pull up with its passengers. Maria's first words were how handsome and strong looking Eugenio appeared. Philomena's first words were that his jaw was too large, his hands were too big and she thought he looked like a typical man from Basilice, all brawn and no brain. To say the least, she was not as impressed with Eugenio as he was with her.

Maria and Dominic brought Eugenio and Giovanni into the house and introduced them to their two nieces. Giovanni explained that he had to leave in two days to go back to Olean and his job. They all sat around that evening, reminiscing about Italy, eating all their favorite foods... manicotti, prosciutto, cheeses, meatballs and drinking some good homemade Italian vino.

Two days later, after a tearful goodbye, Giovanni left for Olean. Eugenio started to work in the steel plant and his courtship of Philomena began, even though Philomena did not know it. Eugenio lived with them for two months before he was able to get a small apartment in the Old Village. For the next six months, he won Philomena's heart with his personality, work ethic, dry sense of humor and his strong feelings of love for her.

The year 1913 was bittersweet for Eugenio. He married Philomena Paolozza, making her Mrs. Eugenio Galanti. That same year he received a letter from Basilice telling him that his mother and father had passed away from an epidemic that devastated central Italy. Eugenio was brokenhearted. For him, Italy would be gone forever.

On November 25, 1914, their first child Raphael (Ralph) was born. The family expanded with daughters; Mary, born in 1916, and Josephine, born in 1918. In 1922, the final member of the family arrived, a son whom they named John.

Suddenly Eugenio's dreaming about his past was interrupted. He heard a distant shout of, "Eugenio, Eugenio." This startled him, waking him from his dream. Again he heard, "Eugenio, Eugenio" and he recognized that it was his wife's voice. He quickly got up from his cushioned chair and went into the front of the store. There he saw his wife, Philomena, and Crystal with worried looks on their faces. Standing near them at the counter were two policemen.

Eugenio thought...*oh my God, what now!*

Chapter 8

Eugenio recognized the two young policemen and said, "Hello Joe, Pete, whatsa up?"

The two officers said hello to Eugenio and told him there was a little problem at the Park Theater that involved his son Ralph, Coco, the Marrano girls and the head usher, Sal Lenti. Philomena and Crystal quickly asked if everyone was all right. They said everyone was OK except for a few bruises. Eugenio asked, "Whata happened?"

The police explained that a group of Ralph's friends tried to get into the show without paying. Apparently, Ralph and Gunther Dochester were to let them in through the emergency door behind the screen. Somehow, Ralph convinced the young Marrano girl, Gracie, to get the usher out of the theater and into the lobby while he let his friends in the theater.

Officer Pete stated, "It seemed like everything was alright until the end of the movies when everybody was leaving. This is when the problem began. Evidently, Sal Lenti, the usher, was told by Gracie that her sister Carmela had the 'hots' for him. When Sal went over to Carmela and gave her a pat on the fanny and a kiss on the cheek, she turned around and slapped him. He became very angry. He grabbed her and asked her why she did that since she had sent her little sister over to tell him that she had the crush on him. Carmela told him he was crazy. That's when some of Ralph's friends started laughing at him and said it was a 'con' and he fell for it."

Police Officer Joe chimed in stating, "This incensed Sal even more and he grabbed Gracie Marrano and threw her on the ground calling her a little bitch. That is when all hell broke loose. The Marrano kid got up, tried to kick him in the balls and he slapped her. Your son then grabbed Sal, turned him around and punched him in the nose and broke it. This sent Sal flying over the counter, knocking over the candy stand and the popcorn machine, bleeding all over the floor."

"Pappy Amadori, the owner of the theater, called us right away. To his credit, your son did not leave and Coco stayed with him. The rest of the boys ran but we have an idea who they were. The Marrano girls, Josephine and Carmela were crying, but Gracie was still going after the usher."

The officer continued stating, "Mr. Amadori is not pressing charges because he knows you but he wants payment for the damages. Sal Lenti, the usher, is also not pressing charges. We convinced him that if he did, there was a good possibility that charges would be brought against him for assaulting a young girl."

Eugenio asked where his son and Coco were. The two policemen said they had them in the car and wanted to explain what happened before they brought them in. Eugenio thanked the two officers and gave them both a pack of Camels for their help and understanding.

The cops left and in came Ralph and Coco looking very worried, especially Ralph. Eugenio did not say a word but just stared at both of them. Finally, Ralph said, "Sorry, Pa. I know I disappointed you. I will talk to Mr. Amadori and tell him I will work for free at the theater until damages have been paid. Everything would have been OK if that big son of a bitch Sal didn't grab and slap little Gracie. I just lost it then." Eugenio still did not say a word but only stared.

"Mr. Galanti," Coco said, "we are all to blame. Raffs was the only one that had enough guts to stand up for that little girl. The rest of them ran out of the theater faster than lightning."

The only thing Eugenio said was, "Raphael, youa come with me. Say good-bye to Coco and Mrs. Freeman." Ralph did what he was told and followed his father into the back room of the store.

Chapter 9

In the large back room of the store there was a big table and several chairs. The back room was a sanctuary for some of the men or boys in which they could play cards, smoke some stogies or just "bullshit." As he was walking behind his father, Ralph thought he was going to get the beating of his life, especially after he was warned by his father about the last debacle with Virgilio.

Eugenio told his son to sit down and to Ralph's surprise he pulled up a chair and sat next to him. He started to speak in Italian. This was unusual for his father because like most immigrants, he believed that the first language their children should learn fluently was English. Their native tongue was only spoken in the house as a second language.

"Raphael," Eugenio started, "I am speaking to you in Italian because I want to express myself and make sure you understand me. I want to tell you a story about how I caused my cousin's death and how I almost killed a man. It was because of my temper and not realizing the consequences of my actions. Today, you and your mother might have been visiting me in prison instead of me being here talking to you."

Eugenio began telling his son the story of how he came to America and how his cousin, Giovanni, gave him a home in Olean and helped him get a job with the railroad. He spoke of the day they were at a tavern and a big-mouthed bully and his friends were challenging the people in the bar to arm wrestle for drinks. Giovanni, minding his own business, happened to look at the bully and the bully challenged him.

Eugenio said, "To his credit, Giovanni ignored him and started to talk to me at the bar. Then the big mouth got angry and called Giovanni and me faggots. When I heard that, I got angry and instead of ignoring him, I accepted his challenge. I was so angry that as soon as we got in the arm wrestling position and they said go, I squeezed his hand so tight that I heard some bones crack and I quickly slammed his arm to the table. I broke his arm and he was crying in pain. Big mouth was crying like a little baby! I was the happiest man in the bar."

"The next day I found out that the big mouth was the nephew of the general foreman. That day I lost my job. The following month, with the help of my cousin, I came to Lackawanna. If that was all that happened, I would have been grateful, but instead tragedy followed."

"Two years later, when you were only a baby, Giovanni's girlfriend, Sarah, sent me a telegram saying that Giovanni was dead. I was devastated. I quickly sent her a telegram back saying that I would take the next train to Olean and be there the following day. When I got to Olean, I asked Sarah what happened."

"Sarah told me that he was killed in a fight in back of a local bar by a big railroad man called Hans. The story that the police told Sarah was that Giovanni challenged the big man to arm wrestle for a few drinks. The police said Giovanni lost and had to buy drinks for everyone. He became mad because he didn't have that much money. He challenged the big railroad man to a fight and when they went outside, the police said Giovanni pulled a knife."

"Through the scuffle, somehow Giovanni was stabbed in the abdomen and he died before the ambulance arrived. Sarah told me that she could not believe it because Giovanni was a gentle man who would never start a fight and especially would never carry a weapon. She told that to the police but they said there were a couple of eyewitnesses that vouched for the big man's story."

"Raphael, I never believed it for a second. I knew Giovanni like a brother and he would never hurt anyone. From what Sarah told me, I knew immediately that it was the same 'bully' who, two years ago, called us 'faggots' and challenged us to arm wrestling. This bully tried to get even and because I was not there, I believe he went after Giovanni."

"Right after the funeral, I met this Hans in an alley and challenged him to a fight. I beat him badly. It was my anger, my hatred and my anguish for my cousin's death that made me keep on hitting him. If I did not get tired, I would have probably killed him. I left him in the alley and fortunate for me, he never reported what happened."

Eugenio did not tell Ralph the complete story. What really happened is that he waited for Hans outside the bar he frequented and when he came out, Eugenio whispered his name in a menacing tone. Hans, a bully, walked confidently into the alley and asked who was there. When Eugenio stepped out from the shadows, Hans said, "Oh, it's you... you bastard faggot. I have waited for you for two years but I got my satisfaction from your Dago cousin and now, I'm going to have special satisfaction with you."

With that, the big man pulled out a knife from his pocket and lunged toward Eugenio, but he wasn't quick enough. Eugenio sidestepped the big man and came down with a hard chopping motion with his hand and broke the man's wrist. The next instant he hit the man flush on the nose, breaking it. With each blow, he kept on saying, "this is for Giovanni." After only a few minutes, the big man was lying on his back, bleeding profusely from every part of his face, which looked like hamburger meat. There were no teeth left in the front of his mouth and his eyes were swollen shut. The only reason Eugenio knew he was still alive was because he was moaning quietly.

Eugenio did not have a mark on him but he was breathing heavily from all the exertion of hitting the man over and over again. He knew that he was lucky that he did not kill him but he felt he had vindicated Giovanni's death in a small way.

He leaned over the big man and whispered in his ear, "Can youa hear me?" The big man slowly nodded his head. "Then leta me tell you. If you saya anything about a me to anyone, I swear to God that I will come a back and kill you, you pezzo di merdo (piece of shit). Do youa understand?" The big man nodded.

The bully never told anyone what exactly happened. He just said he was attacked in the alley by muggers and was robbed. He told the police that he did not recognize them for they had hoods on their heads.

Years later, Eugenio found out this big bully became a big pussycat, scared of his own shadow. He was never the same after that evening. He became a recluse and lived in the woods away from people for the rest of his life. Many thought he feared that the men who attacked him would come back, but he knew he feared only one man and that would be for the rest of his life.

Chapter 10

Philomena watched both her husband and son walk from the back room to the front of the store, neither of them saying a word and looking somber. She dared not say a word but saw her husband kiss his son's face and give him a gentle pat on the back as Ralph left the store. She felt both pride and relief. Pride that her son protected a young girl and relief that her husband and son showed affection to each other.

The rest of the summer was calm for the young boys who hung around Galanti's Confectionary. Ralph was still good-natured and fun loving but he remained low keyed. No one knew what his father had said and Ralph would not divulge it, but it had an affect on him.

On the other hand, in the Marrano family, there was mass chaos. Gracie's father, Federico, was irate when he heard what happened at the movie theater. Even though Gracie was only twelve years old, she still received a "licking" from her father's strap. Still defiant, she never cried. Her punishment was mild compared to that of her sisters, Carmela and Josephine. Although they did not receive a "licking," they were not allowed out of the house for the rest of the summer unless they were going to work. Their household chores doubled and their friends were only allowed to visit them one hour a day. What made matters worse was that their mother, Maria, made the two oldest children, Carmen and Anna, who were not even at the show, responsible to make sure Gracie did not cause any problems for the rest of the summer. They were warned that if anything happened, they would be in serious trouble. This did not make for a good summer for the four older children and Gracie.

The only three of the eight children given reprieves were the youngest siblings, Neal, Lou and Rosie. They were too young to understand what happened but they were not too young to notice all the punishments. To say the least, young Gracie was not the favorite sister in the Marrano family that summer.

The dog days of summer 1932 were coming to an end and the start of the school year was right around the corner. The young men were enjoying these last few weeks by playing one of their favorite sports, softball. It was an exciting part of the summer because this was when the playoffs began. The younger children were occupied playing games like kick the can, nip, buck-buck, hide-n-seek and flying homemade kites. The children were enjoying the innocence of youth, unaware of the problems their parents faced. It was the height of the Great Depression, there was political unrest in the country and the world, industrial plants had declining operations with only a few jobs available. Unfortunately, crime was becoming more and more frequent.

In the United States, the presidential race was being hotly contested between then President Herbert Hoover and his Democratic challenger, Franklin Delano Roosevelt. In Europe, Nazism was making its mark in Germany. An upcoming political force, Adolph Hitler, was the leader of the Nazi party. Benito Mussolini was the leader of Italy under its Fascist regime and Japan was making war overtures in the Near East.

Al Capone, the undisputed Mafia leader from Chicago, was convicted and placed in jail in February. His empire began to crumble due to warring Mafia families from across the United States. Although prohibition would soon be repealed, bootlegging was still a quick way to make money. Speakeasies were rampant throughout the country and with them came the criminal elements of prostitution and gambling. The new organization called the Federal Bureau of Investigation and its director, J. Edgar Hoover, issued an "all out war" on crime.

The city of Lackawanna was not spared. Its multicultural, diverse population of more than 24,000 people were also suffering during the Great Depression. The largest employer, Bethlehem Steel, was laying off its workers and only bringing a few back on a daily basis to work the mills. Many of the men were drowning their sorrows at local speakeasies with the few dollars they had left in their pockets. Crime was up in the entire Western New York area; there was very little hope and much despair. Only one man was the shining light that gave people hope. His name was Father Nelson Baker.

Chapter 11

In front of the great statue of the Blessed Virgin Mary located on the altar of the Basilica of Our Lady of Victory, knelt a fragile 91-year-old man. It was past midnight and no one was in the Basilica but this frail holy man. This was part of his daily routine for it was the only time he could have a private conversation with the Great Lady whom he adored. His name was Monsignor Nelson Baker, but to most he was known as Father Baker, Padre of the Poor.

"Blessed Mother, please forgive me if I ask another favor of you," Father Baker began. "I know throughout the years you have granted me so much that I can never repay you. The only repayment I can give is my devotion to you and your son, Jesus Christ, my Lord and Savior. Last night, a young girl of only sixteen came to our rectory. She was pregnant and ready to have child. She was poor, unwed and had nowhere else to go but here. We took her in and it was a good thing because she was about to bring another young life into this world. There were complications because the girl was so emaciated that the doctors could not save the baby. She is now in intensive care and the doctors say that she may not live through the night. Our Lady, it is with sincere humility that I ask you to please help this young girl. If needed, I will gladly take her place to be with you and our Blessed Lord in heaven. She is so young and has so much to live for and I am old and have lived so long that I am ready if it is God's will to join you."

It was not unusual for the Padre of the Poor to converse in this manner with the Blessed Mother. He had been doing this for close to sixty years. This man, who did not become a priest until 1876 when he was thirty-four years of age, had a profound relationship with Mary, the Blessed Mother of Jesus. Through the years, Father Baker knew there were many favors bestowed upon him through the intercession of the Great Lady. It had been rumored throughout Lackawanna, Western New York and even the United States that Father Baker was responsible for many miracles. Only he did not recognize them as miracles but as the works of the Heavenly Mother watching over her flock.

It was close to 2 a.m. when the fragile old man grew a little weary and after saying his prayers to the Blessed Mother, he bid her a good night and went to his quarters next to the grand Basilica. Two hours later, he heard a light knock on his door. In came Brother Sebastian who quietly said, "Monsignor, Monsignor, are you awake?" Father Baker in his good humor said, "I am now."

Brother Sebastian, who was a stocky, good-natured aide to Father Baker, smiled and said, "Sorry, Monsignor for this intrusion so early in the morning, but Dr. Sullivan said I should inform you that the young mother who we brought in yesterday is requesting to see you. I would not have disturbed you but Dr. Sullivan insisted and said that she may not last through the early morning hours."

"I am glad that you have awakened me because if Dr. Sullivan insisted, the young girl must be in grave condition and I definitely would like to be there to give her comfort. But let me tell you, there is no need to worry about the young girl, she will be taken care of by Our Lady."

With this, Father Baker rose from his bed, and with the help of Brother Sebastian, began to get dressed. They walked across the street to Our Lady of Victory Hospital, where the young mother was being treated by Dr. Sullivan and a few nurses. Father Baker came into the room and gave a nod to the good doctor and stated, "Is she awake?" Dr. Sullivan said, "Yes, Monsignor. She's been asking for you for the last hour. I was going to wait until later in the morning, but I have a feeling she may not last that long. She is very weak and has lost much blood. I have not told her that her baby did not survive. I believe that this might cause her anxiety and stress which may worsen her condition." Father Baker nodded and went to the bed where the young mother was lying.

"Child, the doctor said that you wanted to see me." The young mother opened her eyes and said, "Father Baker, is that you?" He whispered, "Yes." She proceeded to say, "Father, how is my baby? Is it a boy or a girl? I feel weak but I have to know that if I do not survive, you will take care of my baby." With this, tears started to roll down her cheeks.

"Child, you will survive and you will be here for many, many years. Your baby was a boy." As he gently held her hand, he quietly said, "He is now with the angels in heaven for I baptized him as soon as he was brought into this world. Our Lord wanted your child with Him in heaven with the other children so they could play and never have to endure worldly hardships. He is in a far better world and is happy. For you, Our Blessed Lady will watch over you and guide you throughout your life, if you believe."

The young mother started to sob and Father Baker placed his hand on her head and with his other hand, placed a medallion of the Blessed Mother on her chest. He leaned over and whispered something in her ear that the others in the room could not hear. He blessed her and left the room. The nurses in the room were crying, for they felt the young girl would not survive the morning.

Father Baker turned to Dr. Sullivan and said, "As soon as the young girl is healthy enough, I want to have a memorial Mass for her child in the Basilica." Dr. Sullivan said, "But Monsignor, the young girl will not be with us for more than a few hours." Father Baker looked deep into the eyes of Dr. Sullivan and said, "I will be here at 9 a.m. to have breakfast with the young girl. Please make the necessary arrangements." With that, he turned and with Brother Sebastian went back to his quarters across the street.

Chapter 12

At 7 a.m., like clockwork, Father Baker woke up and wished the Virgin Mary a good morning. This had been his custom in the morning for over half a century. He knelt and recited his morning prayers in front of the statue at the side of his bed. After he said his prayers, he would give the Great Lady a wink and he knew that she would give him strength to face each day.

At 7:30 a.m., Brother Sebastian gave his knock on the door to see if Father Baker was awake. But instead of his usual knock, this was more like a pounding on the door. Startled, Father Baker went to the door and opened it to see an excited Brother Sebastian beaming with happiness. "Brother Sebastian, have you just inherited a million dollars?" said Father Baker.

"No, no, no," stammered the Brother. "I'm here to tell you that Dr. Sullivan said that breakfast has been arranged for you and the young mother. He said he didn't know how you did it, but she took a turn for the better and is doing well this morning." Father Baker smiled and said, "Did you ever doubt I was going to have breakfast with her this morning?" Brother Sebastian just blushed and smiled. He then helped Father Baker get dressed and walked him across the street to the hospital.

"You never cease to amaze me, Monsignor," said Dr. Sullivan, who met them there. "Last night, this young mother defied all medical odds of surviving but, somehow, she is with us this morning, and again she is asking for you. It seems that all her vital signs are getting stronger and she is no longer in critical condition. Whatever you said to her last night had a profound affect on her."

Father Baker smiled at Dr. Sullivan, who was affectionately known as one of the "Baker Boys." "How soon we forget, Michael, the power of the Virgin Mary," Father Baker said. "Was it not just a few years ago that you were an infant, left on our doorstep wrapped only in a blanket? The Blessed Mother took you under her wing and guided you through the years and now you are here as a doctor helping to take care of her children."

"I remember. It was with your help and Our Blessed Mother that I was able to reach hopes and dreams that few children in my situation could ever have the opportunity to accomplish. But Monsignor, I am still mystified and surprised at how you can defy the laws of medicine."

The doctor led Father Baker into the young mother's hospital room, where he had ordered the nurses to set up breakfast for both of them. The young girl looked so different for now she had color in her cheeks and a smile on her face when she saw the kindly priest. "My child, you look well this morning. I am happy that you have decided to have breakfast with me." Today, he was going to have whatever the young mother ordered for both of them. Usually, he would have only a piece of toast and fruit that would last him until dinner. While they were eating, Father Baker asked, "Child, what is your name?"

"Elizabeth Donner." Still probing, he asked where she came from, how did she get to Lackawanna and did she have any family. She hesitated for a moment, looking embarrassed and finally, after taking a deep breath, told her story.

"I'm from Trenton, New Jersey. I lived with my mother. I never knew my father because he left as soon as I was born. My mother tried to raise me as good as she could but because there was no work for her, she had to do things for food and clothing that I am not proud to say. I love my mother but the last couple of years, she changed so much that I did not recognize her anymore. She drank and started to bring men into our house. One night while I was in bed, I heard them singing, drinking, yelling and doing other things that scared me. After a couple of hours, there was silence in our small apartment and then I heard my bedroom door quietly opening. In came this large man that I had never seen before and he told me that my mother wanted him to see if I was all right. Before I could say anything, he got into my bed and placed his filthy hand over my mouth and told me that my mother said for three dollars more, he could have me for his dessert. I was petrified and the next thing I knew, he was on top of me ripping my night shirt off and keeping his filthy, smelly hand on my mouth.

"After he was finished, he told me that if I made a sound, he would kill me and my mother. Father Baker, I was hurting so much and bleeding that I wanted to die. He left my room and I heard the apartment door slam. The next morning, my mother came into my room screaming at me, asking what I had done to make him leave. I told her what happened and she slapped me across the face and called me a whore.

"During the next several months, I started to feel a change in my body. I was frightened to tell my mother because I did not know what she was going to do. I started to wear larger clothes because I was gaining weight and my stomach was protruding. After seven months, one day when my mother was sober, I finally told her that I was going to have a child. She screamed at me and told me that we could not afford another mouth to feed. She ordered me to go to the clinic down the street to have an abortion.

"I left the apartment crying and went to the clinic but I could not do this to my child. I came home late at night and my mother was drunk as usual. She asked me if I went to the clinic. I told her no and that I was going to have this child. She became crazy and told me that I was not going to have this baby. She called me a whore again and came at me with a coat hanger and said she would drag the little son of a bitch out of me if it's the last thing she did. As she stumbled toward me with the coat hanger, I was so scared that I started to reach around for anything to protect my baby. I grabbed a pan from the stove and swung it and hit my mother on the side of the face. Then I ran out of the apartment as fast as I could and that was the last time I saw my mother. I don't know if she is living or dead.

"I walked for miles during the night not knowing where I was going. I saw a small church with a light on and I went inside. There was no one there. I just wanted to rest so I laid down in one of the pews and fell asleep. Later that evening, a kindly priest found me and asked me what happened. I told him the story and told him I will never go back home. That is when I found out about you, Father. He said there was a place in upstate New York, near Buffalo, called Lackawanna where there was a protectory for unwed mothers and orphans. He said it was part of Our Lady of Victory Institutions and that it was headed by a great holy man called Father Nelson Baker. He told me that I should go there and I would be safe. I stayed with him for a week until I got my strength back and prepared myself to travel. The kind priest gave me most of the money that he had so I could buy a train ticket to Buffalo and some food. He brought me to the train station, gave me the directions to Our Lady of Victory Basilica and handed me a rosary. He blessed me and my unborn child and bid me a safe journey.

"Somehow, I got off the train at the wrong station and I got lost. I had been traveling for over three weeks to get here. I was able to get rides from wagons, cars, anything that could help me and my baby get to Lackawanna. When I finally arrived, I was somewhere in North Buffalo and I asked for directions to the Basilica. I walked all night until I got here. All this was for nothing! My child died and he never had a chance. Father, it is so unfair." And she started to sob uncontrollably.

Chapter 13

"Elizabeth, Elizabeth," Father Baker whispered as he tried to console the grieving young girl. "Your child is happy in heaven. For you, I believe Our Lord and Our Lady have special plans. Come and eat your breakfast and after you rest, I will come back and we will talk again." With that, he slowly got up, blessed her and left the room.

He met Dr. Sullivan in the hall and told him to take good care of her for he believed that Our Lady had brought her here for a special reason. He would come back and visit with her in the evening. He gave Dr. Sullivan a smile, a wink and left with Brother Sebastian to go across the street to his office.

During their walk, Brother Sebastian had a thousand questions. Who was the young girl, what was her name, where did she come from, how old was she? He asked a dozen other questions before Father Nelson crossed Ridge Road to the Basilica. As he reached the other side, Father Baker stopped, looked at Brother Sebastian and chuckled. "By the time I answer all your questions, I will be dead and buried."

With that, Brother Sebastian blushed and stammered, "Sorry, Monsignor, sorry, Monsignor," and took the arm of Father Baker and helped him up the stairs into the Basilica. "Brother Sebastian," Father Baker said. "You are my pillar of strength, my confidant and my happy-go-lucky, cherished friend." Brother Sebastian's face lit up, chest puffed out and his stride was that of a proud peacock.

As they entered the Basilica, they were met by Father Herman Gerlach, Father Baker's right-hand man who helped him operate the Basilica and OLV Institutions. They went to the office where Father Gerlach gave the Monsignor an overview on the general status of the parish, updated him on the schedule of the day and gave him reports on the finances of the OLV Institutions, which included the Basilica, protectory, infant home, hospital, orphanage and meals served to the poor and needy.

Father Gerlach reported that the last several months they had served more than 30,000 meals to the needy. They had provided well over $3,000 a month in simple hand-out-of-pocket donations to people who could not afford rent. The bread lines were becoming unmanageable as they were stretching over half a mile long. He also informed him that there were several local politicians and businessmen in the waiting room requesting to meet with him.

Father Baker sat there and took in all the information and asked if they still had enough money to serve and meet the needs of the poor. Father Gerlach nodded in the affirmative. "Well, let's deal with the local politicians and businessmen. Do you know what they want?"

Father Gerlach stated, "There seems to be a problem with us housing the homeless at our South Buffalo property and here at the OLV Institutions. People in the community are complaining that they are low life transients who just want a free handout from us. They say that they don't wash, are belligerent and are not the kind of people that our good community should have." Father Baker smiled and said, "This should be interesting. Please bring these gentlemen into the room."

In came a group of well-dressed community leaders; three politicians and four local businessmen. Father Baker greeted the men and in return the men bowed and wished him a good morning. In spite of his small physical stature, Father Baker was a very intimidating man. He smiled and waited for them to speak. There was a long pause and a sense of uneasiness in the room before Edward Wadsworth Wellington, a heavyset businessman dressed impeccably, stepped forward and said, "Monsignor, with all due respect, we come for your help. These people that you provide shelter and food for are nothing but floaters and drifters who are here for a free handout. They're filthy, ill mannered, lazy and are taking advantage of your kindness. Neighbors are afraid to let their children out to play, businesses are losing money because people will not go into their establishments when they see these vagrants in front of their buildings and there is a general sense of fear of them in our community."

Father Baker stared at him and did not say a word. The heavyset man started to sweat profusely while the room stayed silent and no one else in the entourage spoke to support him. Finally, after a minute, which seemed to be an eternity for the people in the room, Father Baker replied, "Yes, what is your point?" The room went silent for another minute as no one knew what to say. At this point, one of the Lackawanna politicians had enough courage to say, "Monsignor, please help us for we do not know which direction to take."

Father Baker stated, "I understand your concerns but what would you like to have me do? Send these people out into the streets where they will not have shelter, food or money? Don't you think this would cause more problems? Where would they find shelter, food and money unless they broke into the homes of our people? If you have a better solution to meet the needs of these poor unfortunate individuals, please tell me and I will abide by your wishes."

The heavyset businessman, Wellington, became flustered and blurted out, "Well, Monsignor, if you didn't advertise that you would help these people, we wouldn't get these low lives from all over the country coming to our community. I think we should take care of our own first. Anyway, most of these low lives are colored and you know what that means."

Everyone in the room was shocked at the bluntness of this arrogant businessman, all except Father Baker. He looked at the man and smiled.

"Oh, I understand. These people of color cannot be trusted. I must be an imbecile because I dedicated my life to the Virgin Mary and her Son, Jesus Christ. And, do you know, sir, in this day and age, our Lord Jesus Christ would have been considered a man of color."

Wellington was stunned and started to stammer, "Monsignor, Monsignor, I did not mean that...you know what I meant. I did not mean to offend you."

"Sir, you did not offend me, you offended Our Lord." With that, Father Baker looked at the gentlemen and said, "I will try to correct the situation but I cannot turn these people away. Give me a few days with my staff and we will do our best to resolve this problem."

At that point, he bid the seven-man entourage a good day and left the room with Brother Sebastian. Father Gerlach thanked the group for coming and told them he would get back to them in a few days. They expressed their appreciation and each one shook Father Gerlach's hand as they left, especially the heavyset businessman, who kept on shaking and shaking his hand until Father Gerlach thought it would go numb.

After they left, Father Gerlach went into the next office where Father Baker was sitting in his usual chair, looking out the window at his beloved Basilica. "Well, Monsignor, I think we have two problems. One is the complaint about the poor people we are sheltering, the other is the possibility of Mr. Wellington having a heart attack before he goes home tonight. I think the latter will happen before we fix the former!"

"I know we have a problem, my dear friend," Father Baker said. "I have heard rumblings about these individuals for the last several weeks. We definitely have to do something but I will not turn them away into the cold. When I die, Our Lord isn't going to ask me if they were worthy. But he might ask me if I helped." With that, Father Baker, Father Gerlach and Brother Sebastian sat down and discussed how they were going to try to solve this dilemma.

Chapter 14

The year 1932 was becoming a tumultuous one. The Great Depression was taking its toll on America and its people. The number of unemployed workers had reached up to 13 million. There were demonstrations and riots throughout the country. In Dearborn, Michigan, 3,000 demonstrators marched upon Ford's River Rouge factory. They were confronted by the police and an altercation ensued as officers with pistols and machine guns opened fire on the crowd. In the end, fifty were injured and four were killed.

There were even demonstrations in the nation's capital. Thousands of unemployed veterans were demanding bonuses for their services in the armed forces. Instead of receiving bonuses, they were attacked by police and U.S. Army units commanded by Gen. Douglas MacArthur. Many of the demonstrating veterans were injured and two were killed.

In May, Amelia Earhart became the first woman to make a solo flight across the Atlantic Ocean. In the same month, the infant son of American icon Charles Lindbergh was found dead after being kidnapped in March.

Sports became an outlet for those suffering in the Depression. In baseball, the Yankees looked like a shoo-in for the World Series and most likely would be facing the Chicago Cubs. The United States hosted both the 1932 Winter and Summer Olympics at Lake Placid,

New York and in Los Angeles, California, respectively. The U.S. athletes performed very well in the competition. Everyone was anxiously waiting for the collegiate and professional football leagues to start their season in a few weeks.

Politically, in the United States, Franklin Delano Roosevelt was the Democratic candidate for president and his platform of the "New Deal" was the talk of the country. Worldwide, the Nazis took the majority lead in the German elections and Italy was under the rule of the National Fascist Party led by dictator Benito Mussolini.

Locally, in Lackawanna, operations in the Bethlehem Steel Plant had been declining. The company's annual report showed a big decline in full-time employment but many opportunities for part-time employment were available. Small businesses were struggling to make ends meet and any type of employment was at a premium.

To make matters worse, there was a steady influx of hundreds of men, women and children who were unemployed, homeless and in need coming to Lackawanna for help. Father Baker became a household name, not only locally but also throughout the country. He had become the symbol of hope for many of the unfortunate.

Meanwhile, at Our Lady of Victory Basilica, the holy man was praying in front of the statue of Our Lady. Father Baker quietly asked, "Please, Our Lady, give me the strength to do the right thing for these poor, unfortunate people and also find a solution that is agreeable to everyone." He remained there kneeling for hours with his head bowed. Suddenly, he looked up, smiled at his Lady, gave her a wink and a thank you. He was ready and the next morning, he would summon Father Gerlach and Brother Sebastian to his quarters.

Chapter 15

Before Father Gerlach and Brother Sebastian could knock, the door opened with Father Baker smiling and welcoming the two into the room. It always amazed Brother Sebastian that Father had this uncanny ability to see through doors. As the two came into the room, Father Baker said, "I think I may have an idea for the solution to our dilemma with the businessmen and the politicians." Father Gerlach and Brother Sebastian looked at each other and started to smile. Whenever Father Baker said he had an idea for a solution, ninety-nine percent of the time it worked.

Brother Sebastian, who was always over anxious, blurted out quickly, "Monsignor, what is it? What is it?" Father Baker always enjoyed the enthusiasm of his friend, while Father Gerlach gave Brother Sebastian a shot to the ribs with his elbow. He turned to Brother Sebastian and said, "Be patient, Monsignor will tell us when he is ready."

Father Baker chuckled and thought how lucky he was to be blessed with these two wonderful men of God. They always brightened his day with the banter between them. "I think I'm ready," he said, giving Brother Sebastian a wink.

"What I am proposing is that every able man and woman who comes to us for help in turn will help others in our community. In order for them to receive food and shelter from us, they will have to give of themselves to help others. As the good Lord says, it is better to give than to receive and that is going to be our motto."

Father Baker continued to explain his idea. Every person who receives help would be assigned to a business or public agency to donate his or her time to help others. They may be cleaning stores, sweeping walkways, removing snow or debris, painting, minor maintenance or anything that could help the community. Each business owner or public agency would be responsible for these people and the jobs that they would perform.

"What if they refuse to do the work?" Brother Sebastian said. "Then, they will have to deal with me," said Father Baker. Father Gerlach was a little worried by that statement because some of these individuals were big and surly and had no respect for any authority. Father Baker knew what Father Gerlach was thinking and only smiled and said, "They may not respect me, but I will tell you, they will respect Our Lady and her Son. Fear not, my good friend, they will see the light." With that said, he asked his two companions to arrange a meeting for that afternoon with the local businessmen and politicians whom they had met a few days ago. Father Baker emphasized that he especially wanted the heavyset businessman named Wellington to be there.

At exactly 2 p.m., Father Baker walked into the huge conference room where just a few days earlier these businessmen and politicians expressed their grievances about the vagrants that the priest was housing. They all stood up and greeted the Monsignor with reverence. Father Baker motioned them to be seated and started to speak.

"I have given it much thought and I believe I have come up with a compromise that will benefit everyone," he said. "Each individual who receives food and shelter from us will have to provide a service to our community. In other words, every man and woman who comes to Our Lady of Victory for help in turn will have to help others in our community. Each businessman and public agency will be responsible for these individuals in the jobs they are assigned. Our Lady of Victory Protectory will monitor these individuals and make sure that they are performing their duties. In the long run, they will be providing a service for our community and we will be giving them pride and dignity that will help them through these troubled times."

There were nods of agreement throughout the room. Even Edward Wellington, the most ardent opponent to these unfortunate people, was nodding his head in agreement. One of the politicians in attendance asked when this would occur. Father Baker stated that if everyone was in agreement, he would start the program as soon as possible. Everyone nodded in the affirmative.

This is exactly what Father Baker was hoping for. He stated, "This is a good starting point. I would like for you individuals to be the leaders of this new program and give it your full endorsement." He looked straight at Edward Wadsworth Wellington and said, "Mr. Wellington, I would like you to be the beacon of the lighthouse and be the first to accept one of our people in need."

Wellington looked bewildered and started to stammer, "Um, ah, of course, um, um, ah, what exactly do you wish me to do, Monsignor?" "I would like to have you take our first candidate and let him work in your haberdashery. The person could clean the windows, sweep the floors and do any maintenance work you may need. Matter of fact, I have just the individual for you."

Not knowing what to say and having everyone staring at him, Wellington had no alternative but to agree to this crafty little man's plan. "What is the individual's name and when will you be sending him to me?" "I'm glad you asked that," Father Baker answered. "He is in the next room and is excited about the opportunity to work. He is twenty-eight years old and his name is Horatio T. Bottoms II."

Wellington raised his eyebrow. He thought this might not be bad. This Bottoms must be a highly educated individual who probably lost his business because of the crash of '29. This might work out fairly well for him. He said to Monsignor, "I'd be happy to take this young man on a trial basis for at least six months." Father Baker was exuberant and told Brother Sebastian to bring in Horatio.

In came Horatio, who was six foot four inches tall and 260 pounds of muscle. He wore a white shirt and dress pants that probably were given to him by Father Baker. He was a handsome man with powerful biceps and very dark black skin. Wellington was ready to have a heart attack. He didn't know what to say or what to do, but because his mouth was still open for a minute, everyone knew he was very surprised. He started to stammer again, "Ah, ah," and before he got another ah out, Father Baker introduced Horatio to his new benefactor.

"I'm very happy to meet you, Sir," said Horatio in perfect English. "I am so happy you are giving me the opportunity to work. I will not let you or Father Baker down." Wellington kept on saying, "Ah, ah, ah" before Father Baker mercifully ended the conversation with, "Mr. Wellington, you will be remembered as being a pioneer for this program." And with that, Father Baker told the group that he would be in contact with each one of them during the week to assign individuals to them. A bewildered Wellington left the offices in Our Lady of Victory Basilica.

A few weeks after having Horatio come on board, Wellington found out that he was a hard-working individual. At the end of four weeks, he gave Horatio a job with a modest salary; by the end of four months, he made him a manager of one of his haberdashery shops in South Buffalo. More importantly, Horatio probably saved the life of Wellington's young daughter, Dorothea.

Six weeks after Horatio started working as a cleaner in the haberdashery, three thugs came in to the business to rob the store. One had a gun, while the other two had a knife and chain. Dorothea, who was only seventeen years old, was working behind the counter at the cash register for her dad, who had to go to the bank. The three came in, locked the store door and told Dorothea that they wanted everything in the cash register. Terrified, Dorothea gave them everything in the drawer, which amounted to $8.60.

Upset with the small amount of cash, they asked her where the rest of the money was. She told them that her father went to the bank to deposit the money an hour ago. The one thug was so upset that he slapped Dorothea across the face, looked at the others and told them "For this little amount of money, let's make it worth our while." They proceeded to tear off Dorothea's dress and hold down her arms while one tried to mount her. She screamed and screamed and screamed.

In the back room, stocking the shelves, Horatio heard the commotion and when he heard the screams, he ran out to the front of the store. He saw the three men, two holding Dorothea's arms down, the other mounting her. Horatio became enraged, grabbed the thug who was mounting her and with one quick motion, broke his neck. The other two looked up, saw this large black man and became terrified. Their friend was lying dead next to the young girl, who was screaming. The one holding her arm grabbed the gun and shot Horatio in the shoulder but it did not stop him from coming forward. The thug shot him again, this time in the abdomen, but it still did not stop Horatio from moving forward. He picked up the closest thing to his hand, which was a large jar full of candy, and cracked the glass across the man's head. The other one pulled a knife but he was not quick enough. Horatio gave a quick and powerful kick to the man's jaw, snapping his head back. The man was dead before he hit the ground.

Horatio stumbled forward, falling into oblivion. Dorothea got up screaming and ran out of the store into the street. Her father, who was walking from the bank, started running toward her with a group of citizens. Dorothea quickly told her father what had happened and how Horatio saved her. She kept on crying hysterically, thinking that Horatio was dead.

Wellington ran into the store, where he found four bodies lying on the floor. Two of the thugs were dead, the other was lying unconscious. Wellington quickly went to Horatio, who was lying face down and bleeding profusely. He heard the big man's shallow breathing and whispered to him tearfully, "Please, Horatio, hold on, help is coming. You will be okay. Please, hold on. Don't die on me, I need you." The ambulance arrived and rushed Horatio to Our Lady of Victory Hospital.

The next day, Wellington went to see Horatio in the hospital. It was ironic that this was the man whom he originally detested and had been angry at Father Baker for coercing him to take him as a worker. With tears in his eyes, he thanked Horatio for saving his daughter from harm. Horatio looked straight into Wellington's eyes and said, "No, thank you, Mr. Wellington, for giving me a chance to get back my dignity."

From that day on, Horatio and Wellington were inseparable. Their businesses became very successful after the Great Depression and the two men remained close friends until their deaths, four decades later.

Chapter 16

Ralph was lying on the grass in front of Lincoln Annex School, daydreaming and watching the clouds go by on the last Saturday in August. This was his last year in high school and he was wondering what his future would be. He knew he was one of the very fortunate ones during these tough years of the Great Depression because his father was always able to work at least four days at the steel plant on a part-time basis. His father, who had the reputation of being a hard worker, was always being picked by the foremen when they were waiting outside the gates.

He also knew that his father had a successful confectionary store that became a focal point for many young people in the First Ward. His father never turned away anyone who was down on his luck and needed groceries for the family. If the people could not pay with money, they would offer garden vegetables, homemade goods, chickens, rabbits or pigeons that they raised....or anything that would help defray the cost of their bill. Because of these traits, Eugenio became a well-respected and trustworthy man in their community.

Unbeknownst to his father, Ralph's mother, Philomena, was even more generous. Many of the wives whose husbands were too proud would come to her and ask her for help. She never refused anyone and always gave as much as she could without accepting any means of payment. It did not matter if you were Italian, Polish, Negro,

Jewish or any other race or denomination, Philomena treated you as a friend in need.

"Hey, Raffs, when are you gonna come out for the football team?" This woke Ralph up from his daydreaming. Coco was at the end of his run as he was getting in shape for football because practice would start in three days.

"You know Pop won't let me play," Ralph said. "I pleaded with him for three years and it was like talking to the wall. I know for sure, in my senior year, he won't have a change of heart and say, of coursa, Raphael, youa can do anything youa want." Coco chuckled and said, "You speak more like your father every day."

"Anyway, I will be having orchestra practice after school. I'm really into playing the sax and last year Miss Twist said that Cswaykus, Bellini, Nowak and I can play for a football pep rally this year. Geez, geez, just think, me playing the 'Wabash Blues' and having all those girls screaming with their big eyes fluttering over our group. They may forget who won the football game the next day, but I bet they won't forget who played the sweet sax at our assembly," chuckled Ralph.

"Are you ready for the football team?" Ralph said. "You bet," said Coco. "Coach Fisher told me last year that if I come in tip-top shape, I'll be the starting halfback and he thinks if I have a great year, I can get a scholarship to some Negro college down south."

Ralph and Coco heard a voice call out. "Hey you two dipshits; don't you guys have anything to do but lie around and shoot the crap?" They turned and saw Tony and Carmen Moretti, their good friends, approaching them. They did not see too much of the brothers during the summer because they worked as caddies at the Wanakah Country Club.

"How's everything going with you two?" Ralph said. "Where the hell have you been, we haven't seen you all summer. By the way, I thought that you guys would be caddying today, a beautiful Saturday, one of the last few days before school starts." With that, Tony and Carm together told Ralph and Coco their woeful story.

"We were working all summer making good money at Wanakah but we got laid off yesterday because we listened to goddamn Geno Covelli," said Carm. Tony continued, "That son of a bitch convinced us and the other caddies that we should go on strike because they're treating us like shit and the pay is crummy. So, we and most of the guys from Bethlehem Park supported him and we went on strike. Geno said it would probably last no longer than a couple of hours and we would get more money and some 'perks' like free lunches on the days we work. We gathered at the clubhouse, sat down and when the golfers came, we refused to caddy. The golf pro and some of the goddamn high and mighty Wanakah members, you know the big shots that have more money than God, said in no uncertain terms, 'So you guys don't want to work? That's OK. You're all fired.' Then they threw us off the premises.

"The only good thing that happened was that Geno was so pissed off at that jerky golf pro that he hit him squarely in the jaw and knocked the poor bastard out cold. We got him out of there quickly and ran before they called the cops. Anyway, we were going to quit because school is starting and we want to have some free time before we go back."

Ralph retorted, "Geez, only Covelli could come up with an idea like that. Don't you remember last year when he climbed the water tower as a platform to promote the need for unions? And, what happened? The cops dragged him down from the tower and sat his ass in jail overnight until his father bailed him out the next day. Instead of getting a union started, he got a whipping from his old man."

The subject changed when along came some more of their buddies, a group of young men known as the "Galanti Guys." During the long years of the Depression, these young men spent most of their time hanging around Pop and Mom Galanti's confectionary store. The dog days of summer were soon ending and many of them were either going back to school or trying to find work to help their families during these hard times.

"Hey guys, did anyone see that great softball game yesterday at Cazenovia Field?" boasted Carl Covino. "Our man, Lou Fistola, was 4 for 4 with a home run and four RBIs as our First Ward guys beat the hell out of the South Buffalo Hawks team in the championship game." Lou, who was standing next to Carl, gave him a nudge in the ribs because he was embarrassed but it did not prevent Carl from praising him more.

"Is that right, 'True Blue Lou'?" said Ralph, smiling. "Hey, True Blue Lou, was Josephine Marrano there cheering you on? Is that why you did so good, hmnnn?" Ralph was having fun. He knew Lou and Josephine had a crush on each other but both were too shy to express their feelings. It was Ralph who had to be the matchmaker. The only trouble was that he was too embarrassed to go to the Marrano home with Lou because of the recent debacle at the Park Theater.

"Hey, Galanti. I'm going to need your help with your old man," said Gene Staniszewski, another of the Galanti Guys. "With what?" "I was hoping that your pop would let us build a clubhouse in his garage behind the store. He has such a massive garage and all we need is a little space for us to hang out during the winter months. I've been talking to the guys and every one of them thinks it's a great idea and is willing to help to build it. As for materials, many of us have means of obtaining them at no cost, if you know what I mean. What do ya think?"

"That's not a bad idea," Ralph said. "I think my father would go for it because then he could keep an eye on all of us and it might give him a little more business during the winter. I think if we go to see him, it should be you, me, Coco and Tony because I think the three of us are good bullshitters and he always liked Coco. C'mon, let's go see him."

The four of them took off to go to see Pop Galanti. As they were walking, they were making plans on how they were going to ask him for the clubhouse. They were getting excited until Coco stopped and said, "What if he says no?" After a moment of silence, Gene finally said, "No problem, we'll just spend the winter kicking the hell out of Ralph!"

Chapter 17

The four entered Galanti's Confectionary and there they saw Pop Galanti and Santo Bonitatibus carrying on a conversation at the counter. The two adults looked up as the boys approached them.

"Mr. Galanti, can we speak to you for a moment?" Gene said in a quivering voice. He did not know if Eugenio was still mad at him because of the Park Theater incident. "Sure, whatsa up boys?" They all looked at each other and finally Ralph said quickly in one breath, "Pop, can we build a clubhouse in the garage?" "Whata you say, Raphael? You spoka so quick, I could no understand you."

Gene finally got the courage and spoke of a plan they had to build a clubhouse where the guys could go during the winter months. They were hoping to build it in the garage behind the store. He explained that they would do all the work and provide all the materials to build it. All they needed was the okay from him.

Eugenio looked at Santo and asked him what he thought. "You know, Eugenio, that might not be a bad idea. It keeps the kids off the street, gives them a place to have some recreational activities like playing cards and hopefully, stay out of trouble." Eugenio responded, "I dona know." "Listen," Santo said. "If you are worried about them not being able to build something like that, I will help them and oversee the job." This put Eugenio's mind at ease because Santo was an excellent builder by trade. Unfortunately, there wasn't too much building being done during these lean times. Eugenio thought that this might be something that Santo could do to fill his days and feel productive.

Coco chimed in, "Mr. Galanti, we're always here at your store. This is like our second home and we thought it would be nice to stay out of your hair and have a room in the back where we could talk, have fun and not bother you. I promise we will cause no trouble and if, by chance, one of the guys is acting up, we will take care of him in our own way."

Eugenio smiled. Out of all of Ralph's friends, he favored Coco. To him, Coco was loyal, trustworthy and a real friend to his son. "Wella boys, when do we start?" The four of them were elated and started slapping each other on the back. "You tell us when, Mr. Galanti, and we will begin," said Tony.

"Alla right, boys, youa can start as soon as Santo gives the word. Santo and I wanna see plans. When Santo gives the okay, we willa begin." With that, the boys ran out the door to meet the guys who were gathered in front of the store. When they told them that Pop Galanti gave the okay, they erupted in cheers and slapped each other on the back. This was going to be the beginning of a new era.

Upstairs from the store in the living room, Philomena was chit-chatting with Santo's wife, Donata. Suddenly they heard all the shouts coming from below the windows. They quickly went downstairs and asked what had happened. Eugenio said to her, "Philomena, youa have adopted forty more sons." And with that, he went into the kitchen to ponder the decision he had made. Santo then tried to explain to Philomena how she inherited forty plus more sons. Then he gave Donata a wink and said to her, "Don't look so shocked, you just inherited forty plus nephews." And with that, he joined Eugenio in the kitchen while the two women continued to look at each other stunned.

Chapter 18

It was the second week of school and the first week of the building of the new clubhouse. Everything was going smoothly at school for Ralph and Coco. Ralph was practicing the saxophone with his group of musician friends for the big pep rally before the first home football game. The team won its opening game, beating Olean High School 42-17 in Olean. Coco had an outstanding game in which he rushed for 170 yards and scored four touchdowns.

Unfortunately, the building of the clubhouse was not going as smoothly as they had expected. Most of the guys were in high school and when they came home there was little time to help Santo Bonitatibus and some of the older guys work on the construction. The majority of the work had to be done on weekends. That is when the arguments and sometimes fights would break out.

One such incident happened when Al "Harpo" D'Alessandro was working on a frame for the wall with his brother, Arnold who they called "Dynamite." Harpo was holding up a two-by-four to be nailed into the partial frame. He told Dynamite to get a hammer and to lightly tap the nail into the board. Apparently, Dynamite did not understand what tapping lightly meant and swung the hammer with some velocity. That would not have been bad if he struck only the nail head, but instead poor Harpo's thumb and forefinger became part of the two-by-four.   With a howl and a string of obscenities about his brother's gender, girlfriend, and birth, he started to take a swing at him.

Before anyone could stop them, they were rolling around in the sawdust, kicking over cans of nails, wooden sawhorses, boards and a few of the guys. Poor Tommy Pepper was on the ladder painting when suddenly both brothers rolled into the ladder. Down came Tommy with a thump, followed by thick green paint that landed in his hair and on his face. Everyone just stared at Tommy as his face turned all green, with only the whites of his eyeballs showing.

Santo immediately stepped between the brothers, yelling at them to stop. He did not care about their safety but did care about them destroying the work they had done these last five days. The place was silent for a moment until everyone turned to look at Tommy, who was drenched in green paint and looked like a green-faced Al Jolson. At that moment, they all broke out into laughter; even Santo had a smile on his face.

Although Santo liked the boys, he was beginning to doubt if this was such a great idea after all. If they could get this clubhouse built before the winter and without anyone getting injured or killed, then he thought it might be worth it.

Today, the only thing Santo was thankful for was that Pop Galanti was working at the steel plant when this happened.

Chapter 19

"What ama gonna to do with you Gracie," screamed a very angry Frederico Marrano. "Youa drive me crazy." This was the second time in a few weeks that Gracie's father was upset with her. "I have a eight children and youa give me more trouble than the other seven puta together." In the room were Gracie's mom, Maria, and her two oldest siblings, Carmen and Anna. The rest were sent upstairs to their rooms, but the five of them sat at the top of the stairs trying to listen.

"This is the seconda time youa came home in trouble. What ama gonna do with you?" Frederico repeated as his face got redder and redder.

A couple of hours earlier, Gracie was escorted home from school by Mr. McHanon, the assistant principal of Bethlehem Park Elementary School. No one was home except for Gracie's mom, Maria, and two of the younger children, Luigi and Rosie. Luigi was too young for school and Rosie was sick. Federico had just come home after putting in twelve hours of work at the Bethlehem Steel plant and three hours at a part-time job. The prior evening, he went to the steel plant to see if they needed additional workers for the night shift. He was lucky and was picked by the foreman to work the long shift. After his shift, he went to Mazuca's Grocery Store, on Jackson Avenue in Bethlehem Park, where he worked three hours stocking the shelves.

When he got home, the last thing he wanted to hear was that his young daughter was in deep trouble at school.

His wife, Maria, who spoke little English but understood the language, told her husband in Italian what Mr. McHanon had said to her when he brought Gracie home. It seemed that Gracie had an altercation with the young Lenti boy, Mario, who was Sal Lenti's kid brother. Mario made some vulgar remarks to Gracie because of the incident at the Park Theater last month. He called Gracie "a bitch who should know her place and play with dolls instead of screwing around with men."

Neal, who was near Gracie standing in line to enter the school, overheard Mario say this to his older sister. Even though he was a foot shorter and a few years younger, he charged Mario and was yelling at him. Neal was too small for the older boy and with one hard shove from Mario, he toppled head over heels to the ground. Neal's head slammed on the concrete, which caused him to start bleeding.

Gracie, seeing this, went absolutely berserk. Mario was in the same grade as Gracie because he had failed two grades. He was bigger and heavier, but she charged at him fearlessly, swinging both her arms. His back hand met her upper lip, splitting the skin. She was bleeding but still kept coming toward him. He went to pick up a rock for protection when Gracie with all her strength kicked him in the groin, where a man's precious jewels are located. Mario went down like a sack of potatoes, groaning, crying and pleading for Gracie to stop kicking him.

By this time, Mr. McHanon came to break up what would have been a thrashing of Mario by a very angry and feisty Gracie. He quickly found out what happened from the other children and he sent Mario to his office while he took Gracie home.

After Maria told her husband the story, he shook his head and told her in Italian that this could be big trouble. He despised the father, Angelo Lenti, who he considered to be a low life son of a bitch. Lenti had four sons, Angelo Jr., who was in prison; Salvatore, who worked at the Park Theater; Mario, who Gracie had the altercation with at Bethlehem Park Elementary school and a toddler, Romeo.

The reason Federico despised the father was because he was a wife beater who abused his wife, Concetta, on a regular basis. There was not a week that went by that Federico, while working at Mazuca's Grocery Store, did not see Concetta without some sort of bruises on her face, arms or legs. Every time he would ask her what happened, she would meekly say that she fell or had some sort of accident. It was common knowledge that Angelo Lenti Sr. beat his wife for no reason at all except for pleasure.

Federico told his wife that he worried about Gracie because the Lenti men have no respect for women. He felt that what happened at the Park Theater and now at school would only fester in their warped minds. In Italian, Federico said, "If anything happens to my Gracie, I will kill the son of a bitches with my own hands."

Maria said that she was also worried about this family. She knew Concetta and liked her very much. She often told her she should leave her husband but it was to no avail because Concetta had nowhere to go. Unfortunately, this was her sad life.

Chapter 20

Federico stared at his daughter, who had her head bowed down and was very quiet. No one spoke until Gracie's older brother, Carmen, chimed in. "Papa, I know Gracie was wrong by fighting but she had no other choice but to protect Neal. That Lenti family is nothing but trouble. I know the older brother, Junior and he will probably be spending most of his life in jail. The other two will likely take the same path. Only the youngest, Romeo, may have a chance if he can get away from those hoods. As for Gracie, I would have done the same thing in her place."

Anna, Gracie's older sister who had a heart of gold and the patience of a saint, said, "Papa, please do not be mad at Gracie. You know she is a good daughter and very protective of our family, sometimes too protective. I get mad at her many times because of her feistiness and bullheadedness, but she means well and you can always depend on her for help when you need it the most. I do not speak just for me but for all of us."

Gracie's eyes started to swell, not because of what the punishment might be, but because of the love that her brother and sister had shown her during this ordeal. She spoke for the first time, raising her head and looking her father right in the eyes. "I'm sorry, Papa, but I would have done the same thing over again no matter what the consequences may have been."

Federico took a deep breath and looked at Maria, who nodded to him oh so slightly, knowing what he was going to say. "Gracie, I knowa you meant good. Youa tried to help your young brother. I lovea you for that but Ia also worry abouta you. The Lenti family is no like us. They no respect women, authority or their family. I worry more for you than anything."

"I love you, Papa, more than anything. But, if they ever do this to our family, you better worry more about them than about me," Gracie said with a little defiance.

Federico shook his head, looked at his wife and said, "Momma, Ima so tired that I cannot thinka straight. Maybe you shoulda have a talka with Gracie. You knowa woman to woman," as he gave a wink to his wife and young daughter. With that, he left to go to the bedroom to get a few hours of sleep. As he started for the stairs, he heard the shuffling of feet quickly on the landing running to the bedrooms. He smiled as he walked up the stairs knowing that his children were concerned about their sister.

Maria and her three children sat around the kitchen table. No one spoke for a few minutes. Finally, Gracie said, "Momma, I will apologize to Mr. McHanon tomorrow. I will do Neal's and Anna's chores for the rest of the month and I will try my best to behave and make you proud of me."

"You don't have to do my chores, Gracie, but I think you should try your best to behave and stay out of trouble," said Anna.

The only thing Carmen said to Gracie was that if she was approached by any Lenti, she better walk away, no matter what they said. But he also wanted her to tell him if anything did happen. He said, "Do you promise?" Gracie nodded yes.

Gracie's mother spoke in Italian and said, "Gracie, you are becoming a young woman. Young women do not beat up men, they marry them, have children, raise a family and become good mothers. If I wanted you to be a man, I would have named you Georgio."

Gracie, her sister and brother chuckled. Maria continued, "As for your punishment, I want you to go to confession and tell Father Vifredo what you have done. Perhaps his punishment would be worse than I could give."

Maria got up, left the table and went upstairs to make sure her husband was resting comfortably. Meanwhile, the rest of the children rushed downstairs and they all sat around the table gawking at Gracie and asking her what happened. Carmen and Anna told them all to hush up, everything has been settled and to mind their own business.

Everything was quiet for a moment until little Neal spoke up and said, "Gee, Gracie, the kick that you gave Mario would have been a forty yard field goal in football! Wow!" With that, everyone around the table started to laugh.

Chapter 21

The weather was quickly changing as summer had ended and the crisp fall air of October was beginning. The leaves started to change, but there was still some warmth during the daytime.

The clubhouse was nearly finished and there were just a few final touches that had to be made. It was remarkable that no other incidents occurred and that no one "killed" someone else as Santo predicted might happen. The grand opening was planned for November 1 and everyone was excited. Of course, Ralph, Coco, Tony Moretti, Gene Staniszewski, and the rest of core group were planning to have a gala affair.

Santo told Eugenio that he enjoyed working with the boys and thought this was a great idea that would keep them occupied and out of trouble during the winter months. Eugenio was secretly proud of these young men and what they had accomplished by building the clubhouse without money. They all pitched in to get the right materials from so many different places. Some of them brought wooden two-by-fours from old houses that were dilapidated; others would walk along the railroad tracks to pick up any scraps of wood or metal that could be used. Bricks were often found in buildings that were destroyed by fire or condemned by the city. Some of the building material could be credited to the Bethlehem Steel Corporation even though the company was unaware that it was donating to this clubhouse. Some of the young men found a way over or through the fence that surrounded the gigantic steel mill and were able to bring home some materials that they thought the steel plant would never miss.

All in all, they had a great time building the clubhouse at a very nominal cost.

The high school year so far had been uneventful, except for the football team having a tremendous season. Coco was having a fantastic year at running back and the team was 4-0 by mid October. The only glitch that happened was during the first week of October, when they had a pep rally in the high school gymnasium. This occurred when Ralph, Cswaykus, Bellini and Nowak were preparing to play music for the rally.

They had practiced for three weeks and were ready to play the high school fight song and then go into some big band music for entertainment. Ralph, along with John Cswaykus, was on the sax, Al Bellini was on the bass and Ted Nowak was on the piano. The group was excited and ready to bring down the house with their music. They all were a little anxious except for Nowak, who was ready to have a nervous breakdown. They convinced him that this was going to be a great time and that when the pep rally ended, the girls would consider him one of the most popular guys at school.

Miss Twist introduced the group to the audience in the gymnasium. Everyone was excited, not only for their first home football game, but because they were going to have some sweet-sounding music. The group began with the "fight song" of the Lackawanna Steelers. To everyone's surprise, it sounded more like a freight train screeching down the tracks. The group was so out of sync that it hurt the eardrums. Ralph, John and Al stopped, turned and looked at Ted. Without losing a beat, nervous Ted gave a sheepish smile and turned his sheet music right side up. With that, everyone laughed and cheered as they played the "fight song" to the loud singing of the audience.

To the treat of those at the assembly, the group was allowed to play the popular songs of the day such as, *Night and Day*, *Somebody Loves Me*, *How Deep is the Ocean* and everybody's favorite, *Minnie the Moocher*. Everyone was in a festive mood and even the teachers were tapping their feet and humming the songs. Ralph was in his glory as he was the lead sax in the melodies. At the end, they received a standing ovation from the audience. Ralph looked around and gave Nowak a wink and whispered, "Geez, now you're more popular than the quarterback." Ted just smiled and thought to himself that he was so glad this ordeal was over because he was afraid he had wet his pants.

After the assembly, Tony Moretti, Ziggy Pietrocarlo, Coco Freeman, Sobey Sobaszek and many of the female classmates went to the stage to compliment the group. Ralph and his fellow musicians were in "dreamland" and the more accolades they received, the larger their egos swelled. To their surprise, the football team came up to the stage and praised them and said they hoped they would come to the game to cheer them on. As the football team exited the gymnasium, most of the girls followed them out. Ralph turned to Ted Nowak and said, "At least we had a brief moment of glory!"

Chapter 22

The theme of the gala clubhouse opening was going to be "Halloween in November." The guys all voted that they should celebrate their new clubhouse on the first Saturday in November. This was the day after the football game between the two steel city rivals, Lackawanna High School and Scranton High School of Pennsylvania. The suggestion came from Doc and at first everybody thought that it was a dumb idea. They argued why not have the opening on Halloween which was only a week away. Doc then gave his reasons for his suggestion.

For all the crazy things that Doc said in the past, everyone got a new respect for his way of thinking. He reasoned that this would be a great time to have another Halloween party because it would be right after the biggest game of the season in football. If Lackawanna won, the celebration would be fantastic. He also stated that usually everyone is at other Halloween parties on the actual date and that would take some of the glamour away from their grand opening. He continued to state that this would be their own special day and everyone could wear their costumes again. But most of all, he explained, it would be a reason to keep the place decorated with low lighting so it would be hard to see what everybody was doing. He also thought it would be dark enough for him to get a little romance from Penelope in the corner of the room. He said trying to rhyme his words, "I plan to be dressed in a long, dark robe… where it would hide my 'big dong'… waiting for the romantic song." Everyone knew Doc was not a great poet, but he got his message across.

That sold the guys and they all started to have fantasies of this gala event where they would be in costumes and no one would know who was doing what to whom. *Ah… Doc sometimes can have some wonderful ideas*, they all thought.

The preparation started as they were getting their clubhouse ready for the gala event. They hung streamers, brought in balloons, put up Halloween paraphernalia and made sure some of the windows were covered with black paper to ensure that it would be darker than usual. The invitations were sent out by word of mouth and they agreed to make sure that there were more girls than guys invited. Coco was in charge of asking only certain members of the football team since they did not want to have too much competition for the girls.

Ralph and Paul Petti were in charge of the entertainment, which was anything from music and dancing to party games. Tony and Carmen Moretti were in charge of the guest list. Everyone was to report to them and tell them who they invited. The Carestio, Pietrocarlo and Renzi brothers along with Tom Pepper were in charge of the refreshments. This group was given this assignment because their fathers made the best homemade wine in the First Ward. The rest of the guys were assigned to either decorating or cleanup the next day.

Gene Staniszewski and "Boots" Ginnetti suggested that everyone should chip in to get a gift of appreciation for Mom and Pop Galanti and Santo and Donata Bonitatibus for making the clubhouse possible. Everyone thought it was a great idea and gave Steve Popich and Mickey Bracci the job of getting the gifts. Even though no one had much money, they were willing to contribute …that is unless Steve and

Mickey could use their ingenuity to get a great gift at a very low cost. Anything was possible with these two.

Gene, Tony, Coco and Ralph went to see Mom and Pop Galanti to personally invite them to the gala opening. They also went to see Santo and Donata Bonitatibus with the same invitation. They explained that they did not have to spend a long time there but all the members wanted to thank them. They diplomatically told them that there would be no need for them to stay all night long because they knew they probably had better things to do. Their worst nightmare was that Pop Galanti and the others would be having so much fun, they would stay till the end! Ralph suggested that Saturday morning, they each should go to church to say a little prayer that this would not happen. They all agreed!

Chapter 23

It was almost dusk, right around dinnertime, when Angelo Lenti Sr. was looking out from his porch on Madison Avenue. His wife, Concetta, was preparing dinner while their young toddler, Romeo, was taking a nap. Angelo was talking with his two sons, Salvatore and Mario, drinking his homemade Dago red wine and telling them about how he got screwed today at Bethlehem Steel. He was standing in line this morning expecting to be called into work by the foreman. Instead the foreman picked that asshole Galanti. He failed to tell his kids that he was still inebriated from the night before and he could hardly stand.

Crossing the street at Madison Avenue while going home with her sisters was Gracie Marrano. Angelo, who was feeling no pain from the Dago red, smiled at his son Mario and said, "Was that the little bitch that beat the shit out of you?" Mario's face turned red. He had a few glasses of wine so he felt no inhibitions and told his father, "Screw you." In one motion, Angelo turned and punched his son in the face, which sent him flying across the porch. His other son, Salvatore, started laughing hysterically, whereupon the father turned and gave him a backhand across the face that sent him in the other direction.

"What the hell are you laughing about? This is the same little bitch that kicked you in the nuts and sent you crying like a baby." Both

Mario and Sal hated their father but hated Gracie even more for causing this indignity to them.

As they got up, their father pointed and asked, "Wouldn't you like to get even with that little bitch?"

"Yeah, but how?" said Mario.

"Well, Halloween is in a few days, maybe she will give us a trick and we could give her a treat," he said, pointing down to his crotch. Both boys started laughing and forgot about the slaps and only thought how nice it would be to get even with her.

Concetta overheard the conversation and became very frightened. She knew the Marrano family and liked Frederico and Maria, who were always kind to her. As she called her husband and two sons in for dinner, she asked if she could speak to her husband in private.

"Angelo," she said very timidly. "Maybe it is not a good idea to put those thoughts in our sons' heads. I know you were only joking but they might take you seriously."

Without any hesitation, Angelo gave her a very hard slap that sent her to the floor and then for good measure gave her a quick kick in the thigh and told her to mind her own goddamn business and get the dinner on the table.

The two boys, who saw their mother get hit and kicked, just stood there nonchalantly. The only reaction they had was to seat themselves at the table and get ready to eat. Their mother slowly got up, limped to the stove and served dinner. She did not eat with them. As an excuse, she said she had to wake up Romeo and tend to him.

As they were eating, Angelo chastised his sons for what occurred and said that this would have never happened to them if their brother, Junior, was here and not in prison. He said, "Your brother,

Junior, was too smart to be fooled by that little Marrano tramp."
Further, he stated that the Galanti kid would be missing his testicles. He
looked at both of them and said, "I wish you had the balls of your
brother."

The two did not say anything, did not look up or make a sound,
for they knew if they did, he would cause them more pain than what he
did to their mother.

After they finished eating, Angelo proceeded to go out on the
porch again with his Dago red to continue drinking and belching. His
wife came downstairs with little Romeo to feed him and clean up the
kitchen. The two boys did not even acknowledge their mother as she
came in the room with the baby and they went outside in the backyard
to play horseshoes.

Lenti sat on his porch and started to feel sorry for himself. He
thought... *life is really screwing me over*. His oldest son, his namesake
who they called Junior, was more like him. He would be out of prison
in a couple of weeks. He was found guilty of beating his girlfriend.
Apparently, a young man was looking at Junior's girlfriend in a way
that he thought was too friendly. Instead of confronting the young
man, he stormed out of the establishment dragging his girlfriend with
him. After they turned the corner and were on the side of the building,
he began slapping and punching her, telling her that she was a whore
and that she was flirting with that punk. A group of guys leaving the
establishment heard the commotion and went to take a look. They
yelled, "What the hell's going on?" and with one last punch in the girl's
face, Junior turned around and ran. Cops were called and found him
hiding in his father's shed, where they arrested him.

Sitting there reminiscing about his son, Angelo thought how
bitches have caused problems for him and his sons. He thought his

wife was useless and only good for cooking, cleaning and pleasuring him when he wanted his physical needs satisfied. He thought that once Junior came home, things would be looking up for him.

Chapter 24

It was the day before Halloween and Ralph and the guys were getting the clubhouse decorated for the gala opening the following week. The theme "Halloween in November" really became popular with the guys and Doc was receiving accolades from everyone on his ingenuity and creativity for coming up with this great idea.

Gene Staniszewski and Coco were in deep conversation in the corner of the room. Ralph went up to them and asked what was going on. Coco said, "Raffs, we're thinking of giving this club a name and we thought it would be only fitting if we named it 'The Galanti Club' in respect to your father." Ralph was a little surprised by the nice gesture and told them that his father would be very proud.

With that, Gene called out to all the guys working on decorating the clubhouse to stop what they were doing and sit down because he wanted to talk to them about giving it a name. Gene and Coco gave all the reasons why they should call it the Galanti Club. They said that Pop Galanti gave them the room for free, that they always hung around the store and that they would never get kicked out because Ralph is in the club.

They all agreed that this was a great idea. But many wanted to make it more personal. Some suggested the Galanti Fighting Club. Others suggested the Galanti Italian Club or the Galanti "Tough Sons of Bitches" Club. Doc came up with the name the "Galanti Black Hand Club."

"Doc, you dumb son of a bitch," said Ziggy. "That's another name for the Mafia and we will be raided every week and poor Pop Galanti might be thrown in jail."

That name was voted down quickly. Doc, even though he thought it was a great name, didn't get upset because they did like his "Halloween in November" idea.

After a few minutes of going through social club, dance club and a number of other names, Lou Fistola said, "Hey, let's call it the Galanti Athletic Club since most of us play sports." That was music to their ears, for they all thought they were great athletes. Gene chimed in and said, "Let's add social to it and make it an athletic and social club." He also said that he thought the girls would be impressed "because we're not only jocks, but jocks that have some class."

There were mixed feelings about including the word "social" in the name. After a few minutes of discussion, Tony Moretti chimed in and said, "Let's call it the Galanti Athletic Association. I think the word association adds a little class to it."

Stan Sobaszek added, "Tony, I think you got it. That has a ring to it and we could nickname us the 'GAA'." This was the first name that they all agreed upon. Tony made a suggestion that at the next formal meeting, the membership should vote on the name. Everyone was in favor.

Gene told them they would have a meeting two days after Halloween to officially name the club and send out flyers for the "Halloween in November" gala. With that, everyone got up and started to decorate the clubhouse. They wanted to make this a Halloween party that everyone would remember.

In the meantime, Angelo Sr. was talking to his sons Sal and Mario, working on a plan to get even with the Marrano girl, who caused them so much embarrassment. They devised a plan that on Halloween night, when the kids were trick or treating, they would somehow lure Gracie away from her sisters, who usually always accompanied her. The plan was that one of them would dress up in a costume and pretend he was Ralph and lure her into a dark area between the houses. Then the other brother would grab her from behind, muffle any screams with his hand and make sure that she did not make a sound. Then all three would have their pleasure with her, Sal, Mario and Angelo Sr.

The father thought this would be a great plan but they definitely had to make sure that they were dressed in costumes and could not be identified. If Gracie screamed, they would have to punch her and knock her out. Angelo Sr. stated that it might not be as much fun if she is not conscious when they satisfy themselves with her, but they would finally get even with the bitch.

The three of them could not wait until Halloween night.

Chapter 25

It was Halloween night and every child in the city was preparing to go out for "trick or treating." These Halloween customs were celebrated by the Irish and Celtics. Many of these immigrants came to America and settled in Lackawanna and Western New York, bringing their traditions with them. Even though it was not yet popular throughout the United States, it was celebrated in Western New York and especially Lackawanna. Halloween costumes were traditionally modeled after supernatural figures such as monsters, ghosts, skeletons, witches, and devils.

Since this was the Depression era, many children dressed as beggars or in homemade costumes that their mothers made. The most popular costume figures were Frankenstein, Dracula, zombies and mummies, all of which were movie hits during that era. There were also comedy characters such as the Marx Brothers, Charlie Chaplin and, of course, plenty of clowns. It seemed like every other male youngster was dressed up like Al Capone from the popular movie "Scarface." Many of the young girls were dressed up as princesses, angels and movie stars but many still loved to be "monsters" for one night.

Ralph, his sisters and his brother dressed in costumes but did not go trick or treating. They stayed at the store to help their parents pass out candy to all the children who came in with costumes. This was a favorite place for the children because they would be treated with bits of candy from the store. Also, the Galanti children did not mind it because they dressed in costume to celebrate Halloween. They also enjoyed putting on a scary show as they passed out candy to the young children. The only one who was disappointed that he could not go out trick or treating with the other children was Johnny. His parents would not let him go unless Ralph went with him but Ralph was too busy in the store. To remedy this, Pop Galanti promised Johnny that he could have anything in the store he wanted the next day. The only things he said that were off limits were cigars and cigarettes.

In the Marrano household, there was a problem. As usual, Gracie was on a short rope with her father, with all the problems she had caused from the theater and school episodes. Her father wanted her to dress up, not as a monster, but a princess. He was tired of seeing kids look like horror creatures instead of beautiful children. He told Gracie he wanted her to dress up as a princess; Gracie wanted to dress up as a vampire. Her father said, "Youa dress up like a pretty princess that you are or you don't go out to trick or treat." Gracie, being her stubborn self said, "No, I want to be a vampire." Her father said, "No, youa princess." Gracie said, "No Papa, a vampire." That Halloween night, Gracie stayed home.

As the two Lenti brothers were watching the Marrano house, waiting for Gracie to leave, they only saw her two sisters, Josephine and Carmela, leave with their brother, Neal. Gracie was nowhere to be found. They waited near the house for over an hour and finally went home to tell their old man she did not leave the house.

Angelo Sr. said, "God damn it" and continued to swear for the next couple of minutes. He looked at his boys and said, "Your brother Junior should be home in a couple of weeks. Then, not only will we get even with that little bimbo, but also with that melon john lover Galanti."

He turned and yelled, "Concetta, get your ass over here and bring us some of that 'giggle juice' that old man Yano brought over yesterday."

Concetta said, "I'll be right with you Angelo. The baby is starting to cry and I want to see what's the matter." The two boys watched as their father turned around, went into the kitchen and smacked their mother across the face.

"When I tell you now, I don't mean 10 minutes from now! Get your ass downstairs in the basement and bring up the bottle. If the baby cries, let him cry."

Angelo turned around and returned to his sons and said, "Pretty soon, these bitches will want to be the head of families. A little smack always discourages that thought." Then he started chuckling as they sat down waiting for the homemade whiskey.

Chapter 26

The day has finally come... Ralph thought. "Halloween in November" was going to be that night at their new club in back of the store and Ralph was excited. That afternoon, Lackawanna High School played an exciting game against Scranton High School, winning 28-27. Coco ran for four touchdowns in one of the best games in his career. He was excited because there were representatives from the Negro colleges in the South at the game. Coach Fisher gave him the game ball after the victory and said that this was the best game he had ever seen a running back perform. Coco had more than 200 yards rushing and had a kickoff return for a touchdown.

Coco met Ralph around six o'clock that evening in the clubhouse with several of their friends making sure that everything was in order for the big party. The clubhouse was like a haunted house with streamers, skeletons, balloons and Halloween decorations everywhere. Ralph turned to Coco and said, "How do you feel because you look like a wreck?" Coco smiled and said, "If I could have a game like this every week, I would feel like a million dollars and I wouldn't care how I looked. Besides, why do you care how I look, do you want to kiss me?"

Ralph had one gesture. He put his middle finger up and gave Coco the "bird." They both laughed.

The party would begin at seven o'clock and some of the guys were starting to come into the clubhouse. They were going to help set up the beverage areas and bring in the food prepared by parents who volunteered. There was a punch bowl that was filled with fruit juices. Doc looked around and snuck in with two gallons of Dago red that his father made. He poured one gallon into the large punch bowl and hid the other gallon in the corner behind the radiator. He thought that the girls who attended would either be loose for the night or sick to their stomachs. He was hoping for the former because he was dreaming of Penelope. He had a crush on Penelope since grammar school. Penelope was shy but he thought she kind of liked him. Doc thought what she needed was something to loosen her up.

One of the guys brought in his Dad's Victrola (a record player) with several albums of songs. Many were the romantic type for later in the evening but a few were a little more fast paced for the beginning. All the guys had high hopes and made sure that after an hour of music, drinking, eating and fast dancing, the girls would be softened up.

Around 6:30 in the evening, the clubhouse was filled with horny guys looking at each other thinking...*where the hell are the girls?* Ralph said to Coco, "What an embarrassment. We're starting a new club, have a new clubhouse, have all this food and drink and nobody attends but these horny guys. Is this what girls think of us?"

It was like magic. As soon as Ralph said the last sentence, in came six of his female schoolmates. Ten minutes later, a half dozen more came and then the onslaught started. The party began! Definitely the females outnumbered the guys and to no surprise, all the guys had big smiles on their faces. The music was playing, the dancing started and the fun began. Mr. and Mrs. Galanti and Mr. and Mrs. Bonitatibus came in to say hello and everyone gave them a resounding round of applause. Pop Galanti smiled and welcomed everyone to the new clubhouse. With that, he took a cup, scooped it into the punch bowl and gave a salute to everyone. Doc's mouth dropped and he was looking for the quickest exit. He thought that the party would end and that he would be crucified by the guys for spiking the punch.

Pop Galanti raised the toast, said a couple of words and took a sip from the cup. Doc watched his face and to his surprise, Pop Galanti did not change his expression as he downed the punch. He wished everyone a great party and he left with his wife and the Bonitatibus's to go to the front of the store. As he was leaving, Doc came up to him and said, "Sorry, Mr. Galanti. It was me that added the little spirit to the punch." To Doc's surprise, he winked at him and stated, "I wasa younga man too, once a long, long time ago. Justa behave." With that, Doc was so relieved that he shook Mr. Galanti's hand and gave Philomena a kiss.

As soon as the Galantis and the Bonitatibuses left, and the door behind them closed, it was like magic; half the lights in the clubhouse went off. The music was more subdued and the romantic singing of the crooner Bing Crosby filled the clubhouse. Ralph got in the center of the room and asked everyone to get a cup of punch for a toast. He said, "I would like to welcome all our guests to our wonderful new clubhouse. Some of you may not know that we have started a club with members that have been friends for years and years. This is the first of many, many parties we hope to have. I am honored, along with my family, that the members of this new club are calling it The Galanti Athletic Association. Please raise your cups to salute our new club, our members and our beautiful guests and some of the few handsome guys we invited to our inaugural party. Salute!"

With that, everyone raised their cup and drank the whole contents in one gulp. Doc looked around and saw Penelope guzzle the drink down and refill her cup again. He thought… *I hope my "dong" is going to have company tonight*!

Chapter 27

It was 7 o'clock Sunday morning and Ralph woke up with a headache. He quickly went to the john and relieved himself of the excess punch and thought... *what a great party*! The party did not end until midnight and that was late considering most of the girls had to be home by 11:30 in the evening. But nobody seemed to care because everyone seemed to be having a great time, even though a few of the girls and guys were outside the clubhouse puking their guts out. The nice thing, Ralph thought, was that there were no incidences. No fights, no vulgar shouts and no taking advantage of the girls that were drunk. The only one who complained just a little was Doc. After the girls left, he told the guys that he had a good time but it could have been better if his "dong" got acquainted with Penelope's hand. Unfortunately for Doc, Penelope was one of the girls who spent most of her time outside puking.

Ralph went downstairs while his siblings were still snoozing. He was going to have an early breakfast and meet some of the guys who volunteered to clean the clubhouse that morning. As he went into his kitchen, his mom and dad were already having their breakfast and told him how proud they were that everyone at the party last night behaved. Ralph looked at his dad and said, "The reason is because they were scared to death of you." That's when his mom started chuckling and his father said, "That'sa not a nice. I'ma calm and a nice man."

Ralph responded, "I know, Pa… but that's when you're not angry!" His father smiled and told him to eat before he did get angry.

Around 8:30 in the morning, Coco and a group of the guys came in to start the cleanup. Philomena asked Coco where his mother was and he said she would be here soon. Then Coco and the guys followed Ralph into the clubhouse, ready to clean up the mess from the night before.

Crystal came into the store. It was her custom since her husband was killed in a steel plant accident to visit Philomena every Sunday. As they sat in the rocking chairs behind the candy counter, Philomena noticed that something was on Crystal's mind. She said to Crystal, "What's wrong?" Crystal replied that nothing was wrong and why did Philomena think something was bothering her. Philomena said, with a smile on her face, "I have been with you every Sunday for the last few years and I know you like you were my sister. Something is on your mind and it is worrying you."

Crystal started to think that this woman was more of a sister to her than a friend. She knew her better than Crystal knew herself. She said to Philomena, "Well, there is a little thing bothering me. Coco is having a great football season and his football coach, Mr. Fisher, said that he has a good chance of getting a scholarship to one of the southern Negro colleges. He's planning to have him visit Tuskegee University. The university has invited Coco to come down there to see their school and watch the Turkey Day Classic against Alabama State University. The school will pay for Coco's travel expenses and provide him food and board for the few days that he will be there. The problem I have is that I want to send Coco there with the appropriate clothing. He never had a suit except for the clothes his late dad had, which are now too small for him. I do not want to have him be embarrassed. He keeps on telling me that this is not a problem and that they are looking more at his football ability than the clothes he is wearing.

"You know, Philomena, I am so proud of him and I know he would never complain about anything. I just feel so bad because I want to send him there feeling very confident and proud." Philomena responded, "Crystal, clothes do not make a man. Your Coco is more of a man at this age than most of the kids who hang around the store."

Crystal smiled and thanked Philomena for her complimenting Coco but still she felt sad that she couldn't do more for her son. Philomena excused herself and told Crystal that she would be right back as she went upstairs to the living quarters above the store. She came back five minutes later, sat down and told Crystal that there was a store on Abbott Road in South Buffalo called Wellington's Haberdashery. "They sell everything from fedoras, socks and underwear to full suits at a very reasonable cost," she said. With that, Philomena pulled out three ten dollar bills and handed them to Crystal.

Crystal was stunned and started crying but gave the money back to Philomena. She said, "I love you. I consider you family. I did not come here expecting you to do this. I came here because I needed someone who I deeply respect and love to listen to me. I appreciate your kindness but I cannot accept it."

Philomena looked at her and said, "I too think of you as part of my family and family helps family. Whatever Coco does and becomes, we will be proud of him because we think of him as part of our family. Please take the money, go to the store and make us all proud of Coco."

With that, Crystal started crying like a baby, kissing and hugging Philomena, who was also starting to cry.

Eugenio Galanti had just walked into the store from the kitchen and saw the two women crying and said, "What'sa happening, why are you crying? Was the store robbed?"

Both women looked at each other and started laughing hysterically. Eugenio shook his head, said something in Italian and walked into the kitchen to have lunch.

Chapter 28

Crystal walked home after her visit with Philomena. She could not believe what her best friend had done for her. Her eyes were still glassy from all the tears of joy and she couldn't wait to get home to plan her trip to the Wellington Haberdashery that week.

Later that afternoon, Coco returned home after helping clean the clubhouse. He left a little earlier than the rest because he needed to study for an exam that he would be taking later in the week. Coach Fisher told him that it was important that his marks were good because athletic ability will get his foot in the door, but his academics will get him a seat in the classroom.

Crystal said, "I have some great news. I am going to the Wellington Haberdashery on Wednesday to buy you a suit for your trip to Tuskegee University. I want you to look proud, handsome and confident as you meet those coaches and teachers at the college. Do you think you could come with me after school to try on some of the suits?"

First thing Coco said was, "No way, Mom. I'm not going to have you pay for a suit. I'll make do with the clothes I have." Crystal looked at Coco. She was trying to think of how to explain to him how she got the money for the clothes. He was a very proud young man and she didn't know how he would react to her receiving this money from his best friend's mother.

Crystal looked her son straight in the eye and said, "Coco, I love you more than anything in this world. There are things that I can do for you and there are things that I cannot do for you. One of them is to buy you a new suit. I would have worked my hands to the bone if I had enough time to save money to do this but unfortunately, your trip is only around the corner. I was in conversation with your best friend's mom, Philomena Galanti, when she asked me why I looked so sad. Because she is not only my best friend, but also my most cherished confidant, I told her what was bothering me. She's always been a sounding board for me when I have a problem. I love her as a sister and a friend."

The tears were swelling in Crystal's eyes when she told him what Philomena did and why she did it. "Coco, she loves us like we were her family and she gave me money to buy you the suit and clothes that you may need. She told me that she wanted to be as proud of you as I am and there is no way that you are going down there to visit those people at the college without proper clothing. I refused to take the money and she looked me in the eye and said, 'Your family is my family and my family is your family. We do these things for family.'" At the end of the sentence, Crystal was balling like a baby and Coco had tears in his eyes.

Coco said, "Mom, I will not only make you proud but I will make Mrs. Galanti proud too." With that, Coco took his school books and went into the next room to finish his studying. There was no way he would get anything less than straight A's on his exams.

On Wednesday afternoon, Crystal met Coco at the high school. Coco was in a very good mood because he thought he did very well on the exam that day. He felt everything was on the upbeat. Now here he was meeting his beautiful mother to go for a walk to the haberdashery in South Buffalo to buy his first suit.

Crystal and Coco walked through the well-manicured park behind the high school on their way to Wellington's Haberdashery on Abbott Road. The trek would take them about ninety minutes. It was a nice fall day with the colorful autumn leaves still on most of the trees.

Coach Fisher excused Coco from practice that day, telling him that he deserved a break since he has been the workhorse for the team for the last few weeks. Coco did not know that his mother had spoken to Coach Fisher. Crystal explained to Coach Fisher that she wanted to buy Coco his first suit for his trip to Tuskegee University. She wanted her son to look impressive to the university and coaches who were considering giving him a scholarship. Coach Fisher smiled and said it was no problem and that Coco needed a rest anyway for the big game coming up at the end of the week.

During their walk, they talked about so many things, from the Galanti family to what college life would be like and how it would be living away from home for the first time. Before they knew it, they were a block away from the haberdashery and they both agreed that was the fastest ninety minute walk ever. Coco was so excited. He had never bought a suit and he was never in a clothing store.

As they approached the Wellington Haberdashery, the front window displayed so many beautiful items, from clothing to jewelry to shoes on the mannequins in the windows. Coco chuckled and told his mother, "All the mannequins are white, how do you think I would look in them being dark?" Crystal smiled and said, "You could be dark, white, purple, orange and maybe a little avocado and you still would look handsome in those clothes."

They walked into the store. Coco stopped in his tracks when he saw a big, black man standing behind the counter. Crystal was also stunned. She had never seen such a handsome man that could compare to her late husband. They both stared at him as he smiled and asked if he could help them. They were both tongue tied. Crystal finally said, "We would like to have the owner or maybe a salesperson help us buy my son a suit. Could you get us someone who is in charge?" Horatio smiled and said, "No problem." He then walked in the back of the store, came back out again and said, "Can I help you?" with a big smile on his face.

Crystal started laughing so hard that Coco and Horatio joined in. Crystal said that she was sorry but she didn't expect him to be the owner. Horatio said, "No, I am not the owner but the manager of the store. My good friend, Mr. Wellington, is the owner. Can I help you?"

Chapter 29

After the good laugh that they had, Crystal became serious and asked the salesman his name. "My name is Horatio and how could I be of service to you?" Crystal thought... *oh my God, a handsome well-built Negro who speaks educated English and has the first name of Horatio must be from some fairytale.* Horatio said again, "May I help you?" Crystal came out of her daydream and said, "Oh, ah, ah, yes. I would like to buy my son a suit and then she said with pride, "He is going to go on a trip in the next few weeks to visit a southern Negro school to play football on a scholarship. I want him to look handsome, feel confident and to tell you the truth, 'knock their socks off'."

"Your son does not need clothing to look handsome because he is handsome and from what I hear from the football crowd that comes into the store, he is a helluva player." Horatio could not say anything more complimentary to make Crystal beam with pride. Even if Horatio told her how beautiful she looked, she would have taken it with a grain of salt, but talking about her Coco made Horatio number one in her mind.

Horatio turned and said, "Sir, can you step over here and I will start taking some measurements and we can look for suits that will fit you." Coco said, "Please call me Coco and not sir... it makes me feel like an old man who came here with his mom to be dressed." With a smile and laugh, Horatio said, "Okay, Coco, let's get to work and take some measurements."

After the measurements, Horatio went into the back room and brought out four suits that he thought would fit. Two were brown, one being a pinstripe and one solid; one was a dark blue and one was a silk gray that was absolutely beautiful. Coco tried them all on and they all seemed to fit with only minor alterations that would have to be made. Horatio asked both Coco and his mother which one would they liked. Before Crystal could say a word, Coco blurted out, "I like them all but how much does each one cost?" Crystal turned and said, "Hold on, young man, we are not looking at cost but what you look best in," and she turned to Horatio and said, "I love the gray silk suit." Horatio agreed with the choice, telling her that they just got it in the store last week and it probably would have been sold by now if he had it displayed on one of the mannequins. He also stated that this suit fit him the best with only very minor alterations.

"So be it," said Crystal. "It is final. We are going to take the gray silk suit but I will also need a shirt, a tie and a nice pair of shoes to go along with the outfit."

Coco looked at his mother stunned and asked if he could speak to her in private. They went over to the side, out of earshot of Horatio and Coco said with anxiety, "Please Mom, this will cost more than you think. I know Mrs. Galanti gave you some money to help but she did not give you the bank!"

Crystal reassured her son that she had been saving money and with the money she received from Philomena, she would have more than enough. What she told Coco was semi-truthful because she only had ten dollars extra that she had saved and she was hoping that it would be enough. But she knew in her heart that it probably would not be enough and she would then ask Horatio if she could pay him part of the balance every week. Coco was skeptical but he did not want to embarrass his mother in front of the manager so he just nodded and said nothing.

Crystal told Horatio that everything was all set, that they would take the gray silk suit. Horatio told Coco to stand on the little box while he tried on the suit for him to make the correct alterations. After marking where the alterations were to be made, he went into the back room and brought out a few shirts and ties that he thought would go along with the suit. He also brought a pair of size eleven black shoes for Coco to try on.

Crystal picked out a beautiful white shirt with a gray and red striped tie. The first shoes that Coco tried on fit perfectly and they were as comfortable as his football spikes. Horatio took the shirt, tie and shoes and placed them on the side. He said it would be about a week to have the alterations done. Crystal told him that would be all right because Coco would not be leaving until a couple of days before Thanksgiving.

Crystal then turned to Coco and said, "Would you mind going down the street and picking up a few pieces of fruit from the huckster I saw parked on the side? Maybe a few apples, oranges and grapes." She gave him a dollar and told him she would meet him there on her way back. Coco said, "Sure, Mom" and took the dollar and went off to find the huckster.

After Coco left, she turned to Horatio and said, "Can you tell me how much this will cost?" The way she said it, Horatio knew she had some concerns. He began to add up the total of each item and turned to her and said, "It will be $46.40. This is the breakdown, $32.00 for the complete suit; $4.00 for the leather shoes; $1.05 for the shirt; $1.00 for the belt; 85 cents for silk necktie; 75 cents for the socks and the dress coat is $6.75. This was ten dollars less than the actual cost but he did not tell her. Crystal did not say anything and just looked at the items thinking about how she could pay for them. Before she said anything, Horatio asked her how much money she had. Pulling out her purse, she said, "I have $40.00 but I need $2.00 for some grocery items on the way back home. Could I give you $38.00 now and pay you the rest on a weekly basis until it is paid in full?"

Horatio looked at her, not as a manager or a salesman, but as someone who had never seen such a beautiful woman and caring mother in all his life. He smiled and said, "Here's what I will do. I will take $38.00 now and you could pay me the balance a little at a time on a weekly basis. It will be up to you as to how much you can afford each week and how long it will take. You look like an honest woman and by the way, I also want to see Coco knock their socks off at the southern Negro school when he gets there."

Again, Crystal was amazed at how lucky she was. First, with her best friend giving her money to buy the suit and now this wonderful man, whom she did not even know, was willing to help her Coco achieve his dream. Without any more provocation, she thanked Horatio and started crying, to which Horatio did not know what to do!

Chapter 30

It was Saturday morning and it had been one week since the "Halloween Party in November".   Ralph got up, went into the bathroom and looked in the mirror. He looked at himself and thought... *what a week.* The party was a success last Saturday; there were no problems; the guys cleaned up the clubhouse and made it spic and span and he aced the exam on Wednesday. His father and mother were happy that everyone behaved and when he told them on Friday that he had aced his exam, his mother gave him a kiss and his father lit up a stogie and patted him on the back. He then said, "That'sa my boy. I'ma proud of you. Now, go in the back in your new clubhouse and clean up the mess that Teddy made on the floor." Ralph thought...*I knew I should have never gotten that damn flea-bitten mutt for Johnny for his Christmas present last year. That's all I have been doing is cleaning up his crap.*

With that, he went for the pail and filled it with soap and water, got the mop and went into the back room thinking that his brother should be doing this. But since Johnny was young (and according to Ralph, his dad's favorite) these chores were placed on him. His sisters were in charge of cooking and helping his mother with household chores and he ended up doing the rest. Of course, Johnny would be sitting on his father's knee, taking all this in and smiling while eating ice cream. Ralph thought....*one of these days!*

Meanwhile, in Bethlehem Park, there was a celebration at the Lenti family home. Junior was released from prison and was able to hitch a ride back to Lackawanna. His father was excited, along with his brothers, awaiting his return. Although his mother loved him very much, Concetta also feared her son. He had a worse temper than his father and had a mean streak. She remembered several years ago when she yelled at him for pushing her younger son, Mario, into the kitchen table. They were arguing and Junior lost his temper. He not only pushed his brother into the table, but punched him squarely in the face. She stepped in and grabbed Junior's arm, yelled and as he turned to face her, he slapped her across the face, knocking her on the floor next to Mario.

Concetta was stunned but was more upset when her husband came into the room, saw Mario and her on the floor and turned to Junior and said, "You are really becoming a man now." They both turned, laughed and went to the refrigerator for Dago red and went out on the porch. Concetta got up and helped her son Mario, who was crying. She got some ice to put on his eye, which was beginning to swell. She thought in her misery...*I married evil and I gave birth to evil.*

Angelo Sr. was looking down the street and his eyes widened when he saw his son approaching. He ran down the steps toward his son yelling his name over and over. Sal and Mario heard their father yelling and they ran out the door to greet their brother. Only Concetta and the baby, Romeo, stayed in the house. Concetta was holding Romeo and saying quietly to him, "Please, please, please be different. Please love instead of hating. I failed your brothers but I will not fail you."

The four of them entered the house, laughing, yelling and celebrating Junior's return. The father yelled to Concetta, "Hey you, get your son some food. Better yet, get your ass down in the cellar and bring up the bottle of Dago red I've been saving for Junior." And with that, they all went into the living room. Junior did not even say hello to his mother but just nodded. He did not even recognize the baby, Romeo, but instead turned to his father and brother and said, "I'm so horny I could screw one of you." With that, they all laughed.

While they were drinking their Dago red, the father started to say how much they missed him and what had happened while he was gone. Angelo Sr. said that they had a lot of payback to do, especially with that little bitch Gracie Marrano and that asshole Galanti boy.

With that, Sal told Junior what happened at the Park Theater with the Marrano family and the Galanti kid. His version was completely different from what actually happened. In his version, he was the innocent good guy who got screwed by those assholes. Then Mario chimed in on what happened at school and told him how he tried to protect a young boy from that little bitch Gracie Marrano. He said that she was beating the young boy up and he stepped in to protect him when she kicked him in the nuts and hit him over the head with a stick. And Angelo Sr. finally said that he got screwed at the steel plant by old man Galanti. He was about to get picked to work but old man Galanti gave the foreman a couple of dollars so he chose him to work for that week in the steel mills.

Junior, hearing this, became infuriated. He said to his father and brothers, "It's time for payback. Those sons of bitches are going to pay for what they did to the Lenti family."

Chapter 31

The fall season was beginning to end more quickly than anticipated. November was becoming very cold as there was a quick drop in temperature. The northwest winds from Canada were blowing over Lake Erie; the mercury plunged below freezing and snow flurries were visible.

Coco was preparing for his trip to Tuskegee University. Coach Fisher and Coco's mother were able to convince the school administration to allow him to leave on Tuesday morning before Thanksgiving. He would miss all classes on Tuesday and Wednesday but would return to classes the following Monday. Coach Fisher knew how important it was for him to travel to Tuskegee University for a possible scholarship so he told Coco he would not be playing in the Lackawanna game that Saturday. He said that he was going to give Coco's backup, who was a freshman, some playing time in the game on Saturday following the holiday. That made Coco's decision to go a lot easier because he did not want to make the team think the trip was more important than the game. Coach Fisher told him that even if he stayed, Roy Braxton would be playing in his spot. He told Coco he wanted him healthy for the last game of the season against their archrival, the Tonawanda Raiders.

On the Friday before Thanksgiving, Horatio came to Crystal's home to deliver the suit and accessories for Coco. Earlier that week, she went to the haberdashery to make her weekly payment and asked if the suit was ready. Horatio told her almost but not to be worried because he would deliver it personally and make sure it fit properly. If there were any alterations necessary, he would do them at her house.

He arrived late Friday afternoon, driving Mr. Wellington's car. Wellington trusted Horatio and considered him a very close friend, especially after saving his daughter's life. When Horatio drove up in the sedan, the neighbors thought that the car was stolen. How could a black man own such a beautiful car? They continued to look out their windows as he walked up to Crystal's door carrying a large package. She met him at the door, smiled and let him in. Her nextdoor neighbor continued to look out the window for the entire duration of his stay.

Crystal invited Horatio into her living room and told him that Coco would be home shortly. He had a team meeting after school to discuss Saturday's opponent, Niagara Falls High School. She asked Horatio if he would like to have a cup of coffee or tea. Horatio smiled and told Crystal a cup of coffee would be fine. While Crystal went into the kitchen to make the coffee, Horatio started looking at the pictures that surrounded the room. The majority were either of Coco or Coco and her. There was one on the wall that was of a good-looking black man in a T-shirt and overalls. As he was staring at the picture, Crystal came in and said, "That is my late husband, Coco's father."

Horatio was a little embarrassed and said, "I'm sorry. I did not mean to stare at the pictures but I was just thinking what a handsome man he was. I do not wish to pry so forgive me for asking, but how did he die? He looks so young." Crystal put her head down and said very quietly, "He was killed at the steel plant. A steel beam that they were transporting to another section of the plant fell from the crane. It crushed him and he died, thank God, instantly." Horatio said, "Oh, I am so sorry. It must have been very difficult for you and Coco."

Crystal said, "It was very difficult for me but Coco was only eight and it was more difficult for him because he was close to his father." Horatio looked shocked and said, "You have been without a husband for all these years?" Crystal nodded. Just then to Horatio's relief, Coco came through the door yelling, "I'm home."

As he came into the living room, he said hello to Mr. Bottoms and there was a bright smile on his face when he asked if the suit was ready. Horatio smiled and said, "I am here to make sure that it fits perfectly. Here is the box with the suit, shirt, tie, and all the accessories. Go try them on and come in here and let's see how you look."

While Coco went into the bedroom to change, Horatio looked at Crystal and said, "Mrs. Freeman, you are an amazing woman. You have done a great job of raising a wonderful son." With that, Crystal gave a huge smile and excused herself as she told Horatio she was going to go in the kitchen to pour the coffee. She asked him if he would like cream and sugar and he told her just black.

Ten minutes later, Coco came out of the bedroom fully dressed in his new attire. His mother took a look and started crying like a baby. Coco said, "Oh no, not again."

She responded, "You look so handsome and grown up that I can't believe it is you." Coco responded, "It's me, all 205 pounds of football meat, ready to go down to see the coaches at Tuskegee. I hope they see me as a helluva football player and not some handsome black guy in a nice suit from the North."

Horatio told Coco, "Don't worry. They had coaches scouting you the last couple of games and there will probably be a couple of coaches here for tomorrow's game. They know you are a 'helluva football player.' Matter of fact, I believe they are going to stay here for the weekend and travel with you on the train to Alabama on Tuesday."

Coco thanked Horatio for doing such a good job on his suit and getting it ready for him on such short notice. His mother was still sobbing with pride but also turned to Horatio and thanked him for everything.

She asked Horatio if he would like to stay for dinner but he said he'd better get back with Mr. Wellington's car. Coco then chimed in and said, "Mr. Bottoms, I would be honored if you stay and have dinner with us. I would like to ask you some questions about Tuskegee University, especially since one of their coaches came to see me today at school. He mentioned that one of their prestigious alumni who played football for them was living in the area. His name happened to be Horatio Bottoms II."

With that, Crystal stopped sobbing, her eyes opened wide and she exclaimed, "What?"

Chapter 32

Crystal looked at Coco, then at Horatio and then back at Coco and said, "What did you say?" Coco told his mother that Mr. Bottoms went to Tuskegee University and was a star football player. For whatever reason he did not know, Mr. Bottoms quit the football team in his junior year but remained in school and graduated.

"I told the Tuskegee coach that I knew Mr. Bottoms. The coach said to me, 'I know that. It was Horatio who called up the college last week and told us more about you. Our head coach told me to come up to meet you personally and see if all the things that he said were true. So far, your attitude and marks are correct and now we have to see more of your football playing ability.' "

Crystal looked at Horatio and asked him if this was true. He nodded an embarrassing yes and said, "I'm sorry. I did not want to embarrass you and Coco. I told them this was a private matter. Apparently, they do not know the meaning of 'private.' Again, I am sorry."

"Sorry, sorry? Are you crazy?" With that she gave Horatio a big hug and a kiss on the cheek. Then regaining her senses, she backed away and said, "I'm sorry." Coco chimed in, "I'm sorry too. Sorry that we're not eating yet because I'm as hungry as a bobcat." He turned to Horatio and said, "Mr. Bottoms, it would be an honor to have you stay for dinner and besides there is so much I would like to ask you about the university."

Horatio stated, "Well, you twisted my arm and besides, I would love to stay for dinner." With that, Crystal excused herself and told them to relax in the living room and she would begin to prepare dinner. She said it would take approximately an hour. Coco said that would be great since he had so many questions to ask Mr. Bottoms that it would take up most of the time, if not all.

The first thing Horatio said to Coco was, "Please call me Horatio. Unfortunately, I do not have a nickname but you do not have to call me Mr. Bottoms. My momma named me that and I have no idea why. I used to get kidded a lot when I was young about my name, but after I won my first fight at the age of eleven, the kidding stopped and they just called me Horatio."

Coco laughed and thanked him and stated, "Please tell me all you can about Tuskegee University."

Horatio started with, "Coco, it is one of the first black colleges in our country. It had an unusual start. It was started by a former slave owner and a former slave. One of our most famous black heroes, Booker T. Washington, became its first teacher and president. Many times, he was called the founder. There is so much tradition and pride of our culture throughout the halls, buildings and campus of this great university. I am so proud to be a graduate of this school."

Horatio proceeded to describe all the successful graduates from his alma mater. After fifteen minutes of talking about all the educational values of the school, he stopped and took a sip of coffee, asked Coco if he had any specific questions and waited for him to answer, although he already knew. Coco smiled and said, "What about the football program?" Horatio smiled back, "Gosh, I almost forgot about that." And they both had a good chuckle. Horatio continued to say that they were one of the pioneers of football among Negro schools in the country.

The football program is very intense and the Golden Tigers had a winning tradition. He told Coco that the president of the university, Dr. Robert Moton, is so supportive of the team that he comes to every home game and visits the players in the locker room after the game to congratulate them, whether they won or lost. He even has an after season party for the players, coaches and their families.

He told Coco that Coach Cleveland Abbott is one of the finest football coaches in the country. Horatio stated, "Unfortunately, I never had a chance to play for him. The coach I played for was James Gayle. He was also a good coach." Just as he finished the sentence, in came Crystal and said dinner would be ready in about ten minutes and asked Horatio if he would like to have a glass of wine. He said no but he would like to have another cup of coffee if it was not too much trouble.

Horatio continued and said to Coco that he was going to have the thrill of a lifetime going to see the famous Turkey Day Classic. This traditional game against the Alabama State University Hornets started in 1924. It is one of the most famous black college football games in the country. The only thing that is more exciting than going to the game is actually playing in it. "I envy you, Coco, if you go there to play because I never had the chance to play in this game."

Coco asked a few more questions but seemed satisfied with Horatio's answers and was becoming more excited about the possibility of playing at Tuskegee. He thanked Horatio for all the information but said, "I just have one more question, why did you quit the football team?"

As if on cue, Crystal came into the room and said, "Come and get it. Dinner is being served in the kitchen. I hope you like it. Spaghetti made with tomatoes from the Galanti's garden. This is Philomena's homemade sauce recipe. I also made a green salad, fresh bread and for dessert, one of my homemade apple pies." Coco and Horatio not only stood up but bolted to the kitchen for the feast.

Chapter 33

As Crystal, Coco and Horatio sat around the kitchen table, she looked at her son and said, "Coco, can you please give thanks for the food we are about to eat?" Coco smiled and started to give thanks to the Lord for the food and added that he and his mother were thankful that Horatio came into their lives.

If a smile can say a thousand words of gratitude, it could be seen in Horatio's expression. Crystal started passing the pasta and they began to eat. They ate in silence for a few moments before Horatio said, "This is the best pasta I have ever tasted. Not only does it smell superb, but it tastes delicious." Crystal gave a shy smile and thanked him.

They spoke about the upcoming Thanksgiving holiday and made small talk regarding what was happening around town. He told them the story of how he knew Father Baker and how he met Mr. Wellington. He told them about the incident that happened at the store but did not go into detail because he was embarrassed to describe the melee that occurred and didn't want to upset Crystal. Both Crystal and Coco were spellbound with his narrative. The only thing Crystal said was, "Oh my God."

After a few moments of silence, Coco stated, "We did not get into the reason why you quit the football team at Tuskegee University."

Crystal looked sharply at her son and said, "Coco, hush. That is not polite and that is not your concern."

Horatio assured Crystal that this was not a problem and Coco had a right to know especially if he was going to go to that university for his education and to play football. Then Crystal became more brave because she wanted to know more about this man and she said, "Okay, then. Not only tell us why you quit but we would like to know more about you." Horatio looked at her and said, "Man, you two are tough on your dinner guests." Horatio began his story.

"Well, I grew up in a small town in Alabama called Union Springs. As far as a town located in the deep South, the colored and whites got along but we always knew each other's places. Like every town in the deep South, we did have incidents between whites and Negroes but it was not a common occurrence like it was in other southern areas. The town started out as a farm community but it expanded to become a little diversified with railroads and some small time industry. My daddy was lucky because he opened a small store for the Negro sharecroppers and we were able to make a good living from his hard work. My momma did a lot of sewing and cooking for the white folks in the area. She could sew anything that was made of cloth or make anything from yarn. But her main skill was being the best cook in Bullock County.

"My childhood was happy. I helped my daddy in the store and did chores and errands for my momma. There is one thing they made me do when I was a young boy and that was to go to school. That was the best decision they made for me in my life.

"We had a small school for the Negro children in our section of town. It was a one-classroom school, mixed with children of all ages. There were only fourteen of us at the school because many of the

Negro families needed their children to work. Outside of my parents, the most influential person in my life was Miss Abigail Johnson. She was my teacher. She went to a school up North called Oberlin College. It was one of the few schools in the North that accepted Negroes into their white school. She came down to the South after she graduated to teach. It was because of her that not only did I have an education, but also had a chance to go to Tuskegee University."

Crystal and Coco were spellbound with his story. Coco immediately said, "Well, why did you quit the football team?" Crystal turned and said, "Hush" and looked at Horatio and told him to please continue.

Horatio smiled and said, "Coco, I will be getting to that in a few minutes but the reason I am telling you this is because I wanted to let you know how important education is." He continued the story by saying that Miss Johnson took him under her wing because she recognized that he craved for knowledge. He explained to them that she taught him for the next six years until he was at the age of eighteen.

"When I turned the age when my schooling was ending, she came home with me to talk to my parents. She told them that she thought I had a gift for learning and she would like to see me continue my studies at a college. My daddy was in shock but my momma was beaming ear to ear with pride. Daddy told her that there was no way he could afford to send me to college and he appreciated everything that she did for me. Miss Johnson told my daddy that she thought I could get a scholarship to Tuskegee University because of my athletic ability as a runner. She told daddy that she never saw anyone run as fast as me and that she knew several people in the athletic department. She said she would be willing to speak to them on my behalf. My daddy was quiet for a few moments and he looked at my momma who had tears in her eyes and looked like she was pleading with him to say yes. He finally told Miss Johnson to see what she could do but if I could not go to school on a scholarship, he could not afford to send me.

"The rest is history. A coach came down to see me. He was impressed with my speed and asked me if I ever played football. I told him no but that I was a quick learner. He brought me to the university where I had a tryout as a track runner and also gave me a few practices running the football. The next thing I knew is that they offered me a scholarship for one year to run and play football the following year. If I did well academically in school and I did well in track and football that first year, I would be given three more years of scholarship funding. I was the happiest man on the face of this earth. Not only would I get a chance to get an education, which not too many of my friends had, but also I had a chance to have fun playing sports. The other great part was that Tuskegee University was only twenty one miles from where I lived. It was not until I was at the university my first year that I found out that the coach who came down to see me was Miss Johnson's brother. Like I said, outside of my parents, she was the most influential person in my life.

"Now, to answer your question why I quit, I will tell you. At the end of my sophomore year, my momma became very ill with pneumonia. I don't know how she got it but she died within a week after I returned home. My daddy needed me to help him with the store. Again, Miss Johnson became my guardian angel as she talked my daddy into letting me stay in school. She asked him if I could only work on weekends and holidays at the store. And if I were able to bring in a little money to help pay some of the bills, would he allow me to stay in school? My daddy told her yes but he asked her how? She said she would get back to him within a week.

"As she left the store, I followed her out the door. I told her it would be impossible for her to do that because I would have to quit football and then I would have to pay tuition and my daddy could not afford it. She looked at me and asked if football was more important than my education. I said no and she just said that she would handle it.

"I don't know how she did it but that following week, she came to see my daddy and me. She talked to her brother, the head coach and a vice president of the college. They would continue my scholarship even though I did not have to play football. They did want me to continue to run track but only on weekdays or if I had an extra Saturday open. They agreed that I could have a part-time job during the week at the college in the bookstore and when needed in the maintenance department. My weekends and holidays would be free whenever my father needed me.

"To say the least, I was stunned and I was hoping that my father would agree to this proposal. He looked at me and Miss Johnson and back at me. He smiled, nodded his head and gave Miss Johnson a great big bear hug. He turned to me and said, 'This is what your momma would have wanted.' I rushed to my daddy, gave him a great big bear hug and thanked him. I turned to Miss Johnson and told her that my momma always said that I have a beautiful guardian angel watching over me. And now, I have the opportunity to thank her. With that, I went to Miss Johnson and gave her a kiss on the cheek. At the age of twenty, I wept like a baby and I was not embarrassed.

"So that is my long-winded story. I hope I did not bore you but don't forget, you two are the ones who asked."

Coco looked at Horatio and said, "I hope my momma will be as proud of me as your momma was proud of you." And with that, he excused himself from the table and went into the other room to prepare for his trip to Tuskegee.

Crystal just stared at Horatio. For a few minutes, there was silence and Horatio felt a little uncomfortable. She finally broke the silence and said, "I will always be proud of Coco no matter what. But now, I'm also proud of a man that I hardly know."

With that, Horatio touched her hand and squeezed it and said thank you.

Chapter 34

Ralph, his two sisters, brother and mother returned from Mass that Sunday morning before Thanksgiving. Pop Galanti had to stay at the store, which was open on Sundays. Besides, religion was not his forte.

Father Vifredo at St. Anthony's Church gave a nice sermon and asked the parishioners to help the more unfortunate in the parish by donating food items for Thanksgiving Day. They could drop off the items at the rectory on Monday, Tuesday and Wednesday of that week.

Philomena told her husband that she would like to gather a few can goods and loaves of bread to donate to the church for some of the poor families in the parish. She also said she was going to bake some cookies, pizzelles and sugar fried dough to bring. Eugenio looked at her and said sarcastically, "Why not invite them to the store and let them pick what they want?" He then smiled and told her, "Whatever you think," and asked her if she would please leave a few of the cookies home for him.

Ralph went upstairs to his room to change from his Sunday clothes. He put on his old clothes but made sure he was dressed warmly because it was cold outside. He told Ziggy, Gene, Carl, Waddie and the rest of the guys that he would meet them in Bethlehem Park in the vacant lot next to the railroad tracks, where they would play a game of football. Coco was not invited for two reasons. One, he was too good for all of them as a football player and second, nobody wanted to see him get hurt because Coach Fisher would "kill them" since he was leaving for Tuskegee University on Tuesday for a possible football scholarship.

Ralph said goodbye to his mom and dad and told them that he would be back in a couple of hours. He was going to Bethlehem Park with the guys to play a little football. His father turned to his mother and said, "Your son no wanna practice his saxophone so he can become good but wants to get his brains bashed in playing that stupid game." His sister, Mary, yelled out sarcastically, "Ralphie, don't get hurt," while Josephine ran up to give her big brother a hug. His brother, Johnny, could care less as he was playing with their dog, Teddy.

Ralph met most of the guys on the way. They were going through the area that was once the old village and was starting to be torn down. There was a little bridge over Smoke's Creek that they crossed from the Old Village into Bethlehem Park. There were about a dozen of them as they crossed and they would meet the rest of the guys at the vacant lot.

When they got there, Doc yelled out, "Where the hell have you guys been? We've been waiting in this damn cold for a half an hour. Did you guys have to put on your lipstick and your tutus? Is that why you are late?" "Frig you," said Waddie. "We come to kick your ass."

They chose sides. There were thirty-one guys so the teams would be uneven. Since everyone knew that Doc was the least talented of anyone, he would be the swing player and play for both teams when they were on defense. They didn't trust him on offense because he could not run, throw or catch the football. They also did not want to hurt his feelings so they told him he would be playing for both teams because he was the best player and they wanted to give each team a chance to play with him. The only one who believed this bullshit was Doc. Waddie turned to Ralph and whispered, "We all love Doc but he is as dull as dishwater and as talented as a dish rag." Ralph just gave a chuckle and smiled.

The game went on for about an hour, with both sides pounding each other. They were having fun, laughing and kidding each other after every play. That changed when the three Lenti brothers came on the scene with their cigarettes dangling from their mouths and a sneer on their faces.

The three of them were watching on the sidelines about thirty yards away from the players. The group playing football heard them laughing but could not make out what they were saying. A few words that everyone heard because they were loud enough were assholes, jerks, faggots and other uncomplimentary phrases. They did not use anyone's name out loud but Ralph and the guys knew they were talking about them.

Waddie turned to Ralph and said, "What losers those Lenti brothers are. You talk about hitting the bottom of the barrel when you talk about that family. They're not even the bottom; they're the whole putrid barrel."

Ralph turned to Waddie and told him to be quiet. He proceeded to try to be a diplomat as he started to walk over to the Lenti brothers. He tried to be nice even though he could not stand them and said, "Junior, it's good to see you home again. How about you and your two brothers joining us so we could have even teams."

Junior turned and said loudly to his brothers, "This guy is really an asshole! His father screwed our old man out of work at the steel plant, he hits Sal when he's not looking because he has the hots for that little bitch Gracie and he wants us to join them in this stupid game?"

Waddie, Sobey, Ziggy and a few of the others came up to Ralph and said, "Forget these losers, let's play." Ralph turned and said to all of them, "Let's forget about this bullshit and just enjoy playing the game of football." He turned to Junior and said, "Just enjoy and have fun."

Junior said, "Ah fongool you asshole. The only game I want to play with you is to kick your pretty face all over the field so even your momma would cry and say what happened to my pretty baby." It took everything Ralph had to hold back from throwing a punch at him. Although Junior was four years older than Ralph and about two inches taller, they weighed the same. Ralph had an edge; he was very skilled at boxing and it was one of his favorite sports. He turned around and just said, "Too bad you guys don't want to join us because I think you would have a good time being part of the human race."

Junior became infuriated and when Ralph turned his back, he pulled out his switchblade and yelled to him, "Turn around you asshole. I'm going to cut you a new hole for your ass, right below your belly button."

Ralph quickly turned around and before he knew it, thirty guys were running toward him and Lenti. The three brothers became frightened and backed off a little and started to walk away. Junior turned and yelled to Ralph, "Listen prick, there will be a time when you don't have your big gang of jerk offs helping you. It will be just you and me." With that, he gave Ralph a sneer, a laugh and the finger. Ralph did not say a word but just stared at the three brothers leaving the area. Doc yelled, "Hey you palooka morons, if you don't wanna play, we could use you for goalposts." With that, everyone laughed. To be sure, if there was a confrontation, Doc would be the last one behind the guys saying let's go get them.

As the Lenti brothers kept on walking, the three of them raised their right arms high over their heads and with the middle finger of their hands sticking up, gave them a farewell.

Gene turned to Ralph and asked him if he was okay. Ralph turned and said, "I really feel sorry for Mrs. Lenti. To have a husband who is a jerk and three sons who are assholes, she must have a sad life. My mother talks about what a life that poor woman has and she feels so sorry for her. I do not want to cause that woman any grief by knocking the shit out of her sons. Knowing them, they probably would take it out on her when they got home."

They all returned to the open field to finish the football game. The enthusiasm was not the same and the game only lasted twenty minutes more before everyone decided to call it quits. They all started walking back to their homes.

As some of them crossed the bridge over Smoke's Creek, Doc turned to Ralph and said, "You know what? I could not lose today. I was on the winning team and I was on the losing team but since I have a choice, I pick the winning team as the team I wanted officially to be on." They all looked at Doc and tried to understand what the hell he was saying, but Ralph's mind was preoccupied by the threat that Junior gave him. He knew the Lenti family was big on revenge.

Chapter 35

Thanksgiving was a day away. The weather was unusually cold and there was a trace of snow on the ground. Coco left for Tuskegee University by train on Tuesday. He only participated in a few plays that weekend because Coach Fisher wanted to make sure he did not get hurt before his big recruiting trip.

Horatio drove Coco to the train station with Crystal to see him off. As he left on the train, Horatio turned to Crystal and said it would be his honor if she would join him for Thanksgiving dinner. He told her that Mr. Wellington and his wife invited him to dinner and said he could bring a guest. She said she would be thrilled and accepted his invitation.

Meanwhile, the guys from the GAA met in the clubhouse that Wednesday to start to discuss plans for a Christmas party in December. The club was beginning to develop into an athletic and social organization. Everyone was recognizing that this club was growing into something special.

Philomena, with her two daughters, Mary and Josephine, started to prepare the Thanksgiving dinner. Philomena made sure she made enough cookies and pastries to bring to the church Wednesday afternoon to be distributed to the needy parishioners. She was a little disappointed that Crystal would not be able to have Thanksgiving dinner with them but was elated when she found out that she would be having dinner with Horatio.

Pop Galanti had Ralph and little Johnny start cleaning the store while their mother and sisters were baking in the kitchen. He also told them to take care of the store while he left for a couple of hours to see if there would be any work available for him that weekend after Thanksgiving. He had a good rapport with the foreman and since he was such a great worker, they usually would save a spot for him on the crew.

At the Marrano family home, all the girls were helping their mother, Maria, to prepare for Thanksgiving dinner. The girls helped with the baking and preparing of the food, except for Gracie and Rosie. They were the cleaners of the house; besides Gracie hated cooking and Rosie was a little too young to cook. The boys went with their father to their shed where they housed chickens, rabbits and pigeons. Their father took a couple of chickens, one rabbit and two pigeons out back with his oldest son, Carmen. There they slaughtered and gutted them. He prepared a large kettle of boiling water and then had the boys dip the chicken and pigeons in the water and pull off the feathers. In the meantime, their father skinned the rabbits.

Josephine, Carmela and Anna were discussing boys while preparing the pies and pastries for the Thanksgiving dinner. Meanwhile, Mom Marrano was preparing her famous red sauce and meatballs. Her husband, Federico, who worked at Mazuca's grocery store, was able to barter for five pounds of ground meat for the meatballs and three pounds of sausage. He offered two of his rabbits and a large homemade apple pie and told Mr. Mazuca that he would work an extra two hours without pay. Mr. Mazuca was more than happy because he loved Maria's apple pies. He told Federico to forget about the two extra hours without pay but sometime in the future, he could bring him another apple pie.

While Maria was preparing her sauce and meatballs, Josephine turned to her mother and said, "Ma, did you know that the oldest Lenti boy is home from jail? Anna and I saw him, his brothers Sal and Mario near the open field where some of the boys were playing football." Mom Marrano looked at all three and said in Italian, "I do not want you to hang around those boys. They are as evil as their father. I pray for their dear mother, Concetta, every day. She's a good woman and her life is a living hell."

Josephine did not tell her everything. When they were walking up Madison Avenue and the Lentis were on the other side of the street, they saw them starting to cross the street and walk toward them. The three were laughing and talking very animated as they approached them. Anna took Josephine's hand and whispered, "Whatever happens, you keep holding my hand and do not say anything."

The three brothers approached and the first thing Junior said was, "Aren't you the Marrano sisters?" Anna smiled but kept walking with Josephine. This infuriated Junior and he yelled, "Hey bitches, I'm talking to you and it's only polite that you stop and answer me." Anna and Josephine started to walk faster away from all of them. Sal and Mario chimed in and said, "You're typical Marrano bitches. You think your shit don't stink. What you two need is three Lenti sausages in your bun." All three started laughing hysterically.

Anna and Josephine were nervous and they thought the Lenti brothers would follow them. As Josephine turned, she was relieved to see that they continued to walk in the other direction toward their home.

Josephine and Anna definitely did not want to tell their parents. Because they were so protective, they probably would never let them out of the house without a chaperone. It was better not to say anything.

Chapter 36

Although the Depression was still rearing its nasty head around the nation, Thanksgiving and the end of November of 1932 brought some happiness to families in Lackawanna.

Father Baker fed more than 3,000 people on Thanksgiving Day alone. He was averaging from the summer of 1932 more than 30,000 meals a month for the poor and unfortunate. These meals also went to the young children who were homeless and orphaned. This was an amazing feat during an era of joblessness and in many cases, hopelessness. This holy man brought a ray of hope to these people. At the age of 91, he, with the help of his aide and friend, Brother Sebastian, would still walk the long lines where the people stood waiting to be fed, greeting and blessing them. Many times, when he saw a family together in line, he would ask them where they lived. Many did not have a roof over their heads for the night and he would then give them a few dollars out of his vest pocket to rent a room for a few days.

In the Galanti and Marrano households, there was much to be thankful for because there was enough food, not only for family members, but they were able to give some to their less fortunate neighbors.

Crystal had one of her nicest Thanksgivings as she went to the Wellington's home with Horatio. She was amazed at how the

Wellington's treated her and Horatio. To be invited into a white family's home that was very elegant and to be treated as one of their equals was beyond belief to her. She could see there was much love and respect for Horatio from this family. It was not until after dinner when Mr. Wellington and Crystal were sitting in the parlor having coffee and tea that he spoke of how thankful he was to Father Baker for introducing him to Horatio. Horatio had insisted on helping Mrs.Wellington and her daughter clean up the kitchen. Mrs. Wellington had given her housekeeper and cook the day off so they could be with their families on this holiday.

Crystal asked Mr. Wellington how it was that Father Baker introduced him to Horatio. Wellington proceeded to tell her the whole story. He just finished it when Horatio, his wife and daughter came into the room. Horatio looked at Crystal and her mouth was open and she was just staring at Mr. Wellington. Not knowing what happened, he turned to his friend and said, "I hope you didn't say anything bad about me because she seems to be in shock." To that, they all laughed and started to carry on casual conversation.

Believe it or not, Concetta Lenti and her sons Romeo and Mario had a very nice Thanksgiving dinner. That was due to the fact that her husband and her sons Junior and Sal were out somewhere in the city of Buffalo doing whatever and Concetta did not care what. She enjoyed her time with Romeo and Mario. Mario was a changed young boy away from his brothers and father. She wanted to savor this blessed day. Angelo Sr., Junior and Salvatore were also very happy. Even though it was Thanksgiving, they had a meeting at the office of Carl DiJoseph. DiJoseph was the leader of the Italian Black Hand in South Buffalo and communities surrounding the southtowns area. They were looking for work in his organization. After DiJoseph interviewed the three of them, he told them he would think about it and be prepared if he accepted them to start work that Monday. He did not tell them what they would be doing but whatever he wanted, they would do it for sure.

After the meeting, the three Lentis went to a speakeasy in downtown Buffalo to celebrate their good fortune. DiJoseph was one of the most influential crime bosses in the southtowns area of Buffalo. He worked as a "capo" for the most powerful family in Western New York, southern Ontario, Canada and parts of Ohio. The family involved that was more powerful was that of Sebastian "The Baker" Massini. Sebastian was known as "The Don" throughout the crime network. The Lentis thought their future had changed for the better.

They decided to celebrate by getting drunk and going to a local whorehouse. Angelo Sr. said, "This is the life. Finally getting a job with a family, getting drunk, getting laid and knocking around a few whores. This is a great Thanksgiving."

A couple of days after Thanksgiving, on Saturday evening, Coco arrived home from Tuskegee University. His mother and Horatio picked him up at the train station. As soon as he got off the train and saw his mother and Horatio, he ran to them and gave his mother a big hug and kiss and shook Horatio's hand enthusiastically. He said to both of them, "You are now looking at a Tuskegee University Golden Tigers football player." With that, his mother gave a short scream of happiness and Horatio patted him on his back beaming with pride. Coco told them that he was receiving a full scholarship to the university and he turned to Horatio and said, "Thank you. Your recommendation for me as a football player and a person apparently helped seal the deal. You are truly well respected at Tuskegee. Again, thank you."

With that, Crystal turned and kissed Horatio and thanked him. Both Horatio and Coco were stunned but soon laughed. Horatio told Coco, "If I get a kiss every time I give you a recommendation, I will be recommending you for every school in the United States." They all laughed.

The last week of November, the guys from the Galanti Club already started to plan their next event. The Halloween in November party was a great success and they started to think about some Christmas celebrations. They were meeting almost every day in the clubhouse in the late afternoon and early evening. The clubhouse became a focal point for these young men and their camaraderie brought them close as brothers. There were all nationalities represented in this club. They were mainly from the First Ward but many of them came from the Second and Third Wards of Lackawanna. This club would be the beginning of friendships that would last for more than seventy-five years.

The last day of November was ending as Ralph looked out of his bedroom window. He thought it was an up and down November with all the things that had happened but he was glad that it ended on a happy note. He couldn't wait for December to start and the Christmas holidays to come. Unbeknown to him, December would be one of the worst months in his life.

Chapter 37

"Boy, the place is really starting to shape up," said Coco as he was looking around their new clubhouse. Since the Halloween party in November, each member had to bring something into the clubhouse to help furnish it and give it some character identifying it as a "guy's" clubhouse.

Ralph said, "I'm really surprised how well this is working out. Even my father gave us some praise when he and Mr. Bonitatibus came in to have a look." It had been over two months since the clubhouse was opened and the guys were using it every day of the week. It was a haven for them during the evenings and the ones who did not go to school and were not working came there during the day just to hang out and "shoot the breeze."

The clubhouse had ample space. The size of the clubhouse was approximately fifty feet by thirty-five feet. Some of the guys wanted to make it double the size but Pop Galanti told them, "Hella no. Whata do you wanna to make a this bigger than my store?" Santo added that the larger it becomes, the more expensive it will be to build even though most of the supplies seemed to appear magically. He also said that maintaining it and keeping it clean would be a chore in itself. They all finally agreed for two reasons. First, no one wanted to do that much work in keeping it clean and second, no one wanted to get Pop Galanti angry. It was more of the latter than the former that helped make the decision.

The room contained about five round tables of various sizes. Three were excellent to have card games on while the others were good for having a few snacks and drinks. There were a variety of chairs, mostly wooden folding chairs. Fifty of these chairs in the room all looked very similar and had the same markings branded into their backs, "Property of Bethlehem Steel Company." No one asked how they got there; no one admitted to bringing them, they were just there one Saturday morning stacked in the corner. Doc admitted that he was responsible. He said he went to St. Anthony's Church the Sunday before and prayed that we would have furniture for the clubhouse. He told everyone, "God answered my prayers. See, it's a miracle!" With that, someone threw a wet rag that they were using to clean the floor straight into his face and yelled, "Doc, you haven't been to church since your First Communion!"

One of the members brought in an old pot belly stove that belonged to his grandfather who passed away during the summertime. They put it in the corner and with the help of Mr. Bonitatibus, were able to vent it out the side of the building. It was a good stove and it kept the clubhouse warm during the winter. Each week during the wintertime, three members were assigned to gather coal at the railroad tracks to burn in the stove.

There were only two windows in the clubhouse. The reason was that the south side was in the back of the store. The north and east walls were part of Pop Galanti's large garage. He built the garage years before as a rental space for cars. He thought this would be a good way to earn added income. Unfortunately when the Depression hit, most of the people lost their vehicles so he had plenty of space but no cars.

The west wall had the two large windows and they built another side entrance to enter the clubhouse. The main entrance was going through the store to the back room and then they made a doorway into the clubhouse. The doorway to the outside was solid and would only be used for emergency reasons. Each window had a couple of bars on it for security.

There was also a long wooden folding table about ten feet long. Ralph, Coco, Ziggy and Waddie, with the guidance of Pop Galanti, built the table from wood that was left over while constructing the clubhouse.

An old couch was given to them by Mrs. Possitti. She was redoing some of the rooms in her boarding house, which was really one of the First Ward's infamous brothels. She was making money "hands over fists" even in this tough economy. Her philosophy was if she had a nice supply of women and an attractive setting for them to entertain their clients, she knew the clients would come back. Besides, one of the clubhouse members was her nephew whom she favored. He asked and she gave.

The ceiling of the clubhouse was about eight feet high and had five rows of neon lighting running the width of the clubhouse. During the evening, this would give enough light for them to play cards and socialize. The two pieces of furniture that were prize possessions and favorites of the guys were a RCA radio console and an upright player piano. It seemed like the radio was always on, morning, noon and night. There were sports that were broadcast, radio shows, and of course, music. A few of the members could play the piano. Even though Ralph played the saxophone, he picked up the piano by ear and became pretty proficient at it. Those who could not play benefited with having strong legs as they would use the pump pedals to produce music on the rolls that were inserted in the player piano. They did not have a lot of money, but they certainly enjoyed life.

Armondo Ginnetti, Gene Staniszewski, Lou Fistola and Carl Covino got everyone together that evening to conduct their first formal meeting. They announced that they should draw up some rules and regulations for the club. Armondo told them that they also should have officers for the club; a president, vice president, secretary and treasurer. Ziggy yelled out, "Hey genius, why the hell do we need a treasurer, we got no money." Everyone laughed except Armondo who told Ziggy to shut his goddamn mouth before he "got no teeth."

Lou said, "We talked about naming the club the Galanti Athletic Association. We agreed to the name but it was not a formal agreement so we have to take a vote." Everyone voted yes except Ralph who was too embarrassed. Coco turned to him and said, "Raffs, are you nuts? Why didn't you vote for it? It's not your name that they're voting on but your mom and dad's. If they did not give us this clubhouse, we wouldn't be here today voting on anything. Sometimes I think you're too proud. It's not about you, it's about your parents." Ralph turned to Coco and said, "Thank you."

The name of the club was formally established. Now the big question was who were going to be officers and what were the bylaws going to be. After much discussion and some yelling back and forth, it was agreed upon that the first president should be Gene Staniszewski because it was his idea to ask Pop Galanti. Gene graciously declined because at that time he could not dedicate his full attention to the club because he was taking care of his sick parents. He nominated Armondo Ginnetti and it was agreed upon. Gene said he would accept the role as vice president, to which everyone agreed. Someone nominated Ziggy to be secretary. Someone yelled out, "I thought the secretary has to know how to read and write. Ziggy can't do either." Ziggy responded eloquently, " Ah fon gool."

Lou said, "Listen, guys. This is serious. The guy who is secretary has to take the minutes of the meetings and make sure everyone knows what is happening in the club. It is a very important position. I would like to nominate Tony Moretti. He writes for the school newspaper and he is very articulate." Everyone voted yes, including Ziggy.

Armondo said, "The last officer we should vote on is treasurer. This is someone who has to keep account of all the monies that we will have in the club, dues, fundraisers, etc. This person has to be honest and good with numbers. I nominate Lou Fistola." Everyone agreed.

Bill Renzi raised his hand and said that they should have one more officer. "We should have a sergeant-at-arms. This person has to keep the meeting in order, someone who is tough and a no-nonsense guy. I nominate Doc." Everyone was stunned and silent. Ralph looked around and yelled, "I second it. Doc would be perfect." Everyone started to chant, "Doc, Doc, Doc." It was a unanimous vote and Doc was voted in as sergeant-at-arms. They yelled to Doc, "Speech, speech, speech." Doc stuck out his chest with pride and said, "Shut your damn mouths and come to order. We have a fuckin meeting to run." With that, everyone cheered and laughed uncontrollably.

The   Galanti   Athletic   Association   was   born.

Chapter 38

Armondo Ginnetti, the newly elected president, called the first Galanti Athletic Association meeting to order. His first order of business was to appoint a few members to draw up the club's constitution and bylaws. He said, "Since most of you sons of bitches don't know how to read or write, I'm appointing the following members to this task. I want Ralph, Coco, Sobey, Waddie, Lou Fistola and Bill Renzi to serve on the committee. You guys have one month to draw up these laws. Do you guys accept this challenge?" They all said yes.

"The next thing I want to bring up is"...before Armondo got the next word out, someone yelled, "Is this a damn dictatorship?" Armondo turned and said, "Who the hell said that?" Harpo raised his hand and the second order of business for the new club was breaking up the fight between Armondo and Harpo.

Ralph yelled out, "Quit this bullshit or else my father will throw us all out and all the work we did to get a clubhouse will be for nothing." Gene agreed with Ralph and helped settle things down. "Listen, if you want this club to work, we gotta have some rules and regulations even before the guys develop them. Armondo is the president and it is his right to assign committees and run the meetings. If we don't like what he is doing, the next election we will vote him the hell out. So, let's at least get things started in an orderly fashion because I agree with Ralph. If Pop Galanti comes in here, he'll throw us all out by the seat of our pants."

All agreed, some reluctantly. Someone yelled out, "I thought the sergeant-at-arms is supposed to keep these meetings orderly." Before anyone knew it, Doc got up and walked out of the clubhouse. They all thought that he was upset but a few moments later, he came back in the room holding a 2x4. The only thing he said was, "The next nitwit who gets out of line, I swear to Christ, I will let him have it with this piece of wood." They all knew Doc meant it... he definitely was going to take his job seriously.

The meeting went on without a hitch the rest of the way. They talked about setting up some kind of dues, how many times they would meet a month, who would be eligible to join the club and what activities they would do during the year. Lou Fistola brought up an important question. He said, "If we have the word athletic in our club, don't you think we should develop different sports teams with our members and challenge other clubs or organizations?" Everyone thought that was a good idea and the president, Armondo, told Lou to develop a sports program for the club to be interwoven with the bylaws.

Lui Marini, who was considered a dapper dan, brought up the idea of sponsoring dances to bring in money to the club. Lui was a little older than most of them and was one of the few who had a decent job at the flourmill. He loved music and he loved dancing but most of all, he loved women. He told the members that he often went uptown on Main Street in Buffalo to attend dances that were held at the Lafayette Hotel. He said it was jam-packed with people and he knew they made a lot of money. He also stated that he went to other places uptown that were more private and had dances that served liquor. He told the club that they could make a lot of money and it would help make the club financially strong, especially in these tough times. Armondo, who was great at delegating assignments, told Lui, "I'm taking you off of the constitution and bylaws committee and making you in charge of the social events of the club. I'm assigning Paul Petti to help you." Lui had a smile from ear to ear and accepted the assignment. Armondo turned and said, "To show you there's no hard feelings, Harpo, I'm putting your brother Dynamite on the bylaws and constitution committee. Besides, he's the smarter one between the two of you." Harpo, being a great orator, yelled back, "Screw you, Armondo."

The rest of the meeting was pretty orderly. Gene suggested that until they get a constitution and bylaws, they should meet every Sunday at one o'clock in the afternoon in the clubhouse. He also asked Ralph to check with his father for the hours that they could use the clubhouse. Ralph said, "It should not be a problem. I believe Pa will allow us to use it anytime we want. But I think he would like us to go through the store to the back room so he could keep an eye on who is coming and going. The hours will probably be when the store is open. Anything beyond those hours, I think we better clear it with him."

Gene thanked Ralph and turned to Armondo and said, "I think you should call this meeting to an end." Armondo stood up and said, "Okay, gentlemen, the meeting has ended." With that, half the guys got around the tables to play cards, while others gathered in little groups to shoot the breeze. The only one walking around was Doc with his 2x4 telling everyone to quiet down and behave or else. Everyone thought this might have been the biggest mistake, voting him in as sergeant-at-arms. He was going to kill someone!

Chapter 39

Ralph and Coco left the clubhouse and were walking to the front of the store. Coco turned to Ralph and said, "In spite of it all, I think that was a pretty good first meeting. It sure was interesting." Ralph agreed and as they were approaching the front of the store, Ralph noticed that Carmen Marrano and his sister Anna were there buying soda and candy. They often took a little stroll across the Smoke's Creek bridge to go to Galanti's store for some treats and to talk to Ralph and Mary.

Ralph yelled, "Hey Carm and Anna, how are you doing?" Carm looked up and said that he was doing well and asked Ralph and Coco how they were doing. Anna was a little more shy with the boys and all she did was say hello and gave a little smile. While Carmen was talking to Coco and Ralph, Mary and Josephine took Anna in the kitchen for a cup of hot cocoa.

Carmen asked, "What's all the fuss happening in the back of the store?" He heard a lot of yelling and a few swear words. He said, "Good thing your Dad is not here or else I think a few heads would have been rolling from the back of the store." Ralph smiled and said, "Yeah, we're lucky Pa's working and not here and also that Ma might be a little hard of hearing...at least, I hope she is."

Ralph started to tell Carmen about the new clubhouse that they built and the start of the GAA. He went on for the next fifteen minutes explaining how they talked his father into having it in back of the store, how Mr. Bonitatibus helped, the trials and tribulations of building it and finally, how they just started to organize today. Carmen, who knew most of the guys in the club but did not hang around the store frequently, was amazed at what they accomplished. He said, "That's great. It looks like you have a special thing going."

Coco asked Carmen where he had been because he hadn't seen him much. Carmen told him that he was working a lot, helping his father at the grocery store. He said that his father was able to get him part-time work, cleaning the store for Mr. Mazuca and also delivering groceries to the customers. He also told them that since he and Anna were the oldest, they were in charge of making sure that their siblings behaved and did their chores around the house.

Ralph laughed. "You have a large family with all those sisters and two brothers but you must have a handful with your young sister, Gracie." "That's only the tip of the iceberg when you talk about Gracie being a handful," said Carmen. "If she's not getting my father mad at her, then it's my mother being mad at her. And if they're not mad at her, it's usually Anna and I who are upset with her. She will be the death of my father and mother, if not, definitely me."

Coco said, "I know what you mean. Her run-ins with the Lenti family have made her a legend in Bethlehem Park. No offense, Carmen, but if she had testicles, she would be the toughest son of a bitch in our neighborhood." They all started laughing.

Carmen then became serious and said, "Gracie's run-ins with the Lenti family have me a little nervous. My young brother, Neal, told me that one day at school a couple of weeks ago, the young Mario Lenti went up to Gracie and gave her a sneer and called her a bitch. He told her to watch her back. Ralph said, "Wow. What the hell did she do? I hope she ran away from him." Carmen said, "Are you kidding? She gave him a kick in the nuts and as he laid on the ground crying, she called him a baby. Of course, one of the teachers who was in the hallway saw this and Gracie was in the principal's office again. Thank God my father was not home and my mother was busy with the young ones in the family. I had to go to pick Gracie up at the school and listen to a half-hour lecture from the principal."

Ralph and Coco would have laughed but this was serious. Coco told Carmen that the Lenti family was evil and Gracie should stay away from them no matter what. He told Carmen that Sal Lenti is still after Ralph and now that the older brother Junior is back from prison, they think they are "tough and cool."

"I know, I was going to go try to talk to Mr. Lenti and apologize for what Gracie did to Mario. I also was going to ask him to please have his son leave Gracie alone." Ralph chimed in, "Carmen, let it go. That won't help. That family, except for the mother and the baby, are all psychos. Just try to explain to Gracie to stay completely away from them no matter what." Carmen looked at Ralph and said, "Easier said than done. Better yet, why don't you explain it to her; she seems to have a little crush on you." Ralph looked at Carmen and said, "No thank you. I want to keep my testicles intact."

With that, they had a good hearty laugh. Carmen called for Anna and told her they had to go. Ralph then asked Carmen, "How about joining the club? I think you will enjoy it. Plus it could be a great escape for you from your sisters and brothers." As Anna came out of the kitchen and walked toward Carmen, he turned to Ralph and said, "Thank you, I'll think about it." Carmen and Anna walked out of the store just as Pop Galanti was coming in.

Chapter 40

"When the hell are we going to hear from DiJoseph," said Junior to his father. "It is a few weeks since we talked to him and that asshole told us he was going to notify us shortly." Angelo Sr. looked at his son and said, "First, we wait until we get a message from him. Second, watch your goddamn mouth. You never know who is listening. I'll tell you, if DiJoseph heard you calling him an asshole, he would cut your asshole too short to shit." The Lentis were very anxious to hear from DiJoseph.

The crime boss was taking his time in deciding whether to give the Lenti family a job in their organization. He made some inquiries about them in Lackawanna. He was told that they were not the swiftest family when it came to intellect, but they took orders very well.
He was also told that they would have no problem with breaking a few legs or arms or even taking care of things if someone had to be silenced...on a permanent basis. The only bad trait they had was that they liked to beat up women, all three of them. It must run in the family.

Carl DiJoseph made a decision and had two of his men drive down to Lentis' home in Bethlehem Park to pick them up for a meeting with him. As the big black Cadillac approached the Lentis' home, Mario was looking out the window. The Lentis were almost ready for dinner when Mario yelled to his dad, "Hey Pop, there's two guys getting out of this big black car and coming up to our house." Angelo Sr. and his two sons ran to the window. Junior said, "Holy shit....they are here." They all ran to the side door to greet them because they knew why they came. Angelo Sr. was hoping it was good news.

The bigger man with the fedora and heavy overcoat, banged on the door while the small, slim man without a hat and a trenchcoat was looking around taking in the surroundings. Angelo Sr. opened the door and before he could say hello, the big man said, "You and your two sons get your coats on, you're coming with us. The man wants to see you." With that, both he and his partner turned and headed back for the car.

Angelo Sr. quickly told his sons to get their coats and he turned to his wife and said, "We have a meeting to go to, we'll be back later." Concetta said meekly, "What about dinner?" He turned and said to her, "Are you fuckin deaf? I said we gotta go and we will be back later. Just feed Mario and the baby and fill your fat face with whatever you want." With that, he and his two sons ran out of the house toward the black Cadillac.

Angelo and his two sons sat in the back while DiJoseph's men sat in the front. No one said a word for several minutes. It was very quiet and for Sal it was a little scary. Finally, Sal said, "Where are we going?" The smaller man turned and said, "Are you an asshole?" And then he turned to Angelo Sr. and said, "You better tell your son it's better to keep his trap shut. The quieter he is the better it will be." Angelo turned to his son with piercing eyes. There was no need for Sal to know what his father was thinking for the eyes said everything.

The Cadillac was traveling down Main Street in Buffalo when it turned down one of the side streets near Niagara Square. They pulled alongside a small Italian restaurant and parked. They got out of the car and headed for the side door where the big man with the fedora knocked. A wooden piece slid open in the top half of the door and you could see a man's eyes look through the opening. The big man said, "Tell him they are here." One minute later, the door slid open and the five of them went into an office that was located in back of the restaurant. There sat Carl DiJoseph.

DiJoseph was behind a big desk and the three Lentis stood in front of him. Sal started to sit on the seat that was in front of a big mahogany desk. DiJoseph said in a very quiet voice, "Did I tell you to fuckin sit down?" With that, Sal stood straight up at attention while his father again gave him a glaring stare.

DiJoseph looked at the three of them as they stood before him and said, "This is your lucky day. I did some looking into the three of you. You three are definitely not the sharpest pencils in the box but I heard some good things about you." He told them they were lucky because he lost four of his men on a bootlegging caper between Canada and Lewiston. He told them that the four got caught crossing the border with a truckload of whiskey by the Feds. He said he didn't give a shit about them being caught but he was pissed off that they lost thousands of dollars worth of whiskey to the Feds. So he said to them, "As you see, I am shorthanded by four. I will give you a chance to work but you have to prove yourself. I need people that will take orders without question, keep their mouth shut no matter what and have loyalty only to me."

Junior spoke first. "Mr. DiJoseph, you will have our loyalty and I guarantee you my father, brother and me will be loyal to you and will do anything you ask without question." DiJoseph looked at him for a few moments without saying a word. The three of them felt a little nervous. They knew that at the pleasure of DiJoseph, they could be working for him or be found floating in the Niagara River. This was the longest minute in their lives.

"Okay, you three will start working for me next Monday. It'll be a few days before Christmas and that could be my gift to you," he said with a chuckle. "I am going to give you Lucky's car, the son of a bitch won't need it because he'll be doing time in prison. Besides, he and those three others owe me a lot for losing that shipment of whiskey from Canada. I'm not giving you the car for free. You will be paying for it each week from the money that I give you for your services. There are a few things I want you to do that my family has business in. One, there are a few debts that have to be collected from some of these pricks that think they could beat us with the loans we gave them. I need to have you check on a few of the businesses that we protect to make sure that we receive our 'gratis money.' Another area is checking on our whorehouses and making sure that we are receiving our cut.

"Last, I want to start checking on some of these grocery stores that are selling homemade wine on the side. They are not giving us our due for protection and they will either stop selling or we will put them out of business permanently. Your area will be Lackawanna and South Buffalo. But I might need you elsewhere. I want you to know that once you become one of us, the code we abide by is silence. We will take care of your family if you abide by the code. If not, I guarantee you, you will be pushing up daisies and the only thing your family will have is the flowers to remember you by."

The Lentis gave their oath of "silenzio se no morte"...silence or death. They went around the desk and kissed DiJoseph's hand.

The big man with the fedora who was standing near the door with his partner walked up to the Lentis and told them it was time to leave. The three Lentis gave DiJoseph a slight bow and turned to walk out the door and into the car.

The big man with the fedora and his partner got in the front seat. The smaller man turned and said, "We will be driving you home. Tomorrow there will be a car in front of your home with the key under the seat. You will have a few days of enjoying your new toy until we call you back to start working for us. Say it's a Christmas gift from the man."

They drove back to Bethlehem Park in complete silence. Angelo Sr. was thinking that he finally made the big time. Junior was thinking about the money he was going to make and the broads he would be having. Sal was not thinking of anything. He was just scared and thought....*what the hell am I getting into?*

Chapter 41

Christmas was only a few days away. Even though the country was deep in the Depression, there was a sign of hope. President-elect Franklin Delano Roosevelt won by a landslide in November over President Herbert Hoover. Roosevelt's platform was the "New Deal" and it gave Americans expectations that life would be getting better in the near future. Everyone suspected that it might get worse before it got better but that ray of hope would sustain them until it arrived. The majority of the country was expecting that there would be a repeal of the prohibition law and that alone caused spirits to be raised.

In Lackawanna, the holiday season was becoming very festive. It was a time to try to forget your problems and celebrate traditions of Christmas past. The schools were having their annual little Christmas parties in the classrooms and having pageants in the auditoriums. Children were excited about the possibility of Santa Claus bringing them a present; whether it was clothes or toys, it didn't matter. It was just the expectation of receiving a gift.

The Galanti Athletic Association was developing into an organized group of young men who enjoyed the camaraderie of each other and the planning of athletic and social events for the future. The clubhouse became a haven for these young men. There was a place for them to go to talk, play cards, listen to the radio and just hang out being themselves. There was activity in the clubhouse every day of the week from the time the store opened letting the members in until the store closed when Pop Galanti said, "All right boysa, itsa time to leave." It would not be until a year later that he allowed them to stay in the clubhouse even though he and Ma Galanti went to bed. As he told Tony Moretti when Tony asked him if they could stay later: "No, not until you all earna my trust. Thatsa going to be entirely up to alla you."

At the Marrano's household, they were getting ready for their big Christmas dinner with their next-door neighbors, the Moretti family. Between the two families, there were sixteen kids. The preparations for the dinner would last for four days with each family making different types of pasta, meat entrees, salads, homemade breads, vegetables and of course, the famous Italian desserts. Mr. Moretti and Mr. Marrano, with the help of the older boys, prepared the bottles of red wine from the barrels in the cellar. All the girls in both households helped in the kitchen except Gracie and Carmela Moretti. Their expertise was cleaning. Carmela was Gracie's best friend. They were the same age although entirely opposite when it came to dispositions. Carmela was shy and quiet. As Josephine described her sister Gracie and Carmela's friendship, she would say... *Carmela was the china shop and Gracie was the bull in the china shop.*

The romance between Crystal and Horatio was beginning to blossom. Even though they only knew each other for a few short weeks, they became inseparable. Horatio used his whole paycheck plus some money that he saved to buy Crystal a beautiful wool coat for Christmas, this along with a beautiful necklace and earrings. He also bought Coco a Tuskegee sweatshirt that he was able to get through one of the coaches. He was praying that it would arrive before Christmas. He also placed in an envelope some money for Coco and he wrote on the envelope...to be used only during the first semester at Tuskegee

University. Coco was voted the Most Valuable Player on the football team. He was preparing to start basketball season for the high school. He was walking on air for the holidays.

For a change, Angelo Lenti Sr. was in a good mood for the holidays. He thought... *this is going to be the best Christmas I have had in years. I have been accepted to work for Carl DiJoseph, I have a car, I will have status and I will have respect but most of all, I will have money.* He even bought a few gifts for his sons. This was the first time he had done this in ten years. And of course, he bought himself a gift, a watch that he got at the pawnshop. The only thing he did not do was buy his wife, Concetta, a gift. He thought her gift was the boys and him. Concetta would not mind because she hadn't received a gift from him in years. Anyway, the only gift that she would want was for him not to get drunk and beat her on Christmas day.

Father Baker was preparing with Brother Sebastian and Father Gerlach to celebrate the Christmas Mass at the Basilica. This was one of Father Baker's favorite holidays except for the entire month of May, which was dedicated to the Blessed Mother Mary. Because of his age, Father Baker did not say Mass every Sunday in the Basilica but he always attended and assisted Mass at the altar. Christmas was special to him and he would be the celebrant of the Mass with Father Gerlach and Brother Sebastian assisting. This holiday he was especially thankful for all the support that he received throughout the country and the world. This Christmas he was able to feed so many of the poor and unfortunate and also had enough money with donations and contributions to buy gifts for the boys and girls in the orphanage and many of the poor families in the Western New York area.

Ralph could not wait for Christmas. It was always his favorite holiday. He loved spending it with his family and was excited not only to receive presents, but also to give them to his parents and siblings. Everything seemed to be going well this year with only a few bumps in the road. The GAA was becoming a reality, his best friend Coco was getting an athletic scholarship to college, his family was able to make a good living from the store and his father had steady work at the steel plant. He felt so blessed this Christmas holiday. He thought this would be a wonderful Christmas. Unbeknown to him, this would be the worst Christmas of his life.

Chapter 42

Josephine felt so pretty. She had her beautiful Christmas dress on with all the frills of the holiday season. She hadn't felt like this in years. Josephine had just turned 13 and was very excited about becoming a teenager. She had spent many of her childhood years as a patient at the Perrysburg Hospital for children who had polio. She was able to progress to the point where she did not need a brace to walk but she did have a noticeable limp in her gait. She looked at herself in the mirror and smiled because this was going to be a special holiday. Her father, Eugenio, promised her that he would take her downtown to the Shea's Buffalo Theatre, where there was a Christmas pageant with music and dancing.

"Will you quit looking in the mirror and admiring yourself," said her sister Mary. "Pop is taking you to a Christmas pageant, not a debutante ball for all the uppity ups!" "Be quiet," answered Josephine. "Just because you look like a cow doesn't mean I have to," she said, laughing and giving her sister a wink.

"Well, don't spend so much time in the bathroom because you know your dumb brothers want to get themselves ready for the big Christmas party after the pageant."

As Mary left the bathroom and closed the door, Josephine quickly locked it because she did not want her brothers bothering her. She looked into the mirror and felt good about herself for the first time in many months. The dress was made by her mother and had all the frills and ornate embellishments that any girl could want. She felt the holiday spirit even in the bathroom because it was decorated with flowers, ornaments and lit candles.

Josephine peered into the mirror and smiled. This would be the first time she would be going with her father for a special evening, just the two of them. She idolized her dad and was very excited to be spending the entire day with just him.

Downstairs in the store, Philomena and Eugenio were having a glass of wine with Crystal and Horatio. It had been a month-and-a-half since Horatio and Crystal met. Philomena asked her to bring Horatio to the store to have some wine and to introduce him to her husband, Eugenio. Eugenio was a little reluctant when Philomena told him that Crystal was bringing a male black friend over to meet him. He agreed only because his son's best friend was Coco and he liked Crystal. Tensions were eased when they shook hands and Horatio said, "My God, I thought I had big hands but yours overlap mine and your grip is causing a little pain!" Eugenio smiled and said he was sorry and Horatio said, "It's okay, next time we meet let's just nod." And both men began to laugh.

Meanwhile, Ralph, Johnnie and Mary were decorating the tree. It had become a tradition that a huge decorated Christmas tree would be in the center of the store for the holidays. Even at the age of 18, Ralph understood that his family was one of the lucky ones during the Depression. They did not have much, but they had more than many.

Ralph was starting to become irritated with his younger brother, Johnnie. Every time Ralph would put an ornament on the tree and turn his back, Johnnie would take it off and put it back in the box. Johnnie thought this was hysterical. Ralph thought he was a pain in the ass. If it weren't for his dad sitting smoking his stogie and watching his children decorate the tree, Ralph would probably have sent his little brother flying out of the store with a quick kick in the ass.

Suddenly, a piercing, agonizing scream interrupted the decorating. It came from upstairs above the store where the family resided. Ralph looked at his father and watched him look up toward the ceiling of the store. They both knew something horrible happened to Josephine. Instantly, Eugenio and Ralph ran for the staircase leading up to the living quarters. Horatio was a step behind them.

As they ran for the staircase leading to the upstairs living quarters, they heard a shriek of agony and the painful yelling of "Papa, Papa." Ralph was taking three steps at a time up the stairs, following the voice he heard. His father and Horatio were right behind him.

When they reached the bathroom door, they heard Josephine screaming from within and when they tried to open the door it was locked. Banging on the door, Ralph yelled, "Josephine, Josephine, open the door." The only response he heard was more blood curdling screams and cries for help. Ralph tried to put his shoulder to the door and break it down but he was unsuccessful. His father pushed him aside and with one great punch of his enormous hand, he broke a hole in the door. Ralph heard not only the wood break, but also heard bone shattering. He placed his hand through the hole and was able to unlock the door where he saw his little sister, Josephine, lit up like a torch. The flames engulfed her whole body except her face, where he saw her eyes full of terror. Horatio quickly jumped toward her, wrapping himself around her and her flaming clothing trying to smother the fire. Ralph and his dad grabbed towels to wrap around her and Horatio. While his father was smothering both of them with his body, Ralph turned on the faucets and soaked more towels in the water. He tried to cover their bodies with the wet towels as tears started to roll down his face. They were able to extinguish the fire but Horatio and Josephine had severe burns on their bodies.

Josephine went into shock as her father wrapped his arms around her in a towel and kept crying in Italian, "Mio bella figlia, io sono qua." "My beautiful daughter, I am here." Coming into the bathroom was her mother, Philomena, Crystal, Mary and little Johnnie right behind her. Philomena started to scream, "Josephine, my Josephine." Eugenio turned to his wife and said, "She will be all right. Raphael, go downstairs quickly and get the car, we are going to take her and Horatio to the hospital."

Ralph ran down the flight of stairs three steps at a time and went into the garage to get his father's car. He drove it to the front of the store where his father, with Josephine in his arms, came out the front door. Behind them was Horatio being helped by Crystal and Philomena. Eugenio turned around and told Philomena to stay with the children and he, Ralph and Crystal would rush to the hospital with Josephine and Horatio.

Ralph drove up Ingham Avenue and down Ridge Road to OLV Hospital as fast as the Model A Ford Circa would go. His father was in the back seat caressing Josephine and quietly whispering to her that everything would be all right. Josephine was still in shock and was whimpering. Horatio was sitting in the front seat next to Ralph and Crystal. Although his burns were serious, he turned around and told Eugenio that everything would be all right.

Ralph quickly pulled into the entrance of the hospital and rushed out of the car to the front desk yelling that he needed help. The nurses responded very quickly and followed him out to the car. They took Josephine from the arms of her father and quickly carried her into the emergency room. Horatio, with the aid of Crystal and Ralph, was able to walk on his own into the emergency room. The pain from his blistering burns was evident from the expression on his face and he was bleeding profusely in the abdominal area. As the emergency staff came to him, he kept on saying, "I'm okay. Help the young girl."

The nurse in the emergency room told Eugenio to go into the waiting room. They would take it from here. She then looked down at his hand and said, "Oh my God, what happened to your hand?" His hand was twice as big as it normally was and had white bone fragments sticking out from his knuckles. It was also charred with burned skin and dry blood and it looked hideous. The nurse immediately told him to follow her as they went into another part of the emergency room. The doctor came in and began to administer medical treatment to him. He glanced at the nurse and asked if she gave him any sedatives because he didn't seem to be in any pain, even though the wounds were severe. She shook her head no, explaining that he just wanted to know about his daughter. She said, "He didn't even know he was injured."

Meanwhile, Ralph was agitated, pacing back and forth in the waiting room, wanting to know information about his sister, father and Horatio. All three were in separate rooms in the emergency area. He kept on asking the nurses about them and the only thing they told him was that they did not have any information. This was making Ralph very angry. He was ready to rush into the emergency room when he saw his father come through the doors.

His father's arm was in a sling and he had a large amount of gauze wrapped around his hand. Josephine and Horatio were still receiving treatment. "Pa, are you okay?" Eugenio responded, "Noa worry about me. Worry about your beautiful sister and that brave man Horatio."

Chapter 43

Eugenio paced in the waiting room, worried and agitated. He was concerned about his daughter and was upset that he did not know what was happening. Ralph tried to console his father and told him that she was in good hands and that the doctors would come and tell them how she was doing. As Ralph was talking to his father, a doctor came into the waiting room. He asked if there were any family members here for the young girl. He also asked if there was anyone here for the man named Horatio. When Eugenio said that he was the father of the young girl, the doctor told him that his daughter was in shock and severely burned over 80 percent of her body. The burns were severe and it was too early to know if she would survive. The doctor said that they were calling in a specialist to evaluate his daughter. They would have more information in the next 24 hours.

Eugenio just stared at the doctor and could not say a word. Ralph stepped in and asked the doctor to be honest and asked for his professional opinion. He looked Ralph straight in the eye and said, "This poor girl has less than a 50/50 chance of surviving. As I stated, the burns are very severe, especially below her waistline. Her face seems to be the only place that was not severely burned but there will be some scarring." Ralph broke down and started crying. His father just continued to stare at the doctor and did not say a word.

The doctor then turned to Crystal and asked her if she was related to Horatio. Crystal said no but she was a very close friend. He then told her that he was sedated and resting. "We are trying to make him as comfortable as possible. He had severe burns on his hands and some parts of his neck and chest but he will recover in time. We are more concerned with the bleeding from his abdominal area." Crystal thanked the doctor and then began to cry.

The doctor left the waiting room and Ralph said to his dad, "It's okay. Josephine is strong. She'll come back to us." Again, Eugenio just stared at his son, more in shock than anything.

After two hours in the waiting room, Eugenio was approached by a frail older man dressed in a priest's garment and hat. He said to Eugenio, "My son, what is it that distresses you so much?" Eugenio looked into the man's eyes and found a sense of serenity as he told him what happened to his daughter. He said that the doctors do not know if she will survive these severe burns. He continued to get all his frustration out. He asked the priest "Why? Why dida this happen to my Josephine? She wasa beautiful girl and God gave her polio when she wasa young. She wasa taken from us for four years ago and put in the hospital. She never hurta anyone in her life. She finally camea home to us and now God tries to take her away from us again. Why? Why her and nota me?"

Father Baker looked into the eyes of Eugenio and said, "God and Our Lady will take good care of your Josephine. Come with me to the Basilica and we will pray together for Josephine."

Eugenio looked at this saintly priest and said, "No! Ia prayed to Him to helpa my daughter when she had polio and He dida nothing. Now, He torments this beautiful girl witha pain from burns alla over her body. She may die and youa wanta me to pray to Him. Youa pray to Him because my Josephine needs more thana prayer. She needsa to be here witha her family and nota in the hands of a cruel God."

Father Baker understood this man's anger and hurt. He did not say anything for a few seconds but looked deeply into his eyes and finally stated, "My son, I understand your anger. You love your daughter more than anything but also Our Lord loves her too. I cannot question why the Almighty has allowed this to happen but be assured that your daughter is loved by Him as much as you love her. He is watching over her along with our Blessed Mother. I will go into the Basilica and pray to our Lord and Blessed Lady until she gets better." With that, Father Baker placed his hand on Eugenio's shoulder and with the other hand, blessed his forehead. He turned and left the emergency room and headed to the Basilica where he would pray in front of the Blessed Virgin Mary. He would stay there long into the night and early morning, until he heard from the doctors at the hospital.

Eugenio watched this frail priest leave the room. Although his words comforted him, he was still angry at God. He kept on thinking how cruel can this God be and more and more he started to become frustrated and angry. He thought...*how dare this priest ask me to pray when even prayers may not help my daughter.*

As the frail old priest knelt in front of the Blessed Virgin Mary statue in the Basilica, he started to cry and asked the Lady to please take him and spare the young girl's life. He stayed there kneeling and praying until the early morning.

Chapter 44

It was past midnight and everyone left Josephine's room. Her father and brother were sleeping in the waiting room down the hall; Father Baker was saying his prayers at the Basilica and Elizabeth Donner quietly entered her room. Elizabeth, after she lost her baby, was in a suicidal state for a while. The visits from Father Baker brought her comfort and a purpose for life. This gentle and holy man gave her the will to live and the desire to help people, especially the young.

Father Baker convinced Dr. Sullivan to take Elizabeth on at OLV Hospital to intern as a nurses' aide. At first, Dr. Sullivan was very reluctant because of the inexperience of this young girl but after a few talks with Father Baker, he knew this holy man would be getting his own way. He conceded and had Elizabeth on an accelerated but thorough internship. He told Father Baker that he would concede to his wishes only if Elizabeth would sacrifice long hours of learning, studying and working at the hospital under direct supervision. Father Baker smiled and told Dr. Sullivan he would guarantee it.

After Elizabeth was healthy enough to get out of bed and perform everyday activities, Father Baker paid her a visit. He told her that she was destined to be a healer and advocate of the faith. When he told her this, Elizabeth was wide-eyed and said, "How could you know this and foresee my future?" Father Baker said, "Because, my child,

Our Lady told me this in my dreams and she has never led me astray. You are special. Believe me, child, you are special."

Elizabeth, although she had some doubts, agreed to Father Baker's suggestion and became a student in the field of medicine but also a devoted follower of Our Lady of Victory.

As she entered the hospital room, she heard the heavy breathing of a sedated Josephine. She walked over to her bedside and noticed that her whole body was bandaged except for her head and upper neck region. She looked into her face and saw a beautiful child not much younger than she, but at the same time, she felt a strong motherly instinct toward Josephine. She could not understand her feelings but she felt compelled to help this child.

She leaned over and whispered her name. There was no response. She whispered her name again, this time a little louder and again, there was no response. Elizabeth finally leaned over, kissed Josephine on the forehead and said, "Josephine, I am here with you along with Our Lady." She waited for a moment and then Josephine opened her beautiful brown eyes, smiled and said, "Who are you?"

Elizabeth told her who she was and that Father Baker and Our Lady sent her to help her recover. Josephine smiled and said, "That is nice. I know who Father Baker is but who is the Lady you are talking about?" Elizabeth gave a little chuckle and thought this was the first time that Father Baker was recognized before Our Lady of Victory.

Elizabeth said, "Our Lady is Mary, the Blessed Mother of Jesus, who has given me strength to overcome my adversities and she is here to help you to overcome yours.

She loves you as does Father Baker and they want you to recover and to enjoy the life that the Almighty has given you."

Josephine, although in discomfort and pain, wanted to talk to Elizabeth. For one hour, the two of them spoke about many things. Elizabeth told Josephine about the child that she had lost and the healing affect that Father Baker and Our Lady had bestowed on her. Josephine was emotional from what she heard that Elizabeth had gone through and the loss of her child. She did not think of her own suffering but instead sympathized and cried for Elizabeth.

Elizabeth told Josephine, "Do not cry. The Lord, the Blessed Mother and of course, Father Baker have shown me my purpose in life, just as they will show you. Sometimes, I do not understand the reason but I know they love me and my child and one day I will be reunited with him and happy forever."

With that, Elizabeth told Josephine to rest. "I will be back tomorrow and we will talk some more. Father Baker told me that I was a gift from the Lord and now I look at you and say that you are a gift. Sleep restfully, have wonderful dreams for the Lord and Our Lady are with you."

Josephine smiled and slowly closed her eyes and drifted off into a restful sleep. With that, Elizabeth arose from her chair, bent over and kissed Josephine on the forehead and smiled. For the first time, she understood what her life calling was going to be and that Father Baker was truly a prophet.

Chapter 45

It was six o'clock in the morning when Dr. Sullivan and one of the nurses entered Josephine's room. Josephine was sleeping comfortably and Dr. Sullivan was reluctant to wake her but knew that he had to in order to check her vital signs and the condition of her burns. He leaned over and said very quietly and gently, "Josephine, can you hear me? It is Dr. Sullivan." Josephine stirred but her eyes did not open and she seemed like she was in a deep, peaceful sleep. This astounded the doctor because even though she was sedated, he thought she would be in pain and discomfort.

He leaned over once more and said, "Josephine, this is Dr. Sullivan. I need to check you and talk to you." Still, there was no movement from Josephine. Dr. Sullivan turned and looked at the nurse and told her that we need to wake her. "I have to check her vital signs and burns." The nurse nodded and moved to the bedside and gently touched her to see if she could wake her. Again, there was no response.

Dr. Sullivan felt that there was another presence in the room and he turned and saw the frail old priest and the young intern standing in the doorway. He smiled and said, "Good morning, Monsignor, and a good morning to you, Elizabeth."

The nurse was looking at Josephine and was amazed when she saw her open her eyes and smile at the old priest and young girl in the doorway. Although her throat was parched and sore, she was able to say, "Good morning, Father Baker" and gave a slight cough as she smiled and said, "Hello Elizabeth."

Father Baker went to Josephine's bedside, smiled and gave her a blessing. Elizabeth followed the old priest and held Josephine's bandaged hand and said, "I hope you are feeling better." Before she could say another word, Pop Galanti and Ralph rushed into the room and went straight to the bed calling her name.

Josephine smiled and in a soft raspy voice said, "Hello Papa, hello big brother." Pop Galanti gave her a gentle kiss on her forehead, while Ralph stood at the foot of her bed, blowing her kisses in abundance. Josephine looked at Ralph and said, "Don't do that...you look like a jerk." Ralph laughed and said, "Josephine, you're getting better!"

Pop Galanti was speaking very fast in Italian telling his daughter how much he loved her and that her mother and her sister Mary would be coming up shortly to visit with her. He turned and looked at Dr. Sullivan and said, "I hope youa will let my little Johnnie to come up too because I knowa he misses his sister." Dr. Sullivan said, "No problem, Mr. Galanti, this is a special occasion and I want her family to see what a brave, strong and wonderful girl she is."

Eugenio smiled and thanked him. He turned back to his daughter and continued kissing her on her forehead and touching her cheek very lightly. That is when Josephine noticed her father's hand was bandaged and his arm was in a sling. She said, "Papa, what happened to your hand?" Ralph replied, "There was a door that was in Pop's way when you were in the bathroom. If you think Pop's hand is bad, you should see the poor door." With that, Josephine smiled and reached out to touch her father's bandaged hand and brought it to her lips and gave it a soft kiss.

Father Baker and Elizabeth, who were standing by the doorway, looked at each other and smiled. Elizabeth said to Father Baker, "Our Lady blessed us again."

And with that, they both quietly turned and walked down the hospital hall to go to the chapel where they would pray and give thanks to Our Lady.

Dr. Sullivan went by the bedside and quietly said to Eugenio that he needed to have a few moments alone with Josephine to evaluate her and ask her some questions. Eugenio turned, nodded and as he was leaving the room with Ralph to go back into the waiting room, he said to Dr. Sullivan, "Thank you. Youa saved my daughter's life and I willa always remember it." Where Dr. Sullivan responded, "Please do not thank me; this was a miracle. Please thank Father Baker. It was his undying faith and Our Lady and his prayers that saved your daughter."

Eugenio did not know what to say. He just turned and left the room. Instead of going back to the waiting room, they went to see Horatio who was on the floor below Josephine.

They entered Horatio's room where they saw him sitting up, holding Crystal's hand who was seated next to the bed. Horatio, with a worried look on his face, quickly said, "How is Josephine?" Ralph said that the doctor told them it was a miracle that she survived. "We think she has a long way to go for recovery but I know she can do it." Horatio said, "Thank the Lord. I know she will recover. She is a strong young girl with a wonderful family."

Pop Galanti said to Horatio, "Before I aska you how youa are, I wanta to thank you so much for helping my daughter and mya family. Youa are one of the reasons whya my daughter is living. Thanka you, mya friend." With that, Crystal started crying. Horatio turned to her and said, "Oh my God, not again. Eugenio, she's been crying now for two straight hours, and if she continues, she will be in the other bed dehydrated." Crystal looked up and gave him a smile and a little poke with her fist in his arm.

Ralph asked Horatio what the doctor said. Horatio said, "Well the burns will leave some scarring on my hands but otherwise, the burns will be healed. He was a little more worried about the bleeding from my abdominal area. I had a little accident a few months ago and it wasn't completely healed so he wants to keep me in the hospital for a couple more days to evaluate the situation. I'm sure I'll be out in a few days."

After a few moments of conversation, Ralph and his father bid them goodbye and told Horatio they would see him tomorrow. Ralph turned to Crystal and gave her a kiss on the cheek and thanked her for all she did. She nodded and Ralph left the room to go back to the store to pick up his mother and siblings to come back to visit Josephine. Eugenio went into the waiting room, thinking about Father Baker.

Chapter 46

The next several weeks were very hectic in the Galanti family. Everyone wanted to visit Josephine in the hospital and spend as much time as possible with her but there was the store to watch, possible work available at the steel plant on a daily basis, school for Ralph, Mary and Johnnie and Josephine's rehabilitation sessions at the hospital. Crystal, Coco and Horatio became a godsend to the family.

Crystal was able to watch the store whenever Pop and Mom Galanti wanted to visit Josephine. When Pop Galanti was selected to work at the steel plant, Horatio was able to drive Mom Galanti to the hospital while Crystal watched the store. Coco would also help in watching the store after school, which gave Ralph the opportunity to visit his sister. This went on for the whole month of January.

Even the guys in the GAA showed their support by making sure that when they were using the clubhouse, everything was cleaned up afterward. They also kept Crystal company in the store to make sure there were no hooligans coming in to take advantage of her when she was alone there.

Meanwhile, the Lentis were enjoying their first month of work for DiJoseph. They actually were becoming trusted soldiers in DiJoseph's criminal family. DiJoseph had them go to several grocery stores in the southtowns that were making bootleg liquor to demand payment of protection money for this right. They were also given the liberty that if the store owners refused or hesitated, they were allowed to use force to convince them. DiJoseph said that everything was allowed except for killing and only he can give that order.

The other areas where they sought payment for the special protection of DiJoseph was in the whore houses of the southtowns and South Buffalo area. This is where the Lentis loved to work. Not only were they getting monetary payment to give to DiJoseph, but they were able to get some services from the ladies of the bordellos. The madames of these bordellos hated this because each time, more than one of the girls would be beaten up after performing this free service to these three thugs. The madames were afraid to say anything because they didn't know how the Lentis would react to them.

Everything was running smoothly for the Lentis and they were having no problems until the last week of January. Usually, when they went into a grocery store, the owner was an elderly Italian man who knew what the score was if he did not pay. All the Lentis had to do was say they worked for DiJoseph and tell them that he is demanding their payment for his kind services. Very seldom was there a problem and if there was, a quick punch in the stomach by Lenti Sr. while the poor owner was held by the two sons quickly changed their mind.

DiJoseph called the three Lentis into his office late in January. He told them there was a new grocery store that opened up in the heart of an Italian Buffalo neighborhood that was making bootleg liquor but not paying for protection. The owner was some big Polish guy who married an Italian girl. DiJoseph said, "I want to teach this fuckin Pollack a lesson. Not only did he screw up this Italian family by marrying that girl, but he is trying to make us look like idiots because he says he doesn't have to pay. I want you to go there and persuade him any way you could, do you understand?" Angelo Sr. nodded and said he would have the money in two days. With that, he left the office with his sons, got in their car and drove home to discuss how and when they were going to do this.

Junior said, "There's no need to plan. Tomorrow, we wait until he is alone, go in and ask for the money. There are three of us. I don't think this stupid Pollack has the balls to do anything against three. And if so, I will have a bat in the car and I will have my blade on me. I would be able to even persuade the Pope to pay." They all smirked and went to get a glass of wine and bullshit on the porch.

The next day, early in the morning, the three of them drove down Niagara Street to the new grocery store that had opened. It was early enough that there were not too many people in the store and they waited in the car until everyone left. They quickly got out of the car, went into the store, shut the door and Sal flipped the sign that said "closed." To their surprise, the owner was a very big man, over six foot two and weighed approximately 270 pounds. Sal immediately became a little antsy and did not say anything but stayed in the background while his father and brother approached this strapping man. Junior was not as cocky as he was the day before when they planned this caper. The big Polish owner smiled and said, "Can I help you?" He did not notice that Sal locked the door and turned the sign to "closed." Angelo Sr. looked at him and said, "You owe Mr. DiJoseph some money and we're here to collect it."

The owner said, "What the hell are you talking about?" Junior responded, "Listen, you dumb Pollack, we know you make bootleg liquor and you sell it. For you to do that, you have to pay us for not only protection but the right to make it."

The big Polish man looked and said, "You have to be fuckin kidding me. Get the hell out of my store before I throw you out" and took one step toward them. Of course, true to colors, the Lentis backed up and were kind of baffled as to what to do. This was the first time they ever had any trouble and they did not have the bat with them. But Junior was more confident because in his pocket, he had his switchblade and he reached in to caress it. This gave him more confidence.

The big Pole said again, "Get the hell out of my store," and he took another step toward them. Angelo Sr. found enough courage to step forward and to push the man backwards. This was a bad mistake for the big Pole sent a haymaker into the left eye of Angelo Sr., knocking him on the seat of his pants. Seeing this, Junior and Sal ran toward the owner, only to be thrown like ragdolls to each side of the store.

Hearing the racket from the back of the store was the owner's young wife. She ran quickly into the storefront and asked what is happening. That is when Junior had his chance because he was lying on the ground right where she came in. He quickly grabbed her around the neck and got behind her with his switchblade at her throat.

The big Polish owner stopped in his tracks. He dared not move, in fear that this lunatic would do something harmful to his wife. He said in a very controlled voice, "Please let her go. I will give you the money."

Junior smiled and said, "You're goddamn right you will, you asshole." He then proceeded to nestle his mouth on the wife's neck and gave it a lick. He said, "Now isn't this better than having a Pollack tongue on your pretty Italian neck?" He then also pressed the knife a little closer to the neck, nicking it and causing her to bleed. She started crying and kept saying, "Please don't, please don't." The husband was incensed but knew that this crazy man would cause harm to his beautiful wife. His rage was so that he probably would have killed all three of them but instead took a deep breath and pleaded, "Please, please let her go. I will give you as much as you want."

Angelo Sr. got up. His eye was already beginning to swell. He went up to the big man and hit him with everything he had in the side of the jaw. Then Salvatore rushed in and kicked the man in the groin and as he went down, kicked him in the head. The big Pole was stunned and was hurting but still was conscious and kept on pleading, "Please let go of my wife."

Angelo Sr. told the owner to get up and bring him the money that he owed. The owner said, "How much?" "Well, because of all the payments you missed and because you are stupid enough to cause us this trouble, I think $20 will cover payment for Mr. DiJoseph for this month and just because of the trouble you gave us, it will cost you $15 more." The big man said he doesn't have $35 but could give him $20 and they could take whatever they wanted out of the store to make up the rest.

Junior just smiled and said, "How about a little piece of this Italian dark meat for me and my brother and we will call it even." With that, the wife started to cry hysterically. Angelo Sr. said, "No, I'd rather have the money. We can get a piece of ass anywhere. Anyway, she is damaged goods, she got that Pollack's Polish sausage in her and that spoiled her." The three laughed.

There were a couple of people trying to get into the store, looking through the window. This got the Lentis edgy. They told the big man to get the money quickly and while he went to the back to get it, Angelo Sr. and Sal started to take things that they wanted from the store, like cigarettes, soda, and candy. Junior still held the wife by the neck with the knife close to her throat. He was starting to getting a hard on and she could feel his bulge against her thigh. He kept on sniffing her neck and licking her wound. She could do nothing but tremble and quietly sob.

The owner came back limping slightly with the $20. He gave it to them and said, "Please let my wife go." Before Junior let her go, he told the big man, "The next time you do this to us when we ask you for payment, I will carve your wife's face so that not even Frankenstein would want to fuck her. Do you understand?" The owner nodded and Junior threw the wife at the feet of the owner. While the big Pole picked up his wife, hugged her and kissed her, the three Lentis backed up, turned and walked out the front door. Before Junior closed the front door, he blew the wife a kiss and warned the owner one more time.

The three got into the car. By this time, there were a half dozen neighbors milling around the front of the store. No one helped. They knew these three came from DiJoseph and nobody had the courage to confront them.

The next day the Lentis went to DiJoseph with the $20 instead of the $10 that was expected.

Chapter 47

"What the hell happened to you?" said DiJoseph, looking at Angelo Sr. Angelo's eye was half shut, swollen and black and blue. He said, "The Pollack hit me when I was not looking."

"You should have been looking, you stupid son of a bitch. You know you can't trust those Pollacks," said DiJoseph, laughing and winking at his two henchmen who were standing near the door.

Even though Angelo Sr. was a little embarrassed in front of his sons, he still held his temper and said, "Well, boss, we taught him a lesson and we brought you even a little bit more than you expected." With that, he gave DiJoseph $20 instead of the $10 and said that he would have no problems sending his collectors in each week for the payments.

DiJoseph smiled and told them that they did a good job. Angelo Sr. forgot about being embarrassed and puffed out his chest a little bit and told his boss that anything he wanted he and his sons would make sure that he gets it.

DiJoseph started talking about how it's getting harder and harder to get payments because of this damn Depression that the country was in. It's hard to make an honest dollar, he told the group. "There is some talk that this new president, Roosevelt, will be getting rid of Prohibition by next year and if that happens, it might be even harder for money to be coming in. Until then, we just have to be satisfied with this amount of money that we are taking in."

DiJoseph did not tell them the whole truth. He was making well over six figures on a yearly basis with the money from bootlegging, prostitution, protection, speakeasies, loan sharking and gambling. Even though he made this money, it was nowhere near the amount of money that Sebastian "The Baker" Massini was bringing in on a yearly basis. DiJoseph, who was a "capo" in the Massini family, would be considered a pauper compared to "The Baker."

DiJoseph was in a good mood and offered the three Lentis to sit down and have a glass of wine with him. This put old man Angelo into euphoria. Junior finally felt he had made the big time while Sal was still nervous wondering why DiJoseph was being so nice. They toasted to the beginning of a successful new year. Angelo Sr., trying to make points, saluted to the health, prosperity and long life of his boss. The Lenti family thought they were in second heaven.

With this new found courage, Angelo Sr. asked his boss, "You know, we have a grocery store in Lackawanna that I know makes bootleg liquor but does not pay his tribute to you." DiJoseph's ears perked up and he said, "I don't think so. I know most of what happens in Lackawanna and I know all the stores that I want pay me. Who the hell are you talking about?"

Angelo Sr. thought this was how he was about to get even with that asshole Eugenio Galanti. He was going to lie a little bit because the only thing that Eugenio made was homemade wine and he gave it away instead of selling it. He told DiJoseph, "It's Galanti's Confectionary Store. That son of a bitch has been making bootleg liquor for years and selling it behind your back. He is making a fool out of you."

Angelo Sr. should have quit while he was ahead, when he was making and drinking those toasts. DiJoseph stood up and knocked the wine glasses off his desk and said to Angelo, "You fuckin asshole. Who are you saying he is making a fool out of? You work here for a month and you think you know how to run this place. I should kick your ass all the way back to Lackawanna. Get the fuck out of my office and I'll call you when I need you."

With that, the three Lentis stood up shaking as they left the office, not daring to look back. Angelo Sr. and Junior were first out the door with Sal right behind them but unfortunately, the big man with the fedora standing near the door slammed the door before Sal was fully out. He toppled over in the snow, hitting his brother and father at the legs and all three of them were lying in the snow. Angelo Sr. kicked his son, screamed some obscenities at him and told him to get in the car. Junior drove home and not a word was said by any of them. Angelo Sr. kept on thinking... *what the hell happened? That fuckin Galanti did it to me again without knowing it.*

DiJoseph sat behind his desk still fuming. The big man with the fedora came up to him and said, "Boss, what happened? I've never seen you that mad in a long time. Do you want me to get rid of those three on a permanent basis?" DiJoseph regained his composure, sat down and poured himself some anisette. He then looked at the man in the fedora and said, "No, Bruno. We could still use those assholes, even though they are not bright but they follow orders. I'm just pissed off about what they said about Galanti making a fool out of me. Those sons of bitches don't even know that I know more about him than they do." He then proceeded to tell Bruno the story.

"When I was a very young man, I used to live in Olean, New York. I had some family there. I had a young cousin named Sarah who was very beautiful and was the apple of my eye. After I moved to Buffalo, I tried to keep in contact with her and every so often, sent her some money. She met a wonderful guy called Giovanni. She was madly in love with him and was hoping that he was going to ask her to marry him. She wrote me and asked me if Giovanni proposed marriage, would I give her away at her wedding. Her father passed away two years after I left Olean. I was so emotional that I wrote her right away and told her I would be honored to be there and give her away to this lucky man.

It's ironic that Giovanni was a cousin of Eugenio Galanti. He sponsored him to come to America and live with him in Olean. The two became inseparable."

He proceeded to tell Bruno of the bar fight and how this big strapping German was put down by the smaller Italian in arm wrestling. He went on about how Galanti lost his job on the railroad because of that and how he moved to Lackawanna. Bruno was not a big talker but was a very good listener. DiJoseph continued.

"A year or so later the big German took out his frustrations and his anger on Giovanni. He stabbed and killed him in a so called fight outside the bar. Witnesses say that Giovanni started it and pulled a knife on him and the German was only protecting himself. Sarah wrote to me about what happened. She was distraught and I thought she was going to commit suicide. I wrote her back and told her that I would be down there in three weeks. That I had important business up here and I could not leave at that time. Three weeks later, I took a ride to Olean and was going to make things right for Sarah and also for Giovanni. That is when I learned from Sarah that Giovanni's cousin, Eugenio Galanti, came down to Olean. She said that the big German was supposed to have been attacked by three robbers and beat up so severely that he was still in the hospital. Sarah knew it was not three robbers but that it was Eugenio by himself who took care of the German. She said Eugenio came to her that night and said to her that he was so sorry. He gave her an envelope, not to be opened until after he left. He kissed her on her forehead and said that if she needed anything, please let him know and he would be there for her. With that, he left and he has never returned.

She opened the envelope and in it was $50. That was more money than most people make in three months down in Olean. Needless to say, that money helped her move on with her life. After she told me the story, I told her that I hope to meet this Eugenio Galanti because I owe him a debt of gratitude. With that, I kissed Sarah and I drove back to Buffalo."

"I found out a few years later that a confectionary store was opened up in Lackawanna. When I found out it was Eugenio Galanti's store, I made sure we would protect this man and his family. It is a debt I plan to keep and those sons of bitches Lentis better honor it."

Chapter 48

"What the hell did you do?" asked a very irritated Carmen Marrano. Gracie just looked at her older brother, Carmen, and did not say a word. Anna chimed in, "Gracie, Gracie, Gracie. Papa is going to kill you when he gets home. Why did you get into another fight with Mario Lenti? You promised Papa that you would stay away from him and yet this is your third fight you have had with him."

Young Neal blurted out, "Leave her alone. She was helping me against that dope. He kept on calling me a baby who has to have a girl to fight my battles. Then he started mocking me by crying and saying, 'Gracie, Gracie, Gracie, please help little me. I am so yellow.' That is when I ran at him and he shoved me to the ground and got up on top of me and started slapping me. Gracie just jumped in and started swinging, kicking, pulling his hair and saying a lot of bad words which I am not going to tell you. She did get in a good right cross to his eye but he also got a lucky punch in and hit Gracie in her left eye."

Carmen looked at his young brother. "Then you are just as much to blame as your crazy sister. I told all of you do not associate with that Lenti family. If they are around, just go in the other direction. How many times do I have to say this before one of them really hurts you?"

As defiant as ever, Gracie yelled out, "That son of a bitch, Mario, is not going to hurt me or Neal ever. He's the one that's going to be hurting."

Josephine, along with Carmela, was there listening to all this commotion. Josephine said, "Watch your mouth, young lady. If Papa heard you say that, you'd be eating soap for a month."

Gracie said, "I don't care. I am sick and tired of the Lentis, all of them. Especially Mario, who keeps on picking on Neal. The next time he touches Neal, I swear to God, I will hit him over the head with a baseball bat."

Carmela tried to keep peace by saying, "Gracie, please listen to Carmen. He's telling you this because he loves you and does not want to see you or anyone in our family hurt. Also, he is trying to protect you from Papa if he finds out that you got into another fight."

Carmen grabbed Gracie and gave her a hug and told her that Carmela was right. He didn't want to see anything happen to his kid sister. "Please promise me that the next time, and I hope there is not a next time, but if there is, you will grab Neal and run home. Everybody knows by now that you're the Joe Louis of Bethlehem Park School." With that, Neal was jumping up and down with his hands over his head and bouncing around like a pro fighter does when he wins a bout.

Carmen continued, "The real problem now is to keep you away from Papa so he doesn't see your swollen eye or some of your scratch marks. I will talk to Ma and explain what happened again. I think she will listen to me because I will tell her that you had no alternative but to do that or Neal might have been injured. Hopefully, she will help me keep you out of sight for a few days. If not, I do not want you to lie. You will have to tell Pa what you did and prepare for whatever happens." With that, Gracie ran up and hugged her big brother and gave him a kiss and told him she loved him.

Gracie and Neal left the room and went outside to play. Carmen and his three sisters, Anna, Josephine and Carmela, stayed to talk about how to make sure Gracie did not get into any more trouble with their father and mother. Anna said, "It might be easier if we bring her to Father Baker's. He definitely will straighten her out." Josephine said, "I love Father Baker but I think he even would have his hands full with her." Carmela chimed in, "Let's all pray to Our Lady and hope that she can persuade Gracie to become a nun. Then she won't be our problem anymore, but Our Lord's." Everybody got a good laugh since Carmela is usually the quiet and reserved one.

Later that day, the Lentis arrived home after their ill-fated meeting with DiJoseph. Angelo Sr. was miserable. He kept on thinking, that no good Galanti has caused me so much goddamn trouble, I hate that son of a bitch and I will get even with him. The three of them walked into the house around dinnertime. They saw Mario sitting at the table eating pasta. His head was down and he did not look up as they entered. Angelo Sr. said, "Where the fuck is your mother?" With his head down, he told him she was upstairs changing Romeo's diaper.

He told Mario to get his ass away from the table and go upstairs to tell her that they are home and wanted to eat. Mario slowly got up, keeping his head down and turned to go upstairs. His father told him to stop. "What the hell's wrong? Why do you have your head down? Are you embarrassed to say hello to your father and brothers?" With his head still down, he quietly muttered no. "Then look up at me."

Mario looked up. His right eye was swollen shut and he had scratches all over his face and neck. The father stared and said, "What the fuck happened to you?" If Mario had courage, he would have asked his father the same question because his left eye was also swollen shut and blackened. But he did not and just said that he had a fight at school. "Well," Angelo Sr. said, "You better have won. You see my eye? The guy got in a lucky punch but I beat the shit out of him. How did you do?"

"I don't know." "What do you mean you don't know? Either you lost or you won." Mario again said, "I don't know." Trying to keep his anger under control, Angelo Sr. said, "Well, who the hell did you fight with?" Mario looked at his father with tears in his eyes and said, "Gracie Marrano."

It was almost like an explosion in the kitchen. Angelo Sr. became incensed with anger and hate. He screamed, "You let a fuckin girl beat the hell out of you? You are nothing but a yellow piece of shit that I am sorry to call a son. You're more like your fuckin mother every day, useless." He pulled out a strap and with his left hand punched his son on the side of the face and as the son was on the ground, started whipping him with his belt. Concetta heard the screaming downstairs and put Romeo in the crib and rushed to the kitchen. She saw her poor son, Mario, lying on the floor in a fetal position being beaten by his father and being called every vile name that Angelo Sr. could think of. Something snapped in Concetta's mind and she screamed out Angelo's name, grabbed the nearest pan on the stove and ran at him full speed. Her first swing caught Angelo unaware on his left hand, causing him to yell out in pain. She kept on screaming for him to stay away from her son or she was going to kill him and kept swinging the pan back and forth. Angelo Sr. was stunned and started to back away from her and the boy.   Mario was sobbing uncontrollably on the floor and Concetta's motherly instinct took over as she dropped the pan and ran to her son's aid. She cradled him, kissed him on the head and told him everything would be all right.

This was a mistake. With the pan on the floor and her without any defense holding her son, Angelo Sr. went berserk. The noise from the house echoed throughout the neighborhood. Some neighbors came out of their houses to see what was happening. They saw it was coming from the Lenti's home and they knew it was something horrible. Fortunately, one of the neighbors had a phone and quickly called the police. By the time the police arrived, both Concetta and Mario were unconscious on the kitchen floor, bleeding profusely from different wounds on their bodies. Angelo and his two sons were sitting on the porch having a glass of Dago red wine.

Chapter 49

"How are her vital signs?" said Dr. Sullivan to Elizabeth. "She has been steady for the last hour but she does some moaning and I can't quite make out what she is saying. I think she's asking about Mario and Romeo. I believe Mario is her son who was brought in with her but I don't know exactly who Romeo is." It was now early morning of the next day and the staff at OLV Hospital did a superb job in tending to the severe trauma of both mother and son.

"I want her monitored every hour," said Dr. Sullivan. "The trauma to her head and body is so severe that I am very concerned. Her son is in bad shape but not as much as his mother. It seems that she was trying to protect him by covering his body and she took most of the brunt of the beating. I hope they caught the son of a bitch who did this to this poor woman."

Elizabeth stayed in the room after Dr. Sullivan left and was talking softly to her, telling her that everything would be all right and that Mario and Romeo were fine. She kept putting a cold compress on her forehead to make her more comfortable and continued talking very softly to her.

Dr. Sullivan, after he left Concetta's room, went straight down the hall to her son Mario's room. Mario was awake and was staring at the ceiling when he came in the room. Dr. Sullivan went over to the bedside, smiled down on Mario and said, "Son, you will be fine. You have a few bruises and several lacerations but in a few days, I believe you will be able to move around on your own." Mario shifted his eyes to the doctor and said, "How is my mother?"

"It's too early to tell but I believe in time she will be able to recover." He never said to Mario that his mother probably would never have children again since her internal injuries were so severe that they had caused permanent damage.

Mario started to cry, not because he was in pain but because of the way he had treated his mother the last few years. He always wanted to impress his father so he treated his mother with less respect and at times ridiculed her along with his dad. He thought... *What a mistake I made all these years because my father was nothing but a piece of crap.* His mother tried to protect him at the cost of her own body being used as a punching bag and whipping post. His mother was his true hero and he kept on crying and crying thinking of what he had done to her. He promised himself that from that day forward, his mother would be the most important thing in his life and he would protect her against his father, even if he had to kill him.

Dr. Sullivan told Mario that his mother was mentioning his name and also the name of Romeo. "Who is Romeo?"

"That's my baby brother. He's only a couple of years old. I am worried that no one will be taking care of him. Please let me out of the hospital. I have to go home to take care of my baby brother. I know nobody else will."

This upset Dr. Sullivan very much. He told Mario that he would definitely take care of his young brother. The best thing Mario could do now was to get healthy to help his mother and young brother.

Dr. Sullivan left the room and went straight back to Concetta's room where he saw Elizabeth holding her hand and speaking softly to her even though Concetta looked like she was still in a coma. Elizabeth looked up and Dr. Sullivan motioned to her to come and see him.

"It seems that we have a little problem. The Romeo she keeps mentioning is her two- year-old baby. Mario is very concerned about him. I believe he is still at home. The father, I know, they took to the city jail and I do not know much about the other two brothers except that Mario's very concerned for his baby brother's safety. I think we should go see Father Baker for some advice."

The two of them left the room, walked down the staircase and on to Ridge Road. They crossed the street to visit Father Baker to tell him about their concerns and to seek his advice. They told this frail but holy priest the story of Concetta and Mario. Their concern was for the safety of the baby who was at home with the two brothers. According to Mario, this was the worst thing that could happen to his baby brother. Father Baker listened very intently and asked for Dr. Sullivan to summon Brother Sebastian to his office. Brother Sebastian came in and said, "Yes, Monsignor. Of what service can I be to you this wonderful morning?"

Father Baker quickly gave Brother Sebastian the scenario of what happened and told him to give this letter to the chief of police of Lackawanna. Father Baker told Brother Sebastian that it is of the upmost importance that the police chief does this as quickly as possible. He then wrote a quick note, folded it, placed it in an envelope and gave it to Brother Sebastian to deliver.

When Brother Sebastian left the office, the holy priest turned, smiled and told them what he planned. "I have asked the police chief to go to the home, take the child and bring him here to me. I, in turn, would like you, Elizabeth, to take care of the child until his mother is able. It may take a while but I will provide you with all the necessary funds and help that you may need. I told you Our Lady has plans for you and this is one.

"As for you Dr. Sullivan, my dear friend and trusted doctor, I leave the physical healing of the mother and older son in your hands. The spiritual healing of the mother, older son and baby will be in your hands, Elizabeth." With that, he bid them a good day and told them that he had to go into the Basilica to pray to Our Lady and have his daily conversation with her.

Chapter 50

When I get out of this pigsty, I'm going to get even with that bastard Galanti. It's all because of him that I'm in this mess. Him and that little bitch Marrano girl... thought Angelo Sr. as he sat on the cot in the jail cell at the Lackawanna Police Headquarters. The more he thought of how unjust those coppers were to him, the more he became infuriated.

*How could they arrest me? That bitch wife of mine attacked me and I was only protecting myself. My sissy son deserved the whipping because he caused people to disrespect me. How the hell could you get beat up by a girl? Why did they arrest me...*he thought again and again. He got up from his cot and started yelling, "Let me out, I don't deserve to be in here. I didn't do a fuckin thing but defend myself against that wacky bitch. Let me out, let me out."

The Irish cop who was on duty came up to the jail cell and slammed his baton against the bars, almost hitting Angelo's fingers. "Listen you greaseball, the next time you make me get out of my seat to shut you up, you will be not in a jail cell but in a hospital bed. Do you understand, you lowlife guinea?" Angelo backed off a little bit and in a softer voice said, "But I didn't do anything."

"Listen, asshole," said the cop. "If it was up to me, I would let you rot in this jail cell but unfortunately, it's up to your wife if she wants to press charges. I hope she does because I will have a field day with you, you fuckin wife beater."

Angelo Sr. just turned his back on the cop and walked back to his cot and sat down. He kept on thinking what an injustice this was. He thought... *when I get out, there's going to be payback to the Galantis, Marranos and now this Irish potato eater cop.* These thoughts started consuming his mind to almost madness.

The next day, early in the morning at the hospital, Elizabeth first went to visit Josephine and spent over an hour with her talking about things that young girls talk about. This was a very therapeutic session that helped Josephine immensely, more than any medicine that was given to her. After her visit with Josephine, Elizabeth went to see Concetta.

As she entered the room, Concetta was sleeping. She quietly went up to the side of the bed and stroked the side of her face very gently. Concetta's eyes opened up. Elizabeth said hello and in a quiet, calm voice told her that she would be helping her during her recovery. She asked if there was anything that she needed.

In a soft voice, Concetta said, "How is my Mario and how is my baby Romeo?" Elizabeth responded, "Mario is on the next floor and he is recovering. Matter of fact, yesterday all he did was ask about how you were doing. He seems like he is a good son."

"Yes, he is and would it be possible for me to see him? Also, I am very worried about my baby Romeo. He is home alone and there is nobody to take care of him."

Elizabeth answered, "As soon as you are well, either we will bring you to Mario or he can visit you in your room. As for Romeo, Father Baker has made arrangements for the baby's care. Matter of fact, I believe he will be coming here to see you sometime today."

"Oh my God, thank you, thank you, thank you," Concetta cried. With that, Elizabeth stroked her hair and told her to get some rest and that she would be back a little later that day.

Elizabeth started going on her rounds to each room to visit the many patients who were on her two floors. She bumped into Mrs. Galanti, Crystal, Horatio and Coco, who were going to visit Josephine. Horatio drove everyone to the hospital while Ralph watched the store. Eugenio was working at the steel plant; Ralph took the day off from school, as did Coco. Later, after Mrs. Galanti returned to the store, Ralph and his father would come to visit Josephine in the evening.

Elizabeth said hello to everyone and they talked for a few moments in the hallway. She told Mrs. Galanti that Josephine was progressing well, both mentally and physically. She also said that she was a very strong, determined and beautiful girl. Mrs. Galanti thanked her with a sweet smile. Elizabeth then turned to Horatio and asked him how he was doing. "Quite well," he responded. "I received the best care here at OLV Hospital and I owe it to the doctors, staff and you." This made Elizabeth blush.

She excused herself and told them that she had to visit a few more patients and they proceeded to go to see Josephine. During one of her patient visits, a nurse came into the room and told her that Dr. Sullivan and Msgr. Baker wanted to see her immediately in the hospital chapel. Elizabeth left the room a little nervous, thinking that maybe she had done something that may have caused a problem at the hospital.

She rushed into the chapel and stopped dead in her tracks. There was Father Baker, Dr. Sullivan and Brother Sebastian. In Brother Sebastian's arms was a bouncing, energetic, smiling baby boy. Father Baker looked at Elizabeth and said, "Elizabeth, I would like to introduce you to Romeo, Romeo I would like to introduce you to Elizabeth." With that, Brother Sebastian walked forward, held the baby out for Elizabeth and said, "Meet Romeo."

Elizabeth eagerly reached out for the toddler and brought him to her bosom and gave him kisses as he started to laugh and smile. The three men just stood there and smiled. Father Baker told Elizabeth that the baby would be in her care until the mother was able to take care of him. "Please go to the cafeteria in the orphanage and make sure he is well fed." He turned to Dr. Sullivan and said, "Please check on Concetta and if you feel that she is well enough to see him, please let Elizabeth come with the baby."

Dr. Sullivan nodded with approval and told the holy priest, "This will be the best medicine I could ever give her."

Chapter 51

In February, everything seemed to be settling down and lives were beginning to return to some type of normalcy. Josephine was beginning her rehabilitation and her health had improved immensely. There was some talk that she might be able to go home in the early springtime. The Galanti family was elated that the prognosis was so positive and that she might be with them for Easter.

Concetta was recovering from her devastating beating by her husband. Her recovery improved more quickly because she knew that her baby Romeo and son, Mario, were cared for by Father Baker and Elizabeth. One day when Concetta was recovering, Father Baker had a conversation with her and told her of his plan for her and her two boys. The holy priest looked her straight in the eye and told her that after her full recovery, she could not go home anymore for the safety of her baby, her son and herself. He told her that he would like her to stay there with him to help him take care of the orphans. He had a room set aside for her and the baby. Mario would stay with the other boys in the orphanage. She would be able to see him every day and take care of the baby and help with the caring of the orphans. At first, she said no. But Father Baker was a very convincing man and she reluctantly said she would try it for a month. The holy priest smiled, reached into his pocket and placed a medal of Our Lady in her hand.

Mario went to the orphanage, where he received three solid meals a day and was able to attend educational classes. Romeo was the darling with the staff at OLV hospital. Elizabeth took care of him as if he were her own child and the bond they formed was remarkable. Father Baker made sure Elizabeth's first priority was the care of Romeo and when she had free time, she would continue her duties in the hospital. To say the least, Romeo was almost a full-time job.

The best time Elizabeth had with Romeo was when she brought him in to see his mother. The three of them would laugh, have fun and forget about their problems. It was especially fun when Mario came after school and the four of them were in the room talking and enjoying each other's company until dinnertime.

Angelo Lenti Sr. was released from jail a week after being arrested. Concetta refused to press charges no matter how the police urged her to do so. For whatever reason that no one could understand, she did not want to see her husband go to jail for any length of time. In her mind, she probably thought that he would feel sorry for what he did and truly change. This was the wish she had but this was the wish that would never come true.

Angelo Sr. was home with his two boys, Junior and Salvatore. The week in jail did not make him remorseful. Instead, he became more hateful about everyone and everything. While he was in jail, Junior and Salvatore would do the bidding for DiJoseph. The boss did not call them into the office like he usually did before the blow up but now he sent one of his men to the house with a list of things to be done during the week. Nothing was written, everything was verbal. DiJoseph had no idea that old man Lenti had been in the slammer.

The week that Angelo Sr. was not with them, everything went smoothly. They were able to fulfill all the orders that were given to them. This was because of their association with DiJoseph. They were not given any problems and their status on the streets rose. It was not until Angelo Sr. started to go with them on their rounds that things began to get a little hectic. Angelo Sr. was so bitter and had so much hate that it filtered out in his mannerisms and attitude. He would slap one of the grocery store owners or madams of the whorehouses even if they gave him the money. All they had to do was give him a look that he did not like or an answer that he did not care for and he would either slap them or punch them. Knowing their father, the two Lenti sons knew they were headed for future trouble.

In the Marrano family, everything was peaceful. That meant Gracie was kept under wraps and Mr. Marrano did not know of her last escapade with the young Lenti boy. The family did a great job in disguising Gracie's injuries, especially on her face. It seemed that mom Marrano had Gracie either doing chores or watching her younger siblings when Mr. Marrano was in the house. The big news in the family and in Bethlehem Park was the severe beating of Concetta Lenti. Everyone was upset that a man could do this to his wife and young child. Mr. and Mrs. Marrano actually went to see Concetta at the hospital and offered her any assistance that she might need for the baby and Mario. They made sure they said nothing of the father and the other two sons.

Anna, Josephine, Carmela, Gracie and Carmen also went to the hospital not only to see Concetta, but to visit Josephine. All four of them including Gracie also went to see Mario, who was on the floor below his mother. Gracie stayed in the background as her sisters and brother asked Mario if there was anything he needed from school. Mario thanked them but said no; that Father Baker said that he is going to be taking care of him for a while.

They all left but Gracie. She slowly went up to the bed and looked at Mario and said in a quiet voice, "I'm sorry." She quickly turned around and ran out of the room before Mario could respond.

Horatio was recovering from his abdominal injuries and burns at a rapid pace. This was a godsend since his good friend and boss, Edward Wadsworth Wellington, was taken ill with a mild case of pneumonia. Horatio's responsibilities at work increased as he was given the task of running the store along with Wellington's daughter, Dorothea. But he still found enough time to spend a few hours with Crystal and help when the Galantis needed him.

Crystal did her best watching the Galanti Confectionary when needed. She was at ease because she was never alone; there was always someone from the GAA there to help. When Coco was not in school or practicing, he would help his mother in any way he could.

The members of the GAA continued to have their meetings at the clubhouse, but any future events that they were going to host were put on hold. They heard the good news that Josephine might be returning home for Easter. There was some talk of them having a social dance in her honor. They were waiting for the approval of Ralph and of course, his father before they started to plan the event. Ziggy was first to tell Ralph of their plans to "feel him out" about the dance honoring his sister. Ralph said it was too early to tell but he would let them know in a week as soon after he talked to his parents and the doctors.

After both a tragic Christmas and a harrowing month of January, things started to look better for February and the months to come.

Chapter 52

"I am calling the meeting to order," said Ginnetti, the president of the GAA. This was the first formal and organized meeting for the club since Josephine's horrific accident.

"Listen, you dumb bastards, I said I'm calling this meeting to order so keep your mouths shut. Where the hell is our sergeant-at-arms, Doc?" Doc was sitting in the back of the room. The clubhouse was almost filled with at least fifty members present. He raised his hand to let him know where he was. Armondo yelled, "You're the sergeant-at-arms, get these guys quiet and do your job."

Doc slowly got up, looked around and yelled, "Shut the hell up." And with that, he brought up the bat he had beside him and started to slap it in his palms. That immediately got everyone's attention. With the new position as sergeant-at-arms for the club, they were worried that he would probably go overboard trying to keep things in order, even if it meant bashing the heads of a few of his friends. Everyone quieted down and Doc smiled looking at Armondo and yelled, "All right Mr. President, continue."

Ginnetti asked Ralph to give the status on his sister Josephine. Ralph told the members that his sister was still in serious condition but was getting better every day. She had first, second and third degree burns over various parts of her body. The doctors were amazed at how well she was doing at this stage of her recuperation. The doctors said that the biggest problem they were worried about was infection. She would be in the hospital for a while but they were hoping that she might be able to go home for short visits. The doctors thought this would be great emotional therapy for her. If she continued to improve, they said she might be able to go home for a few days during the Easter holiday. This would be around the sixteenth of April.

Ralph did not go into more detail about the burns because he knew his sister would be very embarrassed if people knew the severity and location of the burns. The first and second-degree burns were located on her shoulders, lower neck and below her knees. The third degree burns and most severe were located in her pelvic area and upper chest and back. The doctors were concerned that she might never be able to have children.

After Ralph gave the membership an update on his sister, they all started clapping, cheering and praising Josephine. They started chanting, Josephine, Josephine, Josephine, which made Ralph feel great.

Armondo again called for order but this time did not need Doc's help. Doc was still in the back holding on to his bat and slapping it against his palms. Lui Marini raised his hand to speak. He was recognized by the president and when he got up to talk, everyone listened because he was one of the older more respected members of the club. Lui began to speak, "Now that we have an idea of when our beautiful Josephine will be back with us, I think we should start to think about honoring her. In the past, we have spoken of having a dance to raise money for the club. I suggest that we have this dance with a band during Easter week and have it in honor of Josephine. The money we raise should be given to Josephine and her family for any use they feel necessary to help her." The members went wild and said that was one of the greatest ideas that anyone had. They all started cheering, "Let's do it, let's do it." This irritated Doc a little. He thought it was a great idea and he was all for it. But he thought...*these morons have a short memory....it was just last year that they said the greatest idea they ever heard was when I told them let's have Halloween in November.*

Everyone was talking at once about doing this and giving their opinions. Then Paul Petti yelled, "Before we do anything, let's hear from Ralph." Ralph got up and thanked everyone for that wonderful gesture. He felt that his mother and father would be thankful and agree to this event. He also knew Josephine would be very happy that everyone was thinking of her. He told the club he would have an answer for them as soon as he talked to his parents.

Armondo got up and said, "We will make this one of the best dances we have had in Lackawanna. So, I am going to select Lui Marini, Lou Fistola, Tommy Pepper, Bill Renzi and Paul Petti to head up the committee and get things organized." Everyone cheered.

The meeting lasted for another forty minutes. They spoke about the new constitution and bylaws that were being written and asked for reports; they discussed the sports that the club would be offering and participating in during the spring and summer months; they spoke of adding more furniture to the clubhouse and where they could get it at a cheap rate or better yet, for free. A few minor discussions, a few arguments and a lot of swearing followed until someone said, "I call for an adjournment."

Immediately, everyone agreed and Ginnetti got up and said, "Meeting is over." There was a mad dash to sit around the tables to start playing poker. Two card games started immediately. Within fifteen minutes, there was a lot of yelling and accusations of cheating coming from one of the tables. Harpo said, "You son of a bitch. You're cheating." His brother, Dynamite answered back, "Screw you, Harpo. I'm not cheating. I think you're cheating." The two got up to face each other and before a punch was thrown, Waddie stepped in and said, "What the hell's going on?" Harpo said, "I had three aces and two kings, a full house. This asshole had four aces. He had to be cheating." Waddie looked down at the cards on the table. He turned to both of them and started laughing and said, "You two are morons. You've been playing with a pinochle deck for the last fifteen minutes and didn't even know it." The two brothers blushed and then gave each other a hug.

Chapter 53

While the GAA was having its meeting, the Lenti family minus Concetta, Mario and Romeo were at home drinking and complaining. Angelo Sr. was surly, swearing to his two sons that he had been getting screwed by everyone.

"I can't believe this is happening. A few weeks ago, I was sitting on top of the world, a good job, respected and making more money in a couple of months than I made in the last year. Then all of a sudden, my boss won't talk to me, I was thrown in jail for a week for nothing, I don't have anybody here to cook and clean the house, I haven't screwed in weeks and I'm running out of money. All because of that bastard Galanti, that little bitch Marrano and the slut of a wife that I have. God damn it… I am getting pissed."

Junior and Sal did not say anything but just drank the bootlegged liquor that they took from one of the grocery stores as an added bonus. All they did was nod as the old man ranted on and on.

All of a sudden, Sal looked out the window and said, "We got company." Up pulled a black sedan that was very familiar to them. Out of the car came Bruno and his partner, Slick. They were walking toward the door when Angelo Sr. jumped out of his chair to greet them.

"Hello, Bruno, Slick. What have you got for me?" The two did not respond and walked passed him into the house and upstairs, where the kitchen was located. They turned to Angelo Sr. and said,

"Where's Junior?" This incensed Angelo Sr. He found the courage because of his slight drunkenness to say, "Bruno, I am the head of this household, if anything, Junior and Sal do what I say." Bruno smirked and as he was turning Junior and Sal entered the kitchen.

The sons greeted the two DiJoseph men. "I have your assignments for this week. You will be working your regular route but the boss wants you to go to Niagara Falls. He has a special assignment for you. I will give you details later in the week but it has to do with bringing some products across the border." Bruno then proceeded to tell them what their regular assignments were for that week.

The two men ignored Angelo Sr. completely and spoke only to Junior. Sal could tell that his father was becoming annoyed and that things would not be too pleasant after these two left the house. After giving the assignments, the two started to leave toward the door when Angelo Sr. asked if he could speak to Bruno privately. Bruno just stared and did not respond. Thinking fast, Angelo Sr. told him that he had a little gift for him and Slick; two bottles of excellent bootlegged scotch. With that, Bruno smiled and said, "All right, just for a minute or two."

Bruno told his partner to stay upstairs while he went to the basement with Angelo. Angelo Sr. quickly went to the area where he stashed all the alcohol that he confiscated from the grocery stores, whorehouses and speakeasies that were part of his territory. Just before he gave the two bottles to Bruno, he asked, "Bruno, why is the boss so pissed off at me? I did not mean to offend him. I just wanted to tell him that Galanti was screwing him. What should I do to make things right?" Bruno just looked at him and said, "Learn how to keep your big fat trap shut. Do what you are told and nothing more." Angelo Sr. responded, "I will, I will. Maybe instead of telling the boss that he's being taken advantage of, I will bring him the money that is owed to him."

"Whatever," responded Bruno. He did not dare tell Lenti the story that DiJoseph told him. He thought... *let him find out the hard way.* He turned around, walked up the stairs and yelled out to Slick that it was time to go. Both left the house without saying goodbye. Slick turned to Bruno and said, "What the hell was that about?" Bruno responded in a very diplomatic way, "He's an asshole." Both laughed as they went to the car.

Angelo Sr. looked at his sons but did not say anything about what happened in the kitchen. If it was a few years earlier when they were younger, he would have beaten the shit out of them. But now, all he could think of was how to get on the good side of DiJoseph.

They went back to the living room where they sat down and started to guzzle their booze. It started to affect them quickly since none of them had anything to eat but cheese, olives and prosciutto for lunch and dinner. The bread was too moldy to eat and since nobody knew how to bake bread except for Concetta, there was none available.

After Junior quickly informed his father of their plans for the week, Angelo Sr. said out of the blue, "I'm going to get even with old man Galanti this week. Even though the son of a bitch doesn't sell the homemade wine, I'm going to tell him that he owes money because he makes it and that's reason enough to pay." Both boys looked at him skeptically. Angelo Sr. smiled and said, "I got a plan."

He told them that he knew the old man, Ralph and their melon john friend, Coco, go to see the old man's daughter on Friday afternoons. He learned that because his buddy from the steel plant said that old man Galanti does not take jobs on Fridays because that is the time he spends with his daughter, all afternoon. Angelo Sr. continued to tell them that only the wife and her friend, Crystal, would be watching the store. Usually, nobody goes into the store until mid afternoon after school. If anybody else is there, they would probably be in the back clubroom playing cards. We would go in quickly, right after the old man leaves to go to the hospital, and when the two women are alone, we'll get our money. Angelo Sr. reassured them that the women would be so scared shitless when they saw the three of them, that they would give them the money just to get them the hell out of the store.

The two sons seemed to like that idea. Junior mentioned that the colored woman would make a great piece of ass. "She is a fine looking woman even though she's colored." Sal chimed in, "Hell, we might be able to get some candy, snacks, bread and some goods. Shit, we have nothing here at the house, we might as well stock up over there."

All Angelo Sr. was thinking about was how to get even with Galanti and get on the better side of DiJoseph. There was no question in his mind that once he brought him the extra money and a few things from the store, he would again be in good graces with DiJoseph. He thought...*this will kill two birds with one stone. Screwing Galanti and getting back on good terms with the boss. Then the only other thing left for me is getting even with that Marrano girl and of course, with that bitch I married.*

The three of them drank themselves into oblivion. They ended up falling asleep in their chairs, snoring away. The only regret that they would have the next day was a big hangover.

Chapter 54

It was Friday morning and Eugenio said to his wife in Italian, "Philomena, are you sure everything is going to be all right. I want to spend the whole day with Josephine. I probably won't be back until they make me leave the hospital, probably around nine o'clock in the evening." Philomena responded, "Don't worry. Crystal will be here with me the whole day and Ralph and Mary will help during the evening. I will spend Saturday with Josephine. Tell her I love her very much and I will be seeing her tomorrow.

Eugenio kissed his wife on the cheek and left around ten o'clock in the morning. If he could have left earlier and be allowed in the room, he would have done so but they told him they had to change Josephine's bandages and bathe her in the morning. This would take several hours. He was anxious to see his daughter. She seemed to be getting better every day and he was excited to have her come back home, even if it was for a few days.

Ralph, Mary and Coco were at school and they were going to visit Josephine right after school let out. They also planned to visit Concetta.

In the Marrano family, Carmen told his sisters, Anna, Josephine and Carmela, that as soon as school let out they were going to visit Concetta and Josephine. Carmen said he was going to bring Gracie because he wanted her to talk to Mario. He thought that they could end this constant fighting if they got to know each other and had some decent conversation. The sisters agreed.

Around three thirty in the afternoon, there were an abundance of well-wishers in both Josephine and Concetta's rooms. The Marrano sisters were anxiously telling Concetta that if there was anything she needed, they would be there for her. Carmen was in Josephine's room with Pop Galanti, Ralph, Mary and Coco, making sure that Josephine's spirits remained high.

Mario came into his mother's room and stopped on a dime when he saw all the people there. He became apprehensive when he saw Gracie standing with her sisters next to his mother's bed. Concetta said, "Hello, Mario. Come on in. You see that the Marrano sisters came to pay a visit." Mario came in the room and politely said hello to all the sisters by name except when it came to Gracie. He just said, very sheepishly, "Hi." Concetta told Mario, "Why don't you take Gracie down to the cafeteria and buy her a soda. Anna, Josephine, Carmela and I want to have some girl talk. I think Gracie and you would be bored." She took out thirty cents from her little change purse and gave it to Mario. He hesitantly took it but felt very uncomfortable at the thought of being alone with Gracie. He turned to her and said, "Would you like a soda?" Gracie in her own unique way said, "Sure, Mario, as long as you're paying." That seemed to break the ice and Mario and Gracie left for the cafeteria.

It was quiet as they walked down the halls and down the stairs to the cafeteria, neither of them saying a word. The first words were from Mario. "What soda would you like?" Gracie responded, "Is it an ice cream soda or are you going to be cheap and give me a pop?" "Ice cream, of course. And if I don't have enough money for two, I will ask for two straws for one." Both of them laughed.

As they sat at the table both were very quiet until Gracie said very softly, "Mario, I'm sorry about what happened to you and your mother. I am also sorry for what I did to you." Mario responded, "I accept your apology, except for that kick in my very sensitive area. Not only did you do it once, but you did it twice. Now I think I will never have a chance to have kids."

Again, Gracie said she was sorry but this time with a smile. She did say, "You did get a nice right cross to my eye area. I had to stay away from my father for a week until the swelling went down or else I would have gotten the biggest licking that a girl from Bethlehem Park ever got."

Mario smiled and said to Gracie, "I was a jerk. I did all that crazy stuff because I thought my father would finally accept me as a man. But I found out that I am more of a man than he ever will be." Mario then proceeded to tell Gracie how he felt.

"You know, I always thought my father was a big shot, king of the hill, a real man but he is really an asshole. I treated my mother so badly and I am so ashamed. I thought that this was how women should be treated because this is what my father taught me. It changed in an instant. When I saw my mother sacrifice her own body to defend me and take such a beating by covering me with her body, I finally realized how much love that she had for me and how much hate my father has in his heart. I could still hear her moans as he hit her, kicked her, beat her with the strap as she covered me." Mario was now crying unashamedly. "After I gained consciousness in the hospital, I kept wondering if my mother was okay; I wanted to tell her I love her so much but I did not know if she was alive or dead. I hated my father. I promised myself if my mother dies, the first thing I would do when I got out of the hospital was kill him."

Gracie was very affected by the story and reached out to touch Mario's hand. "Mario," she said very softly, "your mother is going to be okay and so are you. You, your mother and your brother Romeo are good people. You have friends that will take care of you. Your father and older brothers will get what's coming to them. I'm very embarrassed to say this but they are three pigs."

Mario smiled and returned the touching of the hand and said thank you. They finished having their ice cream sodas. Mario was able to buy two because the cafeteria worker knew him and his mother and what they went through. She also gave them an extra scoop of ice cream in their sodas.

Eugenio, Ralph, Mary and Coco were in Josephine's room talking about how the GAA members wanted to have a dance during Easter week honoring her. They would only do it if she would say yes and be able to attend. This made Josephine very happy and she smiled and said, "Of course, and the first dance that I have is going to be with Pa, second dance with you big brother and the third dance with Coco." Smiling at her sister, Mary, she said, "You, sis, can eat your heart out standing on the sidelines as a wallflower."

Mary looked at her sister and said, "Sounds like you're getting better." Her father stepped in and stated, "Noa daughter of mine is a wallflower. Whena I'm not dancing with youa Josephine, I'lla be dancing with Mary. The only walla flowers willa be the ones who do not wanna to dance."

Ralph said to Josephine, "We spoke to the doctors and they said that you are doing so well that they are amazed. If you continue this, they will let you spend a few days home and attend the dance. But, it's going to be up to you to make sure that you are getting healthy. So make sure you eat right, do what they say, and take your medicine."

She nodded and said, "Dr. Rafael, I'm not going to miss this dance. I will be there."

Chapter 55

There was so much laughter coming out of Josephine's hospital room that a nurse had to go in to ask them to quiet down. Ralph apologized and as the nurse left the room, they all started giggling again.

This was very short lived. Within a few seconds after the nurse left the room, Lui Marini rushed nto the room a little out of breath and said very quickly, "Eugenio, can I see you out in the hall?" Pop Galanti looked up and nodded and left the room with Ralph and Coco. Ralph quickly said, "Lui, what's up? Why are you out of breath?" "I ran most of the way to the hospital from your store. I was able to hitch a ride near Center Street. Then I ran up these flights of stairs to see you. I have some bad news for you."

Eugenio quickly responded, "Whatsa matter?" "I'll tell you on the way to your car," said Lui. As they were walking to the parking lot, Lui quickly told Eugenio, Ralph and Coco that there was an incident at the store around an hour ago. "I don't know all the facts but I do know that the Lentis came in the store and asked for money. Your wife and Coco's mom got into an argument with them. I was in the clubhouse playing cards with Sobey, Gene and Harpo when we heard a commotion. There was a lot of yelling and some screaming. We ran out to the front of the store and saw your wife lying on the floor, bleeding from the mouth and Crystal was on top of the back of old man

Lenti screaming and pulling his hair. When the Lentis saw us, they pulled Crystal from Lenti's back and threw her on the floor and all three rushed out the front door into a car and took off. It seemed like your wife was okay and Crystal was comforting her. I rushed out the front door as the car sped away. I told Sobey, Harpo and Gene that I was going to the hospital to get you and that they should make sure the Lentis do not come back."

The only thing Pop Galanti said was, "Son of a bitch." Meanwhile, Ralph and Coco had a thousand questions that they were asking Lui. Their main concern was that their mothers were okay. All Lui said was that it seemed that everybody was not hurt except maybe for a few bruises. Pop Galanti said again, "Son of a bitch."

A few minutes later they arrived at the confectionary store. Before the car even stopped, Eugenio jumped out of the front seat and rushed into the store. Coco was right behind him with Lui. Ralph had to park the car before he could enter the store. When he came in, he saw his father with his mother on the store bench behind the counter. He was holding her, cuddling her and giving her kisses on the cheek. Coco was with his mom, holding her hand and talking to her very fast asking her what had happened. In the store, there were several GAA members milling around making sure that nothing was stolen. They were prepared for "warfare" if the Lentis decided to return. But it was obvious that the Lentis would probably be too afraid to come back.

Eugenio spoke to Philomena in Italian and asked her what had happened. Philomena answered back, "Eugenio, the three Lentis came in the store, the father, Angelo, and his two sons, Junior and I don't know the other one's name. I think it was the one that Ralph got into a fight with at the Park Theater. They said they came to collect money owed to DiJoseph for selling the wine that you make. I told them that we do not sell the wine but give it to our friends as gifts of friendship. They laughed and the father told me that it was bullshit. He said that I had to give him thirty dollars today and he would take the rest from what we have in the store; bread, candy, soda and whatever they wanted. I told him he was crazy and that I don't even know who this DiJoseph man was and who are they to ask for our money. He said a few nasty words to me and said he wanted the money now or else our family, especially our son, Ralph, would not be safe to even walk down the street. I told him no. If he wants to talk about money, he has to talk to you. That is when he slapped me across the face and knocked me down.

"The next thing I knew, I saw Crystal scream at him and rush toward him. She jumped on his back, screaming, pulling his hair and the two sons trying to get her off of him. That is when Lui, Sobey, Harpo and Gene ran in from the clubhouse to see what was going on. As soon as the Lentis saw the four of them, they pulled Crystal off of Angelo Sr. and ran out of the store. The boys were brave and they ran after them but the older Lenti had a big knife and started swinging it back and forth in front of them. They then jumped in the car and drove away with the boys chasing them down the street. Eugenio, you would be very proud of how those young boys protected us. Please check Crystal and see if she is okay because if she did not jump on the father's back, he probably would have hit me a few more times."

Eugenio kissed his wife on the cheek and went over to see Crystal. He asked if she was okay and she nodded yes. He then bent over and put his two large hands on her face and brought her head to his lips and kissed her on her forehead. "Grazia, mia bella amica" (Thank you my beautiful friend).

An enraged Ralph told his father that he was going to the Lenti's house in Bethlehem Park. His father turned and said, "No, mio figlio" (No, my son). We do this the righta way. I'lla report it to the police and we will see whata happens." In Eugenio's mind, he wanted to do this the right way but if nothing happened, he would take matters into his own hands as he once did in Olean, New York.

He made sure that the two women were safe and cared for and he told his son to drive him to the police headquarters. In the meantime, more of the GAA members started coming to the store because it was late in the afternoon and that was the time they usually arrived. For sure, if the Lentis came back, they definitely would have their hands full.

Chapter 56

The Lentis drove the car back to their Bethlehem Park house. They were all nervous and shaky about the debacle that happened at the Galanti's Confectionary Store. Junior turned to his father and said, "What the fuck happened? You said that as soon as the two women saw us, they would give us the money. Instead, they became wildcats and there were more guys in the clubhouse than you said there would be. We're lucky to get the hell out of there before we got killed."

Angelo Sr. shook his head and kept repeating, "I can't believe what happened, I can't believe what happened." Sal quickly interjected that he didn't think that they would be safe at the house. He stated, "Let's get some supplies and get the hell out of here. Maybe DiJoseph can help us especially if we come through for him with this job in Canada."

They started to go through the house and get a change of clothes and a few personal items that they might need since they didn't think they were coming back for a least a week. They gathered all the money that they had hidden in the house. Angelo Sr. kept on saying that he couldn't believe that this was happening. Junior was getting a little irritated and told his father to "shut the hell up." This was the first time that one of the sons actually spoke up against the father. Although Angelo Sr. was a little shocked, he said nothing because he knew he did "screw up."

After they got everything they needed from the house, the three got in the car and went north to Niagara Falls. They decided they would stay at one of the fancier bordellos that was closer to the area where they would have to cross the river to get into Canada. They arrived at a four-story apartment building on Pine Avenue. Junior heard about this upscale whorehouse from one of DiJoseph's henchmen.

They checked in with the madame. Her name was Svetlana, a heavily endowed Russian woman. They told her they would be staying there for at least three days because they had a job to do for DiJoseph. The madame did not question them but gave them rooms and asked them if they needed anything. She knew DiJoseph and took care of his people in the past. Junior told her that they would need things when they get back on Saturday or Sunday and he emphasized that he didn't mean food.

Junior asked for three rooms on the fourth floor. Madame Svetlana was not happy to give up all three rooms. She thought one for all of them would have been enough. This meant that she had less money to make because the rooms were taken up by these three thugs. But she wanted to stay on the good side of DiJoseph so she gave them what they asked for.

The Lentis met in Junior's room. It was obvious that Junior now had become the head of the household. He looked at his father and said, "From now on, you will take orders from me. If you don't like it, there's the goddamn door." Sal was shocked but did not say anything. His father had become more crazy than ever thinking that everyone was out to screw him. Angelo Sr. did not say a word. He just stared at his son and nodded.

Junior started to talk and told them that Bruno said they had to pick up a load of hooch coming across the border from Canada. He said the Niagara River was frozen over and that their truck could cross near the Indian Reservation to go over to the Canadian side, pick up the merchandise and drive back. He also told them that they had to bring it to a bakery in Niagara Falls. They were told not to ask any questions, just to pick up the booze, deliver it to the bakery and keep their mouths shut. After they delivered it, they were free to do what they wanted until Monday when their normal workweek began.

Sal was first to speak and said, "That doesn't seem bad. The only problem I see is if the damn ice breaks and we go through. I'm not a good swimmer." Junior told him that was not a problem. He said, "The ice is over nine inches thick and this has been one of the coldest winters we've had in years. Don't worry."

Angelo Sr. kept on mumbling on and on not aware of what was being said.

Junior turned to his father and told him to shut the hell up. "Don't worry. When we finish this job, we'll go back and get payback. It will start with the Galantis and an added bonus will be the Marranos." Angelo Sr. gave a wicked sneer and added, "There is another woman that I'm going to have payback with and her name starts with a big 'C'." Junior and Sal knew who their father was talking about. It was their mother but they were very nonchalant about it and just shrugged their shoulders.

Junior left the bordello by himself and drove to DiJoseph's place. Bruno let him through the door to see the boss. Junior told DiJoseph, "We're ready. Where do we pick up the truck tonight and exactly where do we have to go."

DiJoseph looked at him and did not know what happened in Lackawanna a few hours ago. If he found out that the three tried to shake Galanti down for whatever reasons, he would have been upset. If he found out that old man Lenti slapped Mrs. Galanti, there would have probably been a hefty price to pay. Junior, at this point, was very lucky that all DiJoseph knew was that the shipment was ready to go at twelve midnight on the Canadian side. He told Junior to be there at midnight and bring the goods to the "bakery" in Niagara Falls and that this was a very important assignment. The shipment would be for Sebastian "The Baker" Massini. When Junior heard the name, he was stunned. He thought… *My God, this is for the Don, boss of bosses.*

DiJoseph then told them that they would be free for the rest of the weekend if their job was successful. He asked Junior where they were staying. Junior told him that they were at the whorehouse on Pine Avenue in Niagara Falls because it was closer to their job assignment.

Junior felt pretty good about himself and the situation. He figured that if DiJoseph did not know what happened in Lackawanna and if they were successful delivering the goods, everything would be okay. This was an assumption that would be deadly.

Chapter 57

It was five o'clock in the morning on Saturday when Father Baker rose from his bed. He quickly knelt at the side of his bed, made the sign of the cross and said a morning prayer. He then went through his ritual of approaching the small statue of the Blessed Mother in his room, greeting her with a good morning and proceeding to say the rosary. After the rosary, he carried on his usual conversation with the Blessed Mother and thanked her for all she had done for him and his flock.

Approximately an hour later, he cleansed himself, put on his cassock and he made sure he had a supply of quarters, holy medals and candy. By six-thirty in the morning, the usual soft knock came to his door. Father Baker quietly said, "Come in, Brother Sebastian." The jolly man came in with a big good morning and said, "I don't know how you do it, Monsignor, but how do you know it's always me at your door?" The holy priest smiled and said, "You have one of the softest and most holy knocks I have ever heard."

He did not want to tell Brother Sebastian that he has been knocking at his door at this time of the morning for the last ten years. He would have been shocked if it was someone other than Brother Sebastian but he wanted him to feel special so he flattered him.

"Well, Monsignor, what are we going to do today after Mass? Are we going to the infant home, orphanage, visit the sick in the hospital, do work in your office or take a walk around Lackawanna visiting our people?" Monsignor gave him a little chuckle and said, "We're not going to do just one of those things, but we're going to do all of them." Brother Sebastian thought... *Wow, this is going to be another busy day!*

Father Baker became a little more serious and told Brother Sebastian that right after Mass he wanted him to go across the street to the hospital and ask Elizabeth to come and see him in his office. "Also, my dear friend, tell her I would like to see the baby Romeo because I want to bless him." "Yes sir, Monsignor. I'll do this right after Mass."

In the large Our Lady of Victory Basilica, Father Gerlach celebrated Mass that morning. In the last few years, because of his deteriorating health, Father Baker assisted in celebrating the Mass during the week. But he always said Mass on Sunday morning at nine o'clock. This was when the church was completely packed with parishioners. Many came not only to honor God, but also to pay homage to their spiritual leader.

After Mass, the frail priest went to his office and waited for Elizabeth and the baby. Brother Sebastian waddled across the road to the hospital. He was short, wide and heavy with a few strands of hair on top of his head. But he was jolly, loveable and everyone's favorite in the church, orphanage and hospital. He definitely was a favorite of Father Baker.

He entered the hospital and went straight to Elizabeth's room, but she was not there. He looked up and down the halls and finally thought she might be in the cafeteria having breakfast with the child. He went there and she was nowhere in sight. Then it dawned on him that she must have been in Concetta's room showing the baby to his mother. He hurried up to the floor where Concetta's room was and he was right. There were the three of them. Concetta in her bed, the baby on her lap and Elizabeth standing by the bedside all laughing and talking.

They saw Brother Sebastian and greeted him with a great big hello and Elizabeth went up to him and gave him a big hug. This made the jolly man blush and he started to stammer. He stammered even more when Elizabeth planted a kiss on his cheek. Everyone laughed, even the baby as Brother Sebastian turned beet red and the only words that came out of his mouth were... ah uh uh uh. When he gained his composure, he smiled, said hello to everyone and told Elizabeth that Monsignor Baker wanted to see her and the baby. Concetta was a little worried and asked if there was something wrong because he wanted to see Romeo. "I don't know why Monsignor wants to see Elizabeth but he told me to also bring the baby because he wanted to bless him." There was a big sigh of relief from Concetta and she kissed the baby on both cheeks and gave him to Elizabeth.

The three left the room and Elizabeth turned and told Concetta that she would bring the baby back after lunch. Concetta said thank you, waved and blew a kiss to the baby.

As they crossed Ridge Road to go back to Father Baker's office, Elizabeth felt a little anxiety. It was unusual for Father Baker to ask her to come to see him. It usually was the other way around; he would visit her at the hospital or in her room. She started to wonder if she did something wrong and if she would not be able to work in the hospital anymore.

The distance between the hospital and Father Baker's office was a few hundred yards. To Elizabeth, it felt like a few hundred miles.

Chapter 58

Brother Sebastian was ready to knock on Father Baker's door when he heard the priest say "Come in Brother Sebastian." Brother Sebastian looked at Elizabeth and said, "I don't know how he does it. He knows that I am at the door before I even knock. He either could see me through the door or he is physic." Elizabeth smiled. She thought... *My dear jolly friend. If you could only hear the racket you make when you walk and talk, you would know that anyone could tell when you are approaching, even if you're fifty yards away.*

The three entered the room and saw the holy priest sitting in his favorite rocking chair near his desk. They went straight to him before he had a chance to get up. They knew that it was becoming more difficult for him to be mobile at this stage of his life.

Elizabeth quickly said, "Hello, Father Baker. I am so glad to see you and by the looks of Romeo, he is too." The baby was smiling with his arms and legs flailing away as he tried to reach out to the priest. Elizabeth was hesitant because she did not want the baby to accidently hurt Father Baker with his arms or legs moving so rapidly. But the priest held out his two hands and asked for the baby. Elizabeth put the baby in his hands and immediately Romeo stopped movement and just smiled at him. Father Baker smiled back, kissed him on both cheeks and placed him on his knee. The baby was relaxed, content and kept smiling.

Father Baker spoke to the child as if they were the only two in the room. Romeo did not move but just listened. After a few minutes, Father Baker asked Brother Sebastian to come and hold the baby. He wanted to get up to bless the child with the Holy Water in front of the statue of the Blessed Mother, which was located in the corner of his room. Brother Sebastian took the baby from the priest and Elizabeth went to help Father Baker out of the rocker. They all went in front of the statue of the Blessed Mother. Father Baker took some holy water that was located at the side of his bed and blessed the child with it. He then asked Elizabeth and Brother Sebastian to join him in prayer asking the Blessed Mother to watch over this beautiful child.

After they prayed, he turned to Brother Sebastian and asked him to bring the child inside the Basilica and show him all the beautiful angels that were located in every part of the giant church. As Brother Sebastian took Romeo out of the room, Father Baker turned to Elizabeth and said, "Sit down, my child. I would like to have a conversation with you about your future." Elizabeth sat down in the chair that was near Father Baker's rocking chair. She did not say a word. She was very nervous and thought maybe she did something wrong and would no longer be able to stay at Our Lady of Victory Hospital.

Father Baker said, "Dr. Sullivan and I have spoken about you over the last few days. At the end of this summer, we would like to send you to college to study medicine and become a nurse." Elizabeth was wide eyed. She thought that they were upset with her work at the hospital and wanted her to leave. She told Father Baker, "I am so relieved Father, I thought you wanted to get rid of me because I did something wrong.

I was very nervous."

"No, no my child. Matter of fact, on the contrary, we are impressed with your dedication, knowledge and handling of patients. We would like to send you to college to further your knowledge in medicine and be an integral part of our hospital."

Elizabeth didn't know what to say. She just looked at Father Baker and started to cry. "My child, do not cry. You should be happy that we think so much of you." She looked at the priest and said, "I am so honored. I pray each day and thank God and our Blessed Mother that you came into my life. But Father, I have chosen a path for my life. I want to enter the convent and become a nun and serve God and Our Lady. Thank you so much but I cannot take your generous offer."

The holy priest just smiled and stared at her for a few minutes. Elizabeth was becoming a little nervous thinking that she had offended him. She was waiting for him to scold her. Instead, he got up from his rocking chair, walked in front of her and kissed her on the forehead. He then told her to follow him. They went into the Basilica and walked to the main altar where there was a large beautiful marble statue of Our Lady holding the baby Jesus.

The two of them knelt down at the railing and Father Baker looked up and started to talk very softly to the Blessed Mother. "My Lady, Elizabeth and I come here for your help and guidance. I would like to send this wonderful young girl to college. She has the gift that you, your beloved son Jesus and Our Lord gave her to help the sick and the poor. With this education that she would receive, your servants Dr. Sullivan and I, think she could fulfill her destiny by helping the unfortunate. But she wants to serve God and you by becoming a nun. This is also a wonderful vocation for promoting the word of God and His teachings. The dilemma is which decision should she choose?

Please, My Lady, guide her, give her the strength and determination to choose the path she should take to serve you and Our Lord."

He then turned to Elizabeth, took her hand and said, "Please say the rosary with me." After the rosary was said, they got up and turned to walk back to Father Baker's office when they saw Brother Sebastian sitting outside on a bench. He and Romeo were eating a cookie in front of one of the statues of an angel. Brother Sebastian stood up very quickly and stammered, "Uh, Romeo was hungry." Both Elizabeth and Father Baker laughed.

Father Baker told Elizabeth to take the baby back to his mother. He told her to pray every night to Our Blessed Lady until she is sure which path she wants to take in life. He told her, "Whatever path you take my child, it will be the correct path as long as you dedicate it to Our Lord and the Blessed Lady." With that, he blessed her and the baby and turned to go back to his office with Brother Sebastian.

Chapter 59

"What are we going to do if the ice breaks? I can't swim," said Sal. Junior looked at him and said sarcastically, "Will you shut the hell up. If you're that concerned, why don't you go back and tell DiJoseph that you don't want to do the job because you're afraid the ice will break and you will drown. If he says okay, then you don't have to come." Sal knew that he could not do that so he just kept his mouth shut and had another drink.

It was nine o'clock in the evening and they were in their room about to leave to pick up the truck at the designated place where Bruno had told them to go. They would be taking the truck north along the Niagara River to the spot where they would cross the frozen water to go to Canada to pick up the bootlegged liquor. The area they were going to cross was isolated but it was patrolled by the Border Patrol on a regular basis. Tonight, the Patrol would be making their rounds three hours later than usual. It just happened that some of the Patrol members were on DiJoseph's payroll.

Junior told Sal and his father to get their coats and that they would be leaving in ten minutes to pick up the truck. He told them of the plan and what they had to do. He waited until the final moment before they left to tell them the whole story because he did not trust either one of them. They had a habit of drinking and becoming very loose-lipped with the women who they tried to impress. The only thing that the two knew was that they had to go over frozen water. Where, exactly when, how and where it was going to be delivered, he did not tell them until now.

They left their rooms, went downstairs and told Madame Svetlana that they would be back early in the morning and to make sure that they keep the back door open. Old man Lenti also stated that if any of the girls are still working, they could visit him for a thrill of their lifetime. He was the only one who was laughing at his little joke.

The three got in the car and drove for about half an hour to pick up the large truck that was waiting for them at a warehouse. It was freezing outside but they were heavily dressed and had a few drinks in them that kept them somewhat warm. Angelo Sr. brought a bottle of whiskey with him. His sons did not know. Junior wanted them to be sober and prepared to make sure they brought the liquor across the river without any incidents.

After picking up the truck, they drove up the road that was parallel to the Niagara River. They arrived at a private fishing hut, which was their designated area from where they would cross the river. They went into the hut but did not light a fire for fear that the smoke would attract uninvited guests. It was eleven in the evening. Junior told them that they would be starting to cross the frozen river at eleven forty-five. He wanted to be on the other side at midnight. At that juncture, the river was less than a mile-and-a-half wide.

Angelo Sr. was cuddled up in his coat and hat in the corner taking secretive swigs from the bottle of whiskey he had. Sal was nervously pacing up and down the small hut still worrying about the ice breaking and him drowning. Junior was walking around outdoors thinking if this was successful, which he knew it would be, he would be sitting pretty in the DiJoseph family. He lit a match and looked at his watch. It was almost eleven forty-five. He called inside the hut and told them, "Let's go. It's time." The three of them got into the large truck. They started crossing the river and the truck held up with no problems because the ice was so thick. Even Sal started to feel confident and thought that "this was a piece of cake." They made good time crossing the river and got there before midnight. On the other side was a large truck with several men standing on the shore. There was a full moon so they did not need to put on the lights of their vehicles. They could see with the moonlight alone.

Junior pulled the vehicle up on shore. The only thing Junior said was "Let's start unloading and loading." The group of men on the Canadian side nodded and they started emptying their truck and loading Junior's. Not a word was said by anyone.

After Junior's truck was completely loaded with cases of bootlegged liquor, he turned to one of the men and said, "We're gone." The other man just nodded. No thanks, no goodbyes, no pleasantries. All business.

Junior, Sal and Angelo Sr. got in the truck and they started to cross the river. They heard a little crack when they got on the ice. Sal became very nervous. Coming across with an empty truck is far different than coming back with a truck full of heavy cases of bootlegged liquor. Even though it was frigid outside, Sal started to sweat profusely. Even Junior was a little nervous. At this point, Angelo Sr. was becoming so intoxicated that he was unaware of the danger. Junior drove very slowly and listened very intently. He left the windows open even though the air was frigid outside.

It took them close to a half an hour to cross the frozen river. Even though there were a few crackles, the ice was so thick that it held the weight of the truck and its cargo without too much difficulty.

When they got back to the fishing hut and drove up on solid ground, Junior and Sal breathed a lot easier. Matter of fact, Sal quickly got out of the truck and urinated. Angelo Sr. got out of the truck and threw up, not because of fear but because he drank the whole bottle of whiskey within that short time. Junior felt exhilarated and immediately lit up a cigarette to relax.

They drove back the same route until they reached the city of Niagara Falls. Junior then took the vehicle to the bakery where Bruno told them a group of guys would be waiting for them. They unloaded the cargo into a few bakery delivery trucks. Afterward, they took their truck back to the warehouse, got into their car and drove back to the whorehouse on Pine Avenue. It was four o'clock in the morning. The back door was open but everyone was asleep. Junior and Sal didn't mind it because they were tired and wanted to get to sleep. Angelo Sr. was pissed that there were no women available.

Chapter 60

Junior got up after a short nap. It was approximately seven thirty in the morning. He felt very relaxed, almost a feeling of euphoria, knowing that everything went perfectly. He heard his brother snoring in the next room. The walls were very thin. He started laughing and thinking of how all the grunts, groans and screams of ecstasy could be heard through these thin walls each night. He did not hear anything from his father's room. He did not know if his father was dead, sick or just sleeping. He didn't care.

He went to the bathroom, cleaned himself up and decided to get some breakfast. He saw a small coffee shop on Pine Avenue about half a block away. He wondered if they would be open this early on Sunday morning. He definitely wanted to have some coffee and pastry. He didn't bother to shave because he thought he looked more masculine with a rough beard. He didn't have any toothpowder so he could not clean his teeth but he didn't care because he thought his good looks would compensate for his bad breath. He did have enough personal pride to wash himself with the soap that was left in the bathroom. After bathing his body, he dried himself off and put on the same clothes that he wore the previous night.

As he left, he heard no noises throughout the bordello except for some slight snoring. He knew that everyone would probably be sleeping later since it was early Sunday morning. The air was frigid as he walked down Pine Avenue. As he approached the coffee shop, the smell of coffee and Italian pastries filled his nostrils. He wasn't that hungry before he left his room, but now he was famished. He went in and saw that the coffee shop had a few tables located in front of the counter. He went up to the old gentleman behind the counter and told him he would like to have one espresso coffee and one regular coffee. He surveyed the baked goods in the counter and selected three Italian pastries. He took a table in the corner, sat down and first drank his espresso, then leaned back waiting for the caffeine jolt. He then relaxed, started sipping his coffee and enjoying his pastries.

A few minutes later, in came three young women, all in their late teens or early twenties. They were dressed up in their Sunday finest. They sat down two tables away from Junior. As they removed their coats, he noticed that two of the girls were cute but had no shapes. The third girl had a phenomenal looking body but was not attractive. Junior just glanced at the two cute girls but stared at the breasts of the third girl. He thought... *I never saw a body like that before. If she had the head to go with it, she would be a movie star. But you don't screw the head, you screw the body. I'm gonna put a hit on this bitch.*

The three girls sat around giggling, having coffee and a slice of warm fresh Italian bread with jam. Junior started staring at the unattractive young girl. She looked up and they made eye contact. Junior smiled and gave her a wink. The young girl sort of blushed and looked down at her bread and coffee. After several seconds, she looked up again and Junior was still staring at her and gave her another wink. She started giggling. One of the other girlfriends looked over and saw Junior looking their way. She commented to her friends that she thought he was handsome. They all agreed.

Junior thought... *what the hell do I got to lose? I'm going for the one with the great body and the big boobs. If I get lucky, she will give me the ride of my life.* He got up from his seat and went over to say hello. He used all his charm and it seemed to work, especially with the one who had the great body. He lied and told them his name was Sergio and that he just came into town from Pennsylvania to see Niagara Falls. He asked them what their names were. The two attractive girls told him that their names were Patricia and Mary Ann. Junior looked at the third girl and asked her again what her name was. She shyly said, "Antoinella." Junior said, "What a beautiful name for a beautiful girl." Antoinella blushed and the other two started giggling.

"Why are you girls here so early in the morning?" he asked. Mary Ann told him that they came here every Sunday morning before going to church. They were all friends who just graduated from high school last year. Mary Ann told him that she was becoming a beautician, Patricia is engaged to be married and Antoinella is going to college. Junior turned to Antoinella and said, "Wow, you must be very smart. And they told me smart girls were not pretty. You definitely are smart and you definitely are pretty." Antoinella did not say anything but again began blushing and her two girlfriends giggled some more and nudged Antoinella's arm.

Antoinella finally spoke and said, "You know, we are going to be late for Mass if we keep on talking." Patricia said, "So what. We go to church every Sunday. I think we can be late one time." Antoinella said, "I don't know about you, but I don't want to be late for Mass," and started to get up from her chair. The two girlfriends also started to stand when Junior put his hand on her hand and asked Antoinella very politely if she could stay just for a couple of minutes more. Patricia and Mary Ann took the hint and told Antoinella that they would wait for her outside at the corner. Junior smiled, thanked them and turned to Antoinella and said, "Please just stay for a few minutes. I'm new in town and I have a few questions I need to ask."

Antoinella was so flattered. She knew that she was not the prettiest girl. She always thought her nose was too big and her eyebrows were too bushy. To have this handsome young man say that to her was like music to her ears. She told him, "I could only stay for a few minutes. I hope I can answer your questions about Niagara Falls."

The two other girls left and Antoinella sat down again to talk to Junior. He looked into her eyes and softly touched her hand and said to her, "I really don't have any questions to ask you except would you go out with me tonight. You are the prettiest girl I have seen here in Niagara Falls in the last two days. I have to leave Monday so I was hoping at least I could have my last day here with the prettiest girl in Niagara Falls." Antoinella blushed even more and instantly fell for his come on, hook, line and sinker. She said that she would but she had to go to church, go home and help make Sunday dinner for her family and she could be free around four o'clock in the afternoon. Junior said, "Antoinella, you made me the happiest person in the world. I will see you here at the coffee shop at four o'clock. Maybe you could show me The Falls and we can talk about what a great world this is."

Antoinella agreed to meet him at four o'clock. She told him it might be a little later because sometimes her mother wants her to do an errand right after dinner. She said, "Sergio, if you're willing to wait for me, I will definitely be there." Junior told her, "I will wait for you till the end of time."

Antoinella thought *I finally met a handsome man that likes me for me. I definitely will be there. Wild horses couldn't stop me from coming.* This was a decision that Antoinella would regret.

Chapter 61

Philomena, Mary and Johnnie were getting ready for nine o'clock Mass at St. Anthony's. Eugenio was going to watch the store while they were in church and when they returned, he and his wife would go to see Josephine in the hospital. Ralph was going to the early Mass at Our Lady of Victory and then after Mass would walk across Ridge Road to the hospital to visit his sister. He then would come back around noon to watch the store.

Around ten o'clock in the morning, one of the Lackawanna policemen came into the store to update Eugenio on the Lentis. "Mr. Galanti, we haven't been able to find the Lentis. We went to their house and no one seems to be home. We talked to some of the neighbors and they said they haven't seen them since Friday. I think they know we're looking for them and they're probably hiding out hoping this will blow over. But I give you my word, we will find them and they will be in a lot of trouble."

Eugenio said, "Thanka you. I knowa you will do a good job in finding them." Then he asked the policeman if he would like to have coffee, soda or something to eat. The policeman gratefully declined and left the store to continue his patrol.

Eugenio thought... *I have to let the police handle this no matter how I feel. I want to kill that son of a bitch Angelo with my bare hands, but that is not the way I want my children to be raised. They have to abide by the laws of this great country.* He took a deep breath to ease his tension about the situation and though... *But if that son of a bitch ever touches one of my family members again...* he let that thought linger in his mind until he heard the bell above the store door ring.

In came Horatio and Crystal. "Hi, Eugenio," said Crystal. Eugenio smiled and said hello as Horatio walked up to him and extended his hand while putting his other hand on Eugenio's shoulder. He asked him if everything was all right. Eugenio, who genuinely liked Horatio, shook his hand with both of his hands. Poor Horatio's hand was engulfed by the huge hands of his friend. Eugenio smiled and said, "I'ma all right. I thanka you for coming over to visit. Philomena willa be coming backa from church shortly. Please sit and have a coffee and pastry witha me."

Crystal said, "Thank you. We will. Matter of fact, we came here to go up to the hospital with you to see Josephine, unless you need us to stay here to watch the store while your family visits." Eugenio told them that Ralph would be watching the store and he would really like to have them come with him to visit Josephine.

Horatio asked if he heard any news from the police about the Lentis. Eugenio mentioned that one of the policemen came and told him that they are still looking but they cannot find them. Horatio said, "That's typical of those animals. They're tough in front of women but scared to death if they are confronted by anyone else." Crystal looked at Horatio and said, "I think Philomena and I put a good scare into those three jerks."

Eugenio invited them into the kitchen where he gave them coffee and some homemade pastries. He was able to see the storefront from where he was sitting. As they were talking, they heard the bell above the door ring and running in came Johnny followed by Mary and

Philomena. Philomena was so happy to see her friend Crystal. She told Mary to take Johnny upstairs, change his Sunday clothes and come down for a bite to eat. She then sat down where the four of them had coffee, homemade pastries and waited for Ralph to return.

Chapter 62

Junior was sitting in his car on Pine Avenue about one hundred yards away from the coffee shop. It was four thirty in the afternoon and Antoinella was nowhere in sight. He was becoming more and more agitated every minute. All he thought about in the last couple of hours was the body of Antoinella and what he was going to do to it. *If that bitch doesn't show up, I'm going to find her somewhere and give her the beating of her life. I can't believe she is going to stand me up...* he thought. The coffee shop closed at four o'clock so he couldn't even get a warm cup of coffee while waiting. He had to stay in his cold car and he was not in the best of moods.

He was ready to leave when he saw Antoinella walking hurriedly down Pine Avenue toward the coffee shop. He was starting to get a hard on. He thought ... *this is it. How could I ever doubt that this girl would not show up? At least now I don't have to beat the shit out of her after I screw her.*

As Antoinella got closer to the coffee shop, Junior started up the car, pulled up by the curb and stuck his head out of the window. Using all his charm, he said, "Hey beautiful, do you need a ride?" Antoinella was ecstatic that he waited for her. She said, "I am so, so sorry that I'm late. My mother had me doing all these errands after dinner. I thought you would not wait." With that, Junior turned all his charm on and said, "I would have waited until the end of the world."

Antoinella quickly jumped in the car and Junior planted a quick kiss on her cheek. He thought… *this is going to be easier than I expected.*

He quickly said to her, "How about showing me Niagara Falls? I was never there and I think it would be great to see it." Antoinella told him that would be great, that she loved The Falls and that it was one of the most romantic spots in the world. She gave him the directions as they drove down Pine Avenue. He told her that it was quite cold out today and he made a little drink to keep them warm. While he was in his room at the bordello, he had a bottle of whiskey, poured over half of it out into another container and placed some soda in it to disguise some of the harsh taste of the liquor. His motive was to get her drunk.

While they were driving, he told her to take a gulp from the bottle. He promised her this would keep her warm. Antoinella took a sip and almost choked as it went down her throat. This was the first time she had hard liquor; the only alcohol she ever had was a taste of her father's homemade wine during Sunday's dinners. Junior chuckled and said, "The first sip is always the toughest if you are not used to it. But I guarantee you it will warm you up as we walk outside to see The Falls." He cajoled her into taking another sip to make sure she would be warm when they got out of the car. Antoinella did not want him to think she was a prude and this time, she took a bigger gulp. She gave a little cough but actually started to get a little warmer.

Junior parked the car and they walked toward the Falls. He had his arm around her shoulders and she was feeling that she finally found a man who really liked her. As they were walking, Junior took the bottle that was in a bag out of his pocket. He took a very small sip but told Antoinella that she should take a bigger gulp to make sure she stays warm as they get closer to the brink of The Falls. After she took a large gulp, he leaned over for the first time and planted a large kiss on her lips. As her lips parted, he found her tongue and she reacted with moans.

They stayed watching the beautiful Niagara Falls, cuddling with each other and sipping the bottle that he had in the bag in his overcoat pocket. The more Junior was cooing in her ear, the more Antoinella was taking sips. She thought this was the greatest day in her life.

After spending over an hour at The Falls, it was becoming dark and colder. Junior whispered in her ear that maybe they should leave and go some place where it's warmer. Antoinella slurred her words and said, "Sergio, anywhere you want to go, I will go." She placed her head on his shoulders as they walked back to the car.

Junior started to get impatient. He had a hard on for the last hour and thought it was about time he took her back to his room. It was around seven in the evening and had become very dark and much colder. As they were driving, Antoinella was leaning her head on his shoulder and relishing this wonderful time she was having. She could not believe that this was happening to her. In her innocence, she was thinking... *this is the man of my dreams, someone who I would like to marry.* This was after he gave her another swig of the bottle, which was almost empty by now.

He thought this was it. He was tired of the bullshit of the last couple of hours and now only wanted to screw her. He kept on imagining what her body would look like naked. Because he had a few drinks in him, she was not as homely as he originally thought.

He told her he was cold and wanted to go to his room to get heavier clothes and maybe another bottle of warmth. He said after that maybe they could go for a bite to eat. She said, "Sergio, I will go as long as I get home by ten o'clock tonight. My parents are very strict." Junior thought... *it definitely has to be now or never. This bitch is starting to drive me nuts. She better be worth it.*

He said, "Anything you say, Antoinella. Perhaps some time in the future, I can meet your parents." Antoinella thought... *this is it. This is the man I've been looking for all my life.*

Junior took the back streets to the bordello. He wanted to go to the back door so Antoinella wouldn't become suspicious of the place. To say the least, going through the front doors with all the red lights blaring out the windows and women sitting near the windows scantily clad would be a dead giveaway that this was not a reputable hotel.

Junior parked the car in the back. They went up the back staircase to his room on the fourth -floor. It was very difficult going up the stairs because Antoinella was starting to feel the effects of Junior's "bottle of warmth." Matter of fact, Antoinella for the first time in her life was inebriated. They entered Junior's room.

Chapter 63

Junior told her to sit on the bed while he went into the bathroom. Antoinella started to sway a little bit and slurred, "I kinda feel dizzy. My head is starting to spin." Junior thought... *Great, this bitch is going to throw up or pass out before I screw her.*

He said in a rough voice, "Take your coat off, I'll be right back after I take a piss." Antoinella was a little taken aback by his tone but took off her jacket because she was becoming warm. She sat on the bed swaying back and forth when Junior came out of the bathroom with only his shorts on. Antoinella was shocked. Before she could say anything, Junior was on top of her, reaching underneath her skirt and pulling down her panties. She resisted and kept on saying, "Please don't, please don't Sergio." That did not stop Junior who told her, "Shut the fuck up." He ripped her panties off and mounted her even with her dress on. He then tore open her blouse and pulled off her bra, exposing her breasts.

Antoinella started to cry more and more and kept on saying, "Please, no; please, no." Junior responded by biting her right nipple so hard that she screamed in pain. He then thrust himself into her, which caused another scream of pain. There was blood all over the bed as he kept on thrusting himself into her. Antoinella was a virgin. After he satisfied himself, he laid on top of her breathing heavy, still caressing her breast with his lips.

Antoinella laid there quietly sobbing in pain, bleeding and not believing that this had happened. Junior got up after a few moments and when he looked down at the bed, saw that there was blood. "I can't believe you were a goddamn virgin! Well, you're not any more." He started laughing at his little joke. He went into the bathroom while Antoinella curled up into a fetal position in the bed, in shock.

Junior came out of the bathroom and told her he was going out to have a cigarette. "I want you dressed by the time I get back and I'll take you back to the coffee shop." He walked out of the room and went down the back stairs to walk outside for a smoke.

Angelo Sr. heard the noise in the next room. He heard a door slam shut. He opened his door to see his son walking down the hall to the back stairs. Angelo Sr. was drunk as a skunk. He drank almost nonstop for the last twenty-four hours. He went to open Junior's door when he heard sobbing from within. As he opened the door, he looked in and saw a half naked girl curled up on the bed. He could not tell what the bottom half of her body looked like because she still had a dress on but he could see her exposed breasts. He just stared for they looked magnificent and he started to immediately get a hard on. He quickly went into the room, closed the door behind him and said slurring, "Now it's my turn."

Antoinella looked up. What happened to her moments ago was shock, surprise, disappointment and embarrassment. When she looked at this old man coming at her unbuttoning his pants, she was in total fear. She curled up into a tight ball as he hopped in bed with her, stripping off the rest of her clothes. She screamed. He punched her hard in her face, almost knocking her out. He went down to kiss her and drool and spit came out of his mouth. She looked in his eyes and saw insanity. She screamed and fought back with all her might, clawing his face with her fingernails. He howled in pain and got up and started punching her in the face, arms and chest. But Antoinella fought back as hard as she could, screaming at the top of her voice.

Madame Svetlana, who was on the first floor, heard the screaming from above. It was chilling. Three of her girls who were sleeping also heard the screams and rushed out of their rooms half naked. Madame Svetlana, with the three girls, rushed up the stairs to see what was happening.

Sal, who was in a deep sleep, bolted up from his bed when he heard the piercing screams from a few doors down the hall. He did not know which room it was but knew it had to be his father's or his brother's since they were the only three on that floor.

Junior was outside having a cigarette when he heard the screams. He looked up at the whorehouse and knew it was coming from his room. He rushed up the back stairs.

Sal was the first one to get to the room and as he opened the door, he saw his father punching, kicking and using his belt on what looked like a half naked woman on the bed. He yelled out, "Pop, stop. You're going to kill her." Right behind Sal came in Madame Svetlana. She was stunned at what she saw and screamed, "You animal. Get away from her," and she charged at him. As Angelo Sr. was turning, her nails tore into his face. They dug deep into his face a few inches below Antoinella's scratches. He yelped and slapped her hard across the face, knocking her down on the floor. She got up quickly, went after him again, but this time with a knife that she always had hidden in her garter. She sliced at his face and he put up his arm to protect it. She put a cut deep into his forearm and hand. He screamed from the pain.

Just as his father was being stabbed, Junior entered the room and grabbed the Madame. He held her wrist so she wouldn't stab him. The other three girls jumped on him to protect not only their employer but their friend. It was mass chaos in the room. Sal quickly ran back into his room and pulled out the gun that Junior told him to keep near him for insurance. He ran into the room and shot the gun in the air. The noise was deafening and everyone stopped.

Madame Svetlana, although she was a little fearful of the gun, told them, "Get the hell out of here you animals." Junior, Angelo Sr. and Sal quickly backed out of the room as Sal held the gun on everyone who was there. Junior told them to leave everything; we don't need the shit that we brought here. The three ran down the stairs to the back alley where their car was parked. They hopped in it and quickly sped down Pine Avenue.

The Madame took the young girl who was on the bed and wrapped her in a blanket. She said, "Sweetheart, everything is going to be okay. Those animals are gone." She told one of the girls in the room to bring in a wet towel and asked the other one to go downstairs and bring up some ice. Antoinella grabbed the Madame around the neck and sobbed uncontrollably in her arms. "Shh...shh honey. Everything is okay."

When she received the wet towel, she started to wipe away the blood on Antoinella's face. She swept her hair back and saw her full face for the first time. "Oh my God," said Svetlana. She recognized the young girl. It was Antoinella Surfarci, the niece of The Don, "Sebastian The Baker" Massini. The Madame quickly turned to one of the girls still in the room and told her to comfort Antoinella and she would be right back.

She went downstairs and made a phone call to one of the patrons who frequented her place and was part of the Massini crime family. She quickly told him what happened. The man on the other end of the phone told her not to do anything, just take care of the girl.

The man hung up the phone, quickly got dressed and went to The Don's house.

Chapter 64

Sunday evening dinner in the Marrano family followed tradition, as most families did during this era. For the Italians it was always a pasta dish with plenty of sauce, bread, salad and a variety of meats such as chicken, sausage, meatballs, pigeon or rabbit. Everyone had some wine, whether it was a sip for the younger children or a full glass for the parents and older siblings.

The family gathered around the table, all ten of them, for a prayer before dinner. Their father, Federico, gave a short prayer in Italian and one of the children gave a prayer in English. After the prayers, Anna, Josephine, Carmela and Gracie would help their mother, Maria, serve the different courses to the family.

As they were dining, many conversations were going on at the same time. It was not until Federico spoke that everyone stopped talking. He asked each of them what was new during the week that he and their mother should know about. He started with the oldest, Carmen. Each one gave a little synopsis of their week and was met with the approval of both parents. This was the scenario all the way through until it got to Gracie. Federico said, "Gracie, now your turn." Gracie turned and said, "Pa, I have nothing to report. Same old things, nothing new." Neal quickly blurted out, "That is not true, Pa. Gracie is now good friends with Mario, who tried to beat me up. Now Gracie will get together with him and they're both going to try to beat me up."

Gracie turned to her brother, gave him a scowl and punched him in the arm, which almost knocked him off his chair. She quickly said, "Shut up, Neal. I don't need anyone's help to beat you up!"

"Aspetta (wait), Gracie," said Federico. "Let Neal talk." He knew that this would be entertaining because as much as Gracie loved Neal, she was always irritated at him because he always told everyone what she was doing, either in or out of school. Neal started his report on Gracie. He went back and told them all the problems he had with Mario in school, picking on him, how Gracie defended him and now Gracie goes to see him in the hospital and they become friends. "I think Gracie likes him more than she likes Ralph Galanti." Gracie turned to him and said, "Shut up." And she gave him another punch in the arm that almost knocked him out of his chair. Their mother, Maria, quickly stepped in and said, "Gracie, get more sauce and you and your sisters bring the chicken and meatballs to the table." Whether Neal knew this or not, this probably saved him from further pain.

At the Freeman house, Crystal, Horatio and Coco were having an old-fashioned Southern dinner. Fried chicken with grits, gravy and plenty of vegetables were on the menu. Dessert was homemade pecan pie. Crystal made this especially for Horatio, who was born in the South. They sat around the table talking about how they were lucky to have friends like the Galantis; Coco's scholarship to Tuskegee University; Horatio's good friend and boss, Edward Wadsworth Wellington and the main topic of conversation, the Lentis.

"I can't believe how those Lentis treat women. They are the most despicable people I have ever known in my life," said Horatio. "I am amazed at how Eugenio kept his composure. I believe that if that man ever had Angelo Lenti Sr. in his hands, he would have broken his neck with one snap." Coco and Crystal agreed that Eugenio kept his composure and they both agreed that if they were found by the police, they would pay the price for what they had done.

"I'm tired of talking about the Lentis," said Horatio. "Let's talk about you, Coco. How are you doing in school and are you anxious about college?" Coco stated that he couldn't believe how fast school was flying by and that within a few months, he would be graduating. He also told Horatio that he really appreciated what he did for him and that he hoped he would be able to live up to the expectations that Horatio had for him. Crystal beamed with pride. She was so happy that her son and Horatio liked each other so much. It had been years since she actually looked at another man and thought that he would be worthy of being a father figure to Coco. She was hoping that Horatio felt this way toward both of them as much as they felt for him.

All the Galantis were celebrating dinner with Josephine in the hospital. Volunteering to watch the store while they visited their daughter was Tony Moretti, Stan Sobaszek and Gene Staniszewski. All the Galantis sat around Josephine's bed and had plates of food from the cafeteria. Although it wasn't the traditional Italian Sunday dinner, it was tasty and plentiful but more importantly, they were together as a family. As everyone was talking to Josephine, Eugenio sat in the background wondering if the police had found the Lentis.

In the hospital cafeteria, Concetta, Mario, Romeo and Elizabeth were having an enjoyable dinner. They spoke about the future. Mario spoke of how he would like to become a steel worker. Concetta always wanted to be a seamstress. Romeo did not speak but just enjoyed the food, especially the dessert, which was an ice cream sundae. Elizabeth did not say much but said that what she wanted to do was to help others as Father Baker helped her.

The holy man was in his room having his dinner. He could have had the best meat, the best vegetables and best dessert but on his plate was fruit, crackers and cheese. Father Baker did not relish what he ate but he was more concerned about what the orphans and his flock had to eat. After he had dinner, he went straight to the Blessed Mother's statue in his room and carried on his normal conversation with her followed by a novena.

It was a peaceful Sunday night in Lackawanna but in Niagara Falls, Sunday night into Monday would be a horrific time for the Lentis.

Chapter 65

"Mio bella nipote (My beautiful niece). I am here. Do not fear, you will be taken care of and I will speak to my sister and your father," said The Don to his niece, Antoinella. On the exterior, he was very calm but looking at his niece's face with her puffed cheeks, swollen lips and a possible fractured nose, he was seething on the inside. He was thinking... *whoever did this to my family will pay.*

"Uncle Sebastian," a sobbing Antoinella said, "I am so ashamed. I thought Sergio was the man of my dreams. I swear I did not want him to do this to me. I always dreamed of marrying a man and he would be the first that I ever made love to." The Don simply said, "Do not worry. We love you and this person will pay the price for hurting you. I will talk to your parents and they will understand." He then kissed her on the forehead and told two of his men to take her to his doctor for treatment. He told them that he did not want her to go to the hospital and to make sure his doctor understands that this is his top priority. "After the doctor treats her, I want you to take her home and tell her parents I will be there a little later. Tell them not to confront her or ask her any questions. Just tell them to comfort her."

He sent off his two men with Antoinella and he went down to meet the Madame Svetlana. He kissed her on both cheeks, thanked her and told her to sit down and tell him exactly what happened. She related the story of the three men who came to stay at her establishment. She said they told her that they worked for Carl DiJoseph and they had to do a job for The Don. She allowed them to stay upstairs on the fourth floor free of charge because they said they were doing a service for The Don.

Svetlana said, "They were three weird people, especially the older one who I think was a psycho. They arrived late Friday afternoon and stayed in their rooms most of the time. They left late Saturday night and came back in the early hours of Sunday. The only thing I heard was the screaming of your niece from one of the rooms about an hour ago. That's when I and three of my girls rushed upstairs to see the older man punching, kicking and hitting your niece with his belt. I jumped in, along with my girls, to help but one of them had a gun and shot it in the air. I screamed at them to get the hell out of my place. They went out the back door into the alley where their car was parked and took off. I believe the older man was the father since he was called 'Pa.'

One of the younger men was called Junior and I do not know the other young man's name."

The Don said quietly, "Was one called Sergio? What my niece said was that Sergio raped her and the old man tried to but instead beat her." The Don described Sergio from the description that Antoinella gave him. The Madame said, "That sounds more like the one they called Junior."

He thanked Svetlana, again gave her a kiss on each cheek and told her that he was in her debt. But he also stated he did not want anyone to know what happened. If news broke out about his niece, he simply and quietly said to the Madame, "I will no longer be in your debt." She assured him that no one would ever know.

He turned and left with the rest of his men to go back home. He planned to send his men to DiJoseph's house to bring DiJoseph to him. Svetlana had the girls clean the room and told them that they were not to say a word about what happened if they valued their lives.

Chapter 66

It was close to midnight when DiJoseph arrived at The Don's house in Niagara Falls. He was, to say the least, very nervous not knowing why The Don wanted to see him this late in the evening. What troubled him most was that four of The Don's men came to his house in Buffalo, woke him up and told him to get dressed and come with them. He was very apprehensive since he was not allowed to make a phone call to bring a couple of his henchmen, Bruno and Slick.

He slowly walked into the study of one of the top Mafioso men in the area, if not in the country. In the room, Don Massini sat in a big leather chair behind a big desk. On each side of him stood one of his soldiers. The rest were scattered around the large room, at least six of them as far as DiJoseph could make out. The men who brought him in waited outside the door and only one of them entered the room with him.

DiJoseph cautiously walked toward Massini, reached out to kiss his hand and stated, "My Don, how could I be of service to you?" In a quiet and controlled voice, The Don told him to sit down. "Do you have a man working for you who's name is Junior and perhaps two others that may be related to him?" DiJoseph was hesitant but he knew if he didn't tell the truth, the consequences could be extremely bad. "Yes, my Don, they are the Lentis from Lackawanna. There are two sons called Junior and Salvatore and the old man is Angelo. I hired them last January. We lost several men to the Feds and I was desperate for replacements. Matter of fact, I had the three of them pick up that shipment from Canada for you on Saturday night. Is there a problem?"

The Don looked him straight in the eye and with a slightly harsher voice said, "I will ask the questions. You will do the answering. Capisce?" Immediately DiJoseph knew he was in hot water. This was very, very serious. He nodded his head as The Don continued speaking.

"Do you know where they are?" "No." "Will you be seeing them anytime soon?" "The one called Junior is supposed to come to see me Monday morning." "Will the other two be with him?" "They usually are with him but they wait in the car." "Do you know what happened tonight?" "No, my Don."

In a quiet, calm but menacing voice, Massini told him what happened to his niece just a few hours ago. He told him how they unmercifully beat her, raped her and if it wasn't for the intervention of a woman he knew, they might have killed her. DiJoseph was shocked. He started to think that The Don was going to blame him because they were his men. He had to think of something very quickly or else he might never leave this room alive.

Trying to control his voice to sound both sympathetic but also businesslike, he said, "My Don, let me have the honor of bringing these animals to our type of justice. I swear that they will pay for every indignity they did to your niece and family. I will also pay for any medical treatment she may need and when she recovers, I will make amends to her and her family. I give you my oath." The Don sat there quietly for a few minutes. You could have heard a pin drop in the room. No one spoke, no one moved and they barely breathed.

"Carl, you have worked for me for many years and you have been loyal to me. I will not hold you responsible for what happened to my niece but I do hold you responsible for hiring these pieces of shit. I will accept your offer including making amends for my sister's child and family. You have three days to fulfill your oath to me." The Don stood up behind his desk, walked around it to DiJoseph and kissed him on both cheeks. DiJoseph stepped back, reached for The Don's hand and respectfully kissed it. He said very quietly and humbly, "I will fulfill my oath to you."

He turned and left with the man who escorted him in. They returned to their cars and the four men who brought him, took him back to his house. Not a word was said by anyone during the whole trip.

When DiJoseph entered his home, the first thing he did was call his top lieutenant, Bruno, and told him to come to his house immediately and bring with him five of his best men. Bruno did not question his boss. He knew something very important was happening for him to be called this late.

By two o'clock in the morning, Bruno and his five top men were at his boss's home. DiJoseph then proceeded to tell them about the Lentis and what had happened. He told them, "I gave The Don my oath and by Wednesday you are going to help me fulfill it."

Chapter 67

The officers of the GAA along with the members of the dance committee were meeting in the clubhouse to discuss the Easter dance at the Dom Polski's Hall. Ralph was in attendance because they needed his advice regarding his sister, Josephine. Coco told Ralph that he would watch the store with his sister, Mary, while his parents were up at the hospital.

The members of the committee spoke first. Lui Marini told them that he contacted the people at Dom Polski's Hall and reserved the hall for the Saturday after Easter for the dance. Lou Fistola told them he was looking at three possible bands to hire. Paul Petti mentioned that he was securing the refreshments for the affair. Doc yelled out, "Are you spiking it?" Paul said he did not intend to do it but if someone wanted to sneak in some special drink concoction, he had no problem with it. But it would be only for one designated refreshment bowl. Doc said, "I'll be the concokin chairman." Paul said, "It's concoction, you wacko."

President Armondo Ginnetti thanked the dance committee for getting things rolling, "We have almost two months to finalize everything. We need to get tickets printed, make a decision on the band, get the publicity out, decide how much we are going to charge and to decorate the hall. I also want to decide what we want to give Josephine with the money we have left over."

Doc blurted out, "How about a dog?" "Listen, you dumb shit," said Armondo, "They have a dog. What the hell are they going to do with another one?" Doc retorted, "Maybe we should've put a collar around you, shithead and give you to her. You're a hairy son of a bitch." Lui was the voice of reason as he interrupted the two and said, "Come on fellas, we have a lot of work to do and we are doing this for Josephine and our club."

Paul Petti said that he knew Josephine always wanted to go to Niagara Falls. "Maybe we should get Josephine and her family a couple of hotel rooms in The Falls for a weekend. If we have enough money, we could also give them a nice dinner at one of those swanky restaurants." The group thought that was a great idea but turned to Ralph to find out his opinion. Ralph said, "That is very nice and generous of you but I think my sister would just love to have the dance in her honor. Maybe you can give her flowers that evening."

"Well, we'll wait and see," said Ginnetti. "It's too early yet to see what we're going to do for Josephine. Let's finalize some of the things we are going to do so that at the meeting on Sunday, we can present it to our membership."

Meanwhile at the hospital, Eugenio and Philomena went to see Concetta for a few minutes before they went to their daughter's room. Concetta was with her sons, Mario and Romeo, along with Elizabeth as they entered the room. They exchanged pleasantries and Philomena went up to give Concetta a hug and kiss. She also gave Elizabeth a hug and patted the two boys on the head. Concetta was getting healthier and the baby and Mario seemed very happy. Elizabeth was very polite but seemed to have things on her mind and was not as talkative as usual. After several minutes, the Galantis said goodbye and proceeded to Josephine's room. Concetta turned to Elizabeth and said, "Those are wonderful people. I hope their daughter gets well and is able to go home."

Josephine was resting with her eyes closed. She heard movement at the door and she opened her eyes and to her delight she saw her parents. "Ma, Pa, hi. I am so glad to see you both." Both went up and kissed their daughter on the face but were still afraid to touch and hold her because of the burns. She asked them what had been happening and to tell her everything. Eugenio said, "Mia figlia bella (my beautiful daughter). We were justa here yesterday. The only thinga that happened is the sun went down and it camea up again." Josephine started laughing and it was contagious because her mother started laughing too. Eugenio could not understand it because he was serious.

Tuesday night was also special at the Freeman home. Crystal made dinner for both Horatio and Coco before Coco had to go to the store to help Ralph out. After dinner, Coco left and Horatio helped with the dishes. Crystal confided in him about her son. "I am getting so nervous about Coco. I know it's only late February but he'll be graduating in a few months, then he'll be leaving in late summer to go to college. I am scared, not only for him but also for me. Since his father died, we have never been apart one single day of his life." Horatio nodded and said very quietly, "Crystal, do not be afraid for your son. He is now a man, not a boy. And do not be afraid of being alone because I will always be here."

She dropped the dish that she was washing and turned around. She started crying as she planted one giant kiss on Horatio's lips. "Thank you, Horatio. I thought I would never feel this way about another man in my life. You and Coco are the most precious things in my life. I don't know how to tell you because I don't know how you will respond but I lo..." before she finished the sentence, Horatio grabbed her in his arms and gave her a long and passionate kiss and said, "Crystal, I love you."

Chapter 68

It was four o'clock Wednesday afternoon when Eugenio came into the store after working in the steel plant. He went there early in the morning and was chosen by the foreman to work that day. As he entered the store, there were two policemen plus the Lackawanna Chief of Police, Steve Darren, waiting there. "Hello Steve." "Hello, Mr. Galanti. Can I talk to you for a few minutes?" "Sure. Let'sa go into the kitchen." Ralph was watching the store. He just got home from school and the three policemen were waiting there for his father. His mother was a little nervous and did not know why they were there but did not question them. The police chief told Ralph he would like to talk to his father when he got home from work. Ralph said, "Is there anything I can do for you?" "No, Ralph. This is something I have to talk to your father about in private."

Ralph told his mother that he would drive them to the hospital as soon as his father came home. But Ralph was too curious and worried so he went in the back and asked Lui, who was in the clubhouse, if he wouldn't mind driving his family to the hospital. Lui told him that it would be no problem.

The police chief and Eugenio went into the kitchen with Ralph following. The two policemen stayed outside in the store. Chief Darren told Eugenio that maybe it would be better if Ralph did not listen to what he had to tell him. Eugenio said, "Mya son is a man. If you coulda tella me, you coulda tella him." The chief said all right and proceeded to tell them that they found the Lentis.

"The three Lentis were found at approximately ten o'clock this morning. They were found at Woodlawn Beach in that small wooded area behind the beach. A woman was walking her two dogs when the two ran into this wooded area. She called but they did not come back. So, she went into the woods and discovered a very gruesome scene. She found the three Lentis. She screamed and started running down the street and was hysterical. A few of the neighbors ran out and tried to calm her down but could not make out what she was saying. After a few minutes of trying to calm her down, she told them there were three dead bodies in that wooded area. They called the Woodlawn police who came down and immediately called us because they knew they were the Lentis and we were looking for them. I personally went down there with four of my policemen. Mr. Galanti, it was the most sickening murder site I have seen in all my thirty years of being in the police department.

"When I arrived, the three of them were bound up. The one who we now know as Sal had just his hands tied behind his back and his ankles were bound. He was beaten up pretty bad but mercifully, they put a bullet in the middle of his forehead. The other two had things done to them that I never saw before in my life. Both were beaten severely. Each had cigarette burns on their faces and upper torsos. They were bound with a rope around their necks, tied tightly to their ankles with their knees bent. Their hands were tied behind their backs. It seemed that if they relaxed their legs and let them down, they would choke themselves to death. They both had something in their mouths but we couldn't tell until the coroner came. He said they were both castrated and their private parts were stuffed in their mouths while they were still alive. He does not know for sure until he examines them whether they choked to death, bled to death or strangled themselves with the ropes that were tied to their bodies. Both men, we later found out, were Junior and Angelo Lenti Sr. Both had carved in their foreheads the word "Maiale" which I found out meant "pig." Mr. Galanti, whoever did this hated these men. There are no clues but all indications are that it was a Mob hit."

Eugenio thanked the police chief for coming to tell him personally. He told him that it was only a matter of time that something like this would happen to them because of the life they led and what they did to people, especially women. Ralph listened intently but did not say one word. He had mixed emotions. He did not like the Lentis but to die the way they did was incomprehensible to him.

The police chief and the two policemen left the store. Eugenio told his son not to say a word to his mother or Crystal. All they needed to know was that the Lentis died and that is the end of the story. He told Ralph to watch the store. He was going to visit Josephine but wanted to stop and talk to Horatio before he went to the hospital. Then his father did something that Ralph was unaccustomed to seeing him do. He took the face of his son in his huge hands and kissed him on both cheeks before he went upstairs to change clothes.

Chapter 69

The month of February was finally ending. The biggest topic of conversation in the Western New York area and especially in Lackawanna was the murder of the three Lenti family members. It was headline news in the Buffalo Evening News for over a week. It even made for a topic on the Walter Winchell radio show nationwide. The police agencies in Western New York did not have any leads on who caused these horrendous deaths.

When the Lackawanna Chief of Police went to OLV Hospital to inform Concetta of the deaths of her husband and her two sons, she broke down and cried hysterically. The death of her husband did not affect her but the murder of her two sons was too much to bear. No matter how they treated her, she was still their mother and she had that motherly instinct to protect her children. Concetta told her son Mario that his father and two brothers had died. He cried for his brothers, especially Sal, who he was close to as they grew up. He felt very little for his older brother Junior because he did not know him that well because of the age difference and Junior was in prison for a couple of years. He hated his father and did not have any remorse for the fact that he died.

The Galantis had mixed emotions about what happened to the Lentis. Philomena cried because of the young man Salvatore. She always thought he was led astray by his father and older brother. Ralph felt the same way even though he had that altercation with Sal at the theater earlier in the summer. Eugenio felt no remorse at all. He despised the father and the two sons because of how they treated Concetta. He thought... *Erano animali e sono morte con animale (They were animals and they died like animals).* He also thought that if this happened in the Old Country, their deaths would probably be more gruesome.

The story of the Lentis spread like wildfire in Bethlehem Park. Carmen was the first to find out what happened and he went to tell his parents. Maria made the sign of the cross and said a prayer while her husband, Federico, told Carmen it was only a matter of time when something like this would happen. He also told Carmen to tell his older sisters what happened but do not go into detail. Carmen asked if he should also include Gracie even though she was much younger. The father said yes but he did not want Neal, Lou and Rosie to know. "Your mother will explain to them in a way they will understand."

Carmen called his sisters, including Gracie, to come with him down in the cellar where the second kitchen was located. He told them to sit around the table and then proceeded to tell them what happened to the Lentis. The sisters were shocked. Carmen looked at Gracie for her reaction but he could not read her facial expression. She just stared at him and said, "I do not feel sorry for them. I feel so sorry for Mrs. Lenti, Mario and Romeo." Carmen nodded.

It had been a few days since Concetta was told of the deaths of her husband and sons. She was sobbing in her room when Elizabeth entered it with Romeo. Elizabeth felt so sorry for this poor woman. She went up to her with the baby and said, "Concetta, I am so sorry that this happened. But, you have to understand that you have two beautiful children that need you." Concetta reached out for the baby and held him very close to her chest. She then reached out for her friend's hand and said, "Thank you, Elizabeth, for everything. You've been my guardian angel throughout this terrible time in my life. I am crying because I know I could have done more for my two boys, Angelo Jr. and Salvatore. But, I was too afraid of my husband. I should have been strong but I was weak and now they are gone."

Elizabeth held Concetta's hand tightly. "You are the strongest woman I have ever met. What happened to your sons was not your fault. They were old enough to make their own decisions on how they wanted to live their lives. Your focus should now be on Mario and Romeo. Give them the life that you know they deserve, which is love, caring and a strong devotion to Our Lord and the Blessed Mother." Concetta nodded and gave Elizabeth a kiss on the cheek. "I am healthy enough now to take my children home. They need their own house, their own rooms, things that are familiar to them and neighbors that care about them. I want to start a new life with them. I am going to talk to Dr. Sullivan and Father Baker and ask them if I can leave the hospital with my children and go home." Elizabeth said it was a wonderful idea but asked her what she was going to do to earn money to feed her children and pay bills.

"I thought of that. I am a pretty good seamstress and I could earn some money doing work for neighbors and friends. Also, I hope Dr. Sullivan can use me to work in the hospital, cleaning rooms and washing linens. I could do this while Mario is in school and I can take Romeo here to play in the nursery."

"That is a wonderful idea. I am sure Dr. Sullivan can use you and I will be able to help take care of Romeo during those days. I really love him and I know I would miss him if you took him home and I couldn't see him for long periods of time. I also know that Father

Baker can use some help in the rectory and orphanage. If you don't mind, I can ask him for you."

"Oh, Elizabeth, that would be wonderful. I love you as a sister and it is great that Mario and Romeo have you as an aunt."

The two women then made plans to meet with Dr. Sullivan and Father Baker. They spoke of everything in a positive vein; that both men would agree to their ideas. Both women felt excited about their future.

Chapter 70

The beginning of March 1933 was extremely cold in much of the nation, but worldwide things were heating up. There were conflicts in Europe and Asia. The League of Nations wanted Japan to pull out of Manchuria; in Germany the Nazi party and Hitler were starting to have a stronghold on the country with major conflicts against the German Communist Party and the German Jewish population; Mussolini ruled Italy with an iron hand and the world was in a deep economic depression.

In the United States, Franklin D. Roosevelt was inaugurated as the 32nd President of the United States. He brought hope to millions in the country with his famous inaugural speech where he pledged to pull the U.S. out of its Great Depression. His famous quote, "We have nothing to fear but fear itself," resonated throughout the country with every citizen. He gave hope to the nation with his "fireside chats" and his "New Deal Program." Although the country was suffering through the Great Depression and one out of three citizens was unemployed, there was a feeling that this president would turn the corner on our economic plight.

Under the new regime of President Roosevelt, Congress was starting to think of revoking Prohibition by allowing wine and beer, up to 3.2 percent alcohol, to become legal throughout the United States.

Many people knew this would be the beginning of the end of Prohibition.

Locally in Lackawanna, many things were happening. Father Baker, by the end of March, served almost half a million meals to the unfortunate in Lackawanna and Western New York. Also during this time, he was able to give tens of thousands of dollars to aid the poor and needy who came to him for assistance. Many considered this a miracle because of the economic situation of the country.

March was a happy month for Concetta and Elizabeth. Elizabeth went to see Dr. Sullivan and Father Baker regarding Concetta working at the hospital. Both gentlemen agreed that this was a great idea and told her that Concetta could start the first week in April after she got settled back home in Bethlehem Park. Elizabeth also confided to Father Baker that she had reached a decision about her future. She told Father Baker, if it's possible, she would like to go to school to become a nurse and then enter the convent to become a nun. She told him that it would be the best of two worlds; helping people both physically and spiritually. Father Baker thought that was a great idea, although he secretly figured out that Elizabeth would come to this decision. If not, he would kind of hint that this was a possibility.

He told Elizabeth that he would speak to Dr. Sullivan to see what college she could attend for nursing and he would go see his close and longtime friend, Mother Mary Anne Burke of the Sisters of St. Joseph for her admission to the convent for her training and vows to become a nun. Elizabeth was ecstatic. She hugged Father Baker so tightly that the old priest gave a little grunt. She backed away very quickly, very embarrassed and she said, "I am so sorry that I hurt you, Monsignor." Father Baker responded, "That was the best squeeze I have had in years and I enjoyed it."

Concetta finally was able to go to her home in Bethlehem Park. At first, it seemed so surreal that only a month ago, she was here with her husband and two older sons. It seemed a little empty but more calm and serene. The boys, Romeo and Mario, adapted as though they never had left. Neighbors and friends from the neighborhood came over with a helping hand and welcomed her and her boys back. News spread throughout Bethlehem Park that Concetta was now in business as a seamstress and if anyone needed alterations or sewing, she was available. There seemed to be, for the first time in years, peace and calm in her home and in her neighborhood.

Horatio was going crazy trying to figure out how to propose to Crystal. He bought an engagement ring from his good friend and business partner, Wellington. Wellington sold him the ring for exactly the same price he paid for it at a pawnshop. It was a beautiful ring he had purchased for his wife but seeing Horatio's excitement about proposing to Crystal, he offered it to him. Wellington told his wife what he did. She scolded him, "How could you even charge this beautiful man the cost of the ring. Go back and give him the money and tell him that is our gift for the upcoming wedding." Wellington was relieved because he wanted to do this in the first place but didn't know how his wife would react. Horatio planned to propose to Crystal on Easter Sunday.

Gracie was secretly happy that Mario was returning to Bethlehem Park School. The kids at Bethlehem Park couldn't understand when they saw Mario and Gracie walking to school talking and laughing. They thought it was a mirage and so did her brother Neal. Neal had a hard time accepting Mario but if his sister, Gracie, accepted him, he definitely would be sociable and nice to him.

Every few days in March, Mrs. Marrano would send food to Concetta and her boys until they were settled in their home and their new life. Anna, Josephine and Carmela would alternate taking the food to the house. All three would spend an hour or two playing with Romeo who they started to become attached to.

During March, Josephine was able to come home once a week for a few hours. The doctors wanted to make sure that she would be comfortable in her home where her accident occurred. They also wanted to make sure that the Galantis knew exactly how to take care of her and her medical needs when she came home for good. It started out as twice a week for a few hours and by the end of March, the doctors allowed her to stay overnight. The date that they had targeted for her complete release from the hospital was the day before Easter in April. Even though she was going to be home, she would still have to go to the hospital twice a week for changing of the dressings and evaluation. Dr. Sullivan told the Galantis of the plan for Josephine. He also told them that because of the severity of her injuries this might not happen. He did not want them to be disappointed. Eugenio and Philomena were very happy but cautious.

Ralph and Coco were enjoying their last year at Lackawanna High School. Both made the Honor Roll and had plans to attend college. Coco was assured of a scholarship to Tuskegee University because of his academic and athletic excellence. Ralph was planning to either go to Canisius College or the University of Buffalo.

The GAA was meeting on a regular basis every Sunday. The meetings were very entertaining, to say the least. If there weren't fights and yelling, there was great storytelling by the members. The main topic of conversation was the big dance that was going to be held the week after Easter. They all agreed that this would be the first of many great events to be hosted by the GAA.

Chapter 71

"I call the meeting to order," said Armondo Ginnetti. There was still a lot of talking going on in the clubhouse. No one seemed to be paying attention. Armondo slammed a makeshift gavel on the table. The gavel was a hammer wrapped in rags and it still almost busted the table. "I said I call the meeting to order, shut the hell up. The next guy who talks I'm going to have Doc throw him out on his ass. Do you hear that Doc?" Doc stood up and said, "I hear ya loud and clear, Mr. President." And then he slapped his bat in his hand. He exchanged the piece of wood he originally had for an old-fashioned baseball bat. The membership quieted down because no one knew to what extremes Doc would go to keep it quiet.

"I would like to have Tony Moretti read the minutes." Tony turned and said, "You told me last meeting not to take minutes because we are talking about the same thing that we did at the meeting before that. When I took this position, we were supposed to have a meeting once a month and now we have one every Sunday. This is bullshit. If you want a secretary, go out and hire some broad to take the minutes because I'm not doing this every week." Someone yelled out, "Let's impeach Tony. We can get a broad with big tits and better looking and she doesn't even have to know how to write." Tony responded, "Frig you." Armondo said, "Let's forget the minutes. Tony's right. We have formal meetings once a month. It just happens that we're having one every week because of the big dance in a couple of weeks. As soon as the constitution and bylaws committee comes up with concrete rules and regulations, then we can have regular formal meetings with reports."

"I would like to have the dance committee give a report of where we are at. Lui, where are we now with the dance?" Lui got up and stated, "Everything is set for Saturday, April 22, at the Dom Polski Hall. I have it booked from nine o'clock in the evening until three o'clock in the morning. We can get in there for decorations at noon on Saturday. The cost to rent the hall will be $8.00 instead of $12.00 as long as we clean up afterwards. They said they're giving us a deal because it's a benefit for Josephine." Someone yelled out, "Good job, Lui."

"Ok. Thanks, Lui. Let's hear from Lou Fistola regarding the band." Lou stood and said, "I got a great deal. Al Brown and his Georgians agreed to play for nothing because he heard about Josephine's accident and he knows the Galanti family very well. He told me it's his contribution but he wants us to know that the next time we have a dance, we'd better book him and his band."

"That's great," yelled Sobey. "I heard them play just last week up in Buffalo and they were jivin. The girls were going crazy." The members gave Lou a rousing cheer. "All right, let's have our next report from Petti regarding the refreshments." Doc was the only one that cheered before Petti got up and spoke. "Shut the hell up, Doc. Let the guy speak for Christ's sake," said the president.

"As you all know," Paul started to say, "President Roosevelt is making the sale of wine and beer legal this month. So by April, we can have alcohol at the dance. I suggest that we offer pop and punch for free and charge for beer and wine. We can make a little extra money if we do this as long as the price is reasonable." Everyone was excited about the prospect of having legal alcohol at the dance. Everyone but Doc. He raised his hand and said he had a question. "What happens with the broads who can't afford alcohol or do not want to drink it? I still think we should have one bowl of punch spiked with booze. I will take responsibility of getting the booze for that one bowl." The members looked around at each other and said that maybe Doc had a point. It would be nice to have a few broads inebriated. Armondo turned to Doc and said, "All right, you're in charge of that one punch bowl. Make sure you put it away from the other bowls and make sure that it is only for the broads and our members. I don't want some of those cheapskate Pollacks or Potato Heads coming to the dance drinking on us for free."

"Listen, you stupid Dago, it's Italians like you who are cheap," said Sobey who was proud of his Polish heritage. "That's right, you son of a bitch," said Tom McCann, whose father was Irish and mother was Italian. "If it wasn't for the Pollacks and us Micks, there would be nobody at the dance." Lui Marini got up and was the voice of reason, saying, "Everyone be quiet. Maybe you don't realize it but this is a club made up of all nationalities, although maybe the Italians have the majority. We are friends, we are brothers, we are GAA members. Let's be proud of that and quit this stupid bickering."

Everyone was quiet for a moment and thought about what Lui said. President Ginnetti apologized for his remarks, as did Sobey and McCann. The meeting became orderly and Armondo asked Tom Pepper about the tickets and how much we were going to charge for admission. Pepper told everyone that he worked a deal with Steel City Printing for producing the tickets. He said that the printers would do the tickets for free if we gave them free advertising on the tickets and allow them to hang a few signs in the hall. They also wanted us to consider them to be our printers in the future for any ticket events we sponsor. "Wow," said Armondo, "How the hell did you make that great deal?" Pepper said, "It took a lot of top notch negotiation and bullshitting but I convinced the owner that this was a great deal for them. Besides, the owner is my brother-in-law. I also told him that a few words from me to my sister could make his life miserable. It only took him a few seconds before he agreed to my proposal."

The guys in the clubhouse gave him a cheer as they were laughing and slapping him on the back. Pepper continued and said, "I think admission should be thirty five cents and I ordered three hundred fifty tickets. If we sell three hundred, we can make over one hundred dollars. I think it would be a good idea to have fifty reserved for freebees for special guests. I also took it upon myself to order the tickets in light blue." Armondo told him he did a great job and told the membership to give the committee a round of applause for their great work.

The members not only gave him a great applause, but gave the committee a standing ovation and started slapping each other on their backs saying this was going to be a great event. Armondo started slamming the gavel hammer on the table trying to get order and yelled, "Quiet, we have one more thing to discuss and it's about Josephine's gift." When the members heard this, they started to quiet down and sat back in their seats.

Armondo asked Ralph to please stand up and give the report about Josephine. Ralph stated, "I talked to my sister and told her what we planned to do. She was so happy that she was in tears. I told her that we wanted to buy her something and asked her what she would like. She told me to tell everyone she is thrilled to have a dance in her honor and to thank everyone but there was no need to buy her anything. The dance was more than enough." Doc blurted out, "I still think we should buy her a dog." "Listen you dumb son of a bitch, we told you last time, she has a dog. We're not going to get her another one," said Ginnetti. "Then let's get her a kitten. Everyone likes kittens." Ginnetti yelled, "Enough is enough with these fucking animals. Shut the hell up and just listen." Before Doc could respond, Ralph quickly chimed in, "Listen, she did say something that she would like to have but she wanted to have it for the club. Josephine noticed that our radio was old and sometimes did not work. She would like us to buy a brand new tabletop radio for the clubhouse and if there's not enough money, maybe a phonograph. That's all she wants."

The members were quite taken with this gesture and were quiet for a few moments. Finally, Ginnetti said, "Well, if that's what she wants, that's what we will do. But I think we should still present her with flowers that night." Everyone agreed. Someone yelled out, "We're going to make this a great event for Josephine. Let's get this rolling."

Chapter 72

It was early Saturday morning, the day of the big dance that the GAA was sponsoring. Coco arrived at the clubhouse at nine o'clock in the morning to meet Ralph and many of the club members who volunteered to decorate the hall. Also arriving were Carmen and Anna Marrano to help decorate and buy tickets for the dance.

"Hi, Ralph," said Carmen. "I would like to buy two tickets for Anna and me for the dance tonight. Since you talked me into becoming a member of the GAA, I want to support the club and your sister, Josephine." "Thanks, Carmen. I'm glad you're a member but I know you're busy and we have more than enough help for decorating. Just being there is support enough. By the way, I'm giving you three complimentary tickets for Josephine, Carmela and Gracie. I owe them for what I put them through last summer at the movie theater."

"Ralph, there's no need. I think we should give you something because of what Gracie put you through. By the way, I don't know if my father would allow Gracie to attend. Even though she is almost a teenager, she is still walking on thin ice with my father." Anna chimed in, "I think I could convince Pa and Ma. I will tell them that we're honoring Josephine and it would be nice for all the Marrano girls to be there for her, except for Rosie, who is definitely too young to be out that late." Ralph gave the tickets to Carmen, shook his hand and gave Anna a kiss on the cheek. "I hope I see you all there tonight."

Ralph went back to the clubhouse, where there were about thirty members gathering around to bring the decorations to the Dom Polski Hall. The brothers Dynamite and Harpo were already starting to argue. "I'm not blowing up the balloons; you blow up the balloons and I'll hang the streamers," said Harpo. "Listen dimwit, the streamers are important and I have experience in putting decorations up for parties. Besides, you have so much hot air that you could fill these balloons in a matter of minutes." "Bullshit, you ain't screwing me again," said Harpo. "The only reason you want to hang the streamers is because it's easier than blowing up the balloons and hanging them up. And don't call me a dimwit, you dipshit." Then the shoving began with both of them grappling each other and falling to the ground. Four or five of the members intervened to separate them and Coco thought ...*Oh my God, I hope this is not a sign of what's going to happen tonight.*

Lou Fistola and Carl Covino got in between the two. Lou said, "That's it. If you two are going to do this, forget about helping with the decorations. Matter of fact, forget about coming to the dance tonight because you two will ruin it. Either shake hands and make up or get the hell out of here." As usual, the two brothers apologized to each other and gave each other a hug. Nobody knew how long this peace would last. Hopefully, at least until after the dance.

They all left the clubhouse and arrived at Dom Polski's Hall, where some members were already setting up chairs and tables. Paul Petti, Sobey and Moretti were bringing in the beverages for the bar. Petti was also taking inventory of the wine and beer because they were charging for these refreshments. Al Brown was looking for an area where he could set up his band for the evening. He wanted to make sure that there was enough area for a good dance floor. Pepper was setting up a table for ticket sales near the door. They had already sold two hundred and twenty five tickets and he expected to sell the rest that evening.

By two o'clock in the afternoon, the hall was decorated and everything was in its place. It looked very festive with all the different colored balloons and streamers. There was also a "Welcome Home" sign for Josephine, made and brought in by the Marrano girls. When they saw the hall, they were impressed. "What a beautiful job you guys did decorating this hall," said Anna. "I would pay the thirty five cents just to come in and admire this room." "Give me a break," said Gracie. "It's nice but I'd rather give them the thirty five cents to dance and listen to the music." Josephine Marrano gave her little sister a little punch in the arm and told her to be quiet or else she would not be going anywhere. "Listen, Gracie. The only reason why you are coming is because Anna talked Ma and Pa into it and also told them that she would take you back by your extended curfew of eleven o'clock. Anna is giving up a good time so you can come. So, behave and act like a young lady." Gracie looked at her sister with irritation but did not dare say a word. She definitely wanted to be at the dance tonight. The thing she loved the most was music and dancing.

Ralph told the Marranos, especially Gracie, that they would have a special guest at the dance. "I gave Elizabeth Donner a complimentary ticket. She has done so much for my sister and my sister really likes her so I thought it would be nice if she was here for the dance. At first, she declined, but when I told her my sister Josephine wanted her here with us, she accepted. Also, to our surprise, she convinced Dr. Sullivan to allow Josephine to stay overnight at our house. She told him that she would stay with Josephine at our house and make sure that she is comfortable and if there would be a problem, she would be there for her. My parents were elated when Dr. Sullivan said that he would allow this. Elizabeth is such a wonderful person. I hope one day I can help her as much as she is helping us."

The Marrano girls were elated. They all liked Elizabeth. Gracie thought ...*This is going to be one great dance and I am so happy I am going to be part of it. I owe my sisters and somehow I am going to repay them, even that dip Ralph who gave me a free ticket. But I have to admit, he ain't bad looking for an old guy.*

The Marranos bid Ralph goodbye and told him they would see him at the dance. Ralph went over to see Coco. "I hope your mother and Horatio are coming. I also gave them complimentary tickets for Mr. and Mrs. Wellington and their daughter, Dorothea. It was nice of them to donate that beautiful bonnet and scarf for Josephine. Do you think they will come?"

"I know my mother and Horatio are definitely coming and I think they are bringing Dorothea. She heard about this dance and begged her dad to let her come. Horatio told Mr. Wellington that he will definitely be her chaperone and bring her home at a reasonable hour. I don't think Mr. and Mrs. Wellington are coming because he has been very ill the last couple of months and I don't think he has the strength to go out."

Ralph responded, "I'm sorry that they can't make it but I'm happy they will let their daughter come. I know Horatio and your mom will have a great time. Coco, are you bringing a date?"
"No! I don't want to get you jealous. Youse know, Master Ralph, that I'm all yours for the taking," laughed Coco. "Very funny," said Ralph as he gave Coco a punch in the arm.

Ralph, Coco and the rest of the GAA members looked around at the hall. Everything seemed perfect. It was three o'clock in the afternoon and they were going to lock the hall up, go home, get cleaned, dressed and ready for the big dance. They all planned to get there at seven o'clock in the evening, two hours before the opening of the doors to make sure everything was ready. They were all excited. This was the first big event for the newly formed GAA; they were honoring Ralph's sister whom they all loved and it looked like it was going to be one great event. They all couldn't wait for the doors to open.

Chapter 73

"Oh my God," said Ziggy, "The line is a half a block long and it's not even eight thirty. I don't know if there's going to be enough room in the hall for all the people." "Don't worry," said Ralph. "The place is big enough and if we see there are too many people, we just won't sell any more tickets at the door and only let in the ones who bought tickets earlier."

Almost all the GAA members were in attendance, making sure everything was ready for the opening of the doors at nine o'clock. Every one of them paid for their tickets. They all agreed that the only comp tickets that would be given out would be from Ralph since he knew all the people who contributed to the dance and helped this club get organized. Doc was excited. He looked out the window and saw waves of girls waiting to get into the dance. He was telling everyone that the ratio had to be three girls to every guy. He hurried into the kitchen where he had his special mix of punch and alcohol in one of the large bowls all prepared. He brought it out and put it near the corner of the hall where he would be sitting guarding the punch and making sure only the prettiest girls would be offered a drink.

Al Brown and his Georgians were set up and tuning their instruments. Ralph thought... *I hope to God they play better than their tuning or else we will not get out of this place alive.* Someone brought in a special chair that was well padded and decorated. It looked like a throne. This was for their special guest, Josephine.

Ralph looked at his watch and yelled to everyone in the hall. "It's fifteen minutes before nine. Are we all set with everything? Are the punch bowls filled, the bar set for drinks, the band ready and the ticket table ready to go?" Everyone yelled that they were all set. Ralph yelled down to Ziggy, "We will open the doors in fifteen minutes. I will give you a call down when you should do this." Ralph looked at Coco and said, "I will need your help. I asked my mother and father to bring Josephine here at ten o'clock tonight. I figured this would be when everyone will be here. I think Josephine will be in a wheelchair and I need to have you and some of the guys carry her up the flight of stairs in the wheelchair." "Raffs, don't worry about anything. We will have her up here. Just relax." "Thanks, Coco. You're always there when I need you." Coco gave Ralph a slap on the back and turned around to make sure everything in the hall was ready to go.

The doors opened at nine sharp. It was chaos for the ticket table. Some had tickets, some wanted to buy tickets and they all were in close quarters at the door. Coco and Lui quickly got to the table and started to give directions. They yelled, "Everyone who has a paid ticket, come in at the left side of the door and hand in your ticket. Everyone who has to buy a ticket, stay on the right side in a single line and we will accommodate you. Anyone who does not abide by the rules will be escorted out." Lui was determined to get some order at the door.

By nine thirty, most of the people were in the hall, dancing, drinking, socializing and having a ball. There was still a line out the door but not as long as earlier. Ralph was getting a little worried because he wanted to make sure there would not be a problem of getting Josephine and his parents up the stairs and into the hall. There was no need to worry because by ten o'clock the place was packed and the line was minimal.

They were dancing and jitterbugging to some great songs of that era. Al Brown and his group had them jumping with *Minnie the Moocher, As Time Goes By, Tiger Rag, All of Me, Night and Day, I Got Rhythm, Stormy Weather*, and many, many more great hits. Gracie was in her heyday, loving every minute. She did not sit down once, dancing mainly with her sisters. She was getting very thirsty and saw there was a punch bowl near Doc that nobody was going to. The rest of the punch bowls were crowded so she walked over to where Doc was sitting and asked him for a cup for the punch.

Doc was hesitant. He knew Gracie was young and he also knew that if anything happened, Carmen would knock the hell out of him so he tried to be diplomatic. He said, "Gracie, you don't want any of this punch." "Why?" said Gracie. Doc had to think quick and the only thing he thought was, "Because somebody had a taste of it and didn't like it and spit it back into the bowl." "Ugh, that is disgusting." And she walked away standing in line for a cup of punch at the crowded bowl.

Since Gracie left Doc's punch bowl, only a few people came for a drink and the few people were mostly GAA members. Only one other female came and when she saw the punch bowl and where it was, she said, "Ugh, I don't want any of this stuff," and turned to leave. Doc reached for her arm and said, "Why don't you want the punch from this bowl? It is a special recipe." She looked back and said, "You gotta be kidding. Yeah, the special recipe is spit from someone else's mouth back into the bowl. I heard what happened. Someone didn't like this stupid punch and spit it back into the bowl. You can keep it."

Doc figured out what happened. He thought... *That damn Gracie told everyone what I said. I can't believe I said it and I can't believe she believed me. Shit, if no one is going to drink it, then I'm going to finish this goddamn bowl.*

It was approaching ten o'clock and Ralph was getting a little nervous that his sister might not be feeling well enough to attend. His mind was at ease when he started to hear applauding and cheering from the people around the front door of the hall. As he turned, he saw Coco, Lui, Ziggy, Sobey and a few others carrying Josephine in her wheelchair. Behind Josephine were his parents, his sister Mary, followed by Horatio, Crystal and Elizabeth. As they placed the wheelchair down and started to push her toward the special chair, the music started playing "Happy Days are Here Again" and everyone started to applaud and cheer. Ralph rushed to his sister and gave her a kiss on the cheek. Josephine was turning red as a beet with all the accolades from the crowd. As they reached the chair, Ralph carefully helped her from the wheelchair into the decorated chair. Josephine looked beautiful with her new dress. She was still bandaged from the neck down to her ankles but it didn't matter. She still looked like an angel.

Ralph took the microphone from the band after they completed the song. They were still cheering and applauding. He raised his arms to quiet them down and gave a short emotional speech about his sister and all the friends who were here to honor her. There was not a dry eye in the crowd. He then gave the microphone to his sister to say a few words. Josephine, who was very shy, hesitated but took the microphone and said a few short words. "Thank you for all of this," as she waved her hand throughout the room. "Some people might feel sorry for me but please don't because I am the luckiest person to have the best family and friends anyone could ask for." With that, she gave a quiet sob and quickly handed the microphone back to Ralph. The applause was deafening. Ralph quickly took the mike and gave it to Armondo Ginnetti. "Josephine, on behalf of the GAA, we would like to present you with these beautiful flowers and we will adhere to your wish about the radio and we thank you." Ralph gave the microphone to Horatio, who made a beautiful speech. He finally stated, "Mr. and Mrs. Wellington, their daughter Dorothea, Crystal and I want to give you this beautiful Easter bonnet, scarf and a dress of your choosing from our store." When he gave the bonnet and scarf to Josephine, she immediately put it on and received more cheers from the crowd.

Ralph was ready to hand the microphone back to the band when Doc ran up and asked him if he could say something. Ralph handed him the microphone. Doc turned to Josephine and said, "I have a special gift from me to you." He reached in to his coat pocket and pulled out a little fluffy baby kitten. He gave it to Josephine, who became ecstatic. "Oh, Doc, this kitten is so beautiful. I can't thank you enough. I love it." She reached out and gave Doc a kiss on his cheek.

Doc turned and walked away as if he was on a cloud. As he passed Armondo, he snickered and said, "Who's the dumb son of a bitch now? I knew she would love a kitten, you asshole." Armondo could not say anything but, "Sorry, Doc, you were right."

The dance went on until three o'clock in the morning. Of course, Gracie had to leave at eleven o'clock with Anna. She was a little reluctant but was grateful that she was able to attend. Before she left, she gave Josephine a kiss, Elizabeth a kiss, her brother Carmen a kiss and said good-bye to Ralph with a handshake. She then went up to her three sisters and thanked each one of them, especially Anna. She left the dance shaking and jiving down the stairs to the music.

Josephine left shortly after Gracie. She left with her parents, her sister Mary, Horatio, Crystal and Elizabeth. They were going back to the store to have coffee and a glass of anisette. Eugenio and Philomena were grateful that Elizabeth was there for Josephine. This would be the first time Josephine would spend a night home in her own bed since the accident.

The dance was a tremendous success. The GAA now had the reputation of sponsoring great social events. All the members stayed to clean up after the dance was over. The hall looked spic and span when they left.

Josephine, with Elizabeth on the couch next to her bed, slept soundly and peacefully. Elizabeth affectionately watched over her until she herself went into a deep sleep. Eugenio held his wife close to him in bed and said to her quietly in Italian, "Now we are a whole family again," and gave his wife a kiss on her forehead.

Chapter 74

After the great success of the GAA dance, the days started to fly by. All the members of the club were floating on a cloud and couldn't wait to have more activities. Their first formal meeting of May was fully packed with members in the clubhouse. Armondo Ginnetti asked for committee reports regarding the dance. Everything was positive except for one incident. Someone became so sick that he was throwing up in the john for most of the night. It seemed that he drank too much of the spiked punch. Everyone turned and looked at Doc who started blushing. "What the hell, since nobody was drinking it because of what Carmen's sister Gracie said, I didn't want it to go to waste." Someone yelled, "Well, it did go to waste because most of it ended up in the toilet." Everyone laughed and someone yelled out, "We still love ya, Doc."

Lou Fistola gave the financial report. He told everyone that after all the expenses were paid, they made $113.75. "We definitely have enough to buy that radio Josephine wanted for our clubhouse. I suggest that we ask Mr. Galanti to place the rest of the money in his safe. We can decide what we are going to do with it later. I know everyone is a little leery of banks but I think it would be wise if we open up an account." The membership agreed.

Before the meeting ended, Armondo had the constitution and bylaws committee give their report. After the report, Armondo told the membership that by the June meeting, he wanted to have a vote to adopt these rules and regulations. He asked for an adjournment and as soon as the meeting ended, half the membership started to get seats around the tables to start playing cards. The rest just enjoyed each other's company, talking and laughing.

Josephine was back at the hospital but Dr. Sullivan was very encouraged with her improved recovery and state of mind. He allowed her to go home every weekend from Saturday morning to Sunday night as long as Elizabeth was able to accompany her. He told the Galantis that Elizabeth would show them how to change the bandages if needed and how to administer medicine for their daughter. After they were comfortable with doing this, there would be no need for Elizabeth to come every weekend. This was a double-edged sword for them because they enjoyed Elizabeth being at their home but knew that she had other commitments in her life, especially at the hospital. Elizabeth enjoyed her whole month of staying at the Galantis during the weekends. She enjoyed it so much that she told Philomena that she gained six pounds from all the pasta, great meals and desserts that she made.

During the month of May, Father Baker, Dr. Sullivan and Mother Mary Ann Burke started to make plans for Elizabeth's future. They decided that she would first go to college that September and after graduating from college, she would enter the convent. They all agreed that if she changed her mind about the convent, she would go straight to the hospital to work on a full-time basis. They conferred with Elizabeth and told her of their plans. She was elated but also told them that she was definitely going to become a nun.

The month also brought wonderful changes in the lives of Concetta, Mario and Romeo. The transition back to their home was smooth and peaceful because of their wonderful friends and neighbors. Concetta was making money as a seamstress and also working at the hospital and orphanage. She was able to pay her bills and provide food and clothing for her family. She even had a few extra dollars for surprise gifts for her boys. Mario was doing better than expected at school. His attitude and demeanor changed immensely. His best friend turned out to be Gracie and nobody could believe it. The two would go to school together, talk during recess, lunch and walk home together after school. Mario never felt more happy and actually enjoyed going to school. Romeo had it made. At home, he was pampered by his mother; at the hospital, he was pampered by Elizabeth. Every night, Concetta thanked the Lord for the blessings she was receiving. She also prayed for her two sons, Junior and Salvatore, and hoped that God would forgive them. Her thoughts and her memory never went to her husband, Angelo.

Horatio and Crystal were making plans for their wedding that summer. Coco was excited and relieved that his mother was marrying this good man. Ever since they told him he would be receiving a scholarship to Tuskegee University, he wondered how his mother would do without him. He was more worried about her than going to college and making the football team. Now, his mind would be at ease knowing that she would be in good hands with Horatio.

Horatio and Crystal wanted to make sure that the wedding date would be before Coco had to leave for college. They thought the first week of August would be good. They also would postpone their honeymoon until November, when they would travel down to Alabama to see Coco play in the Turkey Day Classic football game. Coco was elated. He told them, "Now you really put the pressure on me to make the team. If I don't, you won't have a honeymoon." "Don't worry," retorted Horatio. "You definitely will make the team. Your mother and I will be on a honeymoon for the rest of our lives." Crystal started to cry again and both men groaned.

In the Marrano family, May was a special month. There were three birthdays to be celebrated; Mr. Marrano got a raise and was promoted to assistant grocery store manager; Carmen got a job driving milk wagons in South Buffalo; Anna and Josephine got part-time jobs helping at the hospital and the infants' home at OLV; Carmela was getting engaged to a young man from Italy and the young children were enjoying their childhood. It was even a better month for Gracie. She made a new friend in Mario, was not in trouble with her father, mother or older sisters, was not sent home from school even once and was enjoying her new reputation of being a great dancer.

Ralph was preparing for graduation. His marks were excellent and he thought he had a chance of maybe going to college. He went to his high school Class Day Ceremony, where he received an award for penmanship. He was also recognized with a few other students for their leadership qualities and school activity involvement. Unfortunately, the only one who saw him receive this recognition was his sister, Mary, who also was in school. His father and mother were either working, watching the store or staying with Josephine in the hospital.

Ralph and Coco became inseparable the whole month of May. There were so many things happening to both of them that they needed each other for support and companionship. They both talked about their plans for the future, their hopes, their dreams and of course, if they would ever meet the right girl. Coco told Ralph that he felt so relaxed now that Horatio was in their lives. "Raffs, I can't believe it. A few months ago, I never heard of him or even the name of Horatio.

He told me his story and now I feel like I have known him all my life. It is an unbelievable story but do you know, if it wasn't for Father Baker, this would have never happened. When I was young, I feared Father Baker because my mother said if I didn't behave, she would send me to Father Baker's. I didn't know him or even had ever seen him but the way my mother sounded, he had horns, a pitchfork and ate children for lunch and dinner. Now, I think of him as a great man." Ralph laughed. "Hell, my mother was going to send me to Father Baker's every other week when I was growing up. When I was knee high and she told me that she was going to send me there, I cried and peed in my pants. Matter of fact, after our fiasco in Bethlehem Park with Virgilio, I told my mother when I was tied around the chimney to send me to Father Baker's because he's probably more merciful than my father." Both were laughing.

It was the last evening of May. Ralph was lying in his bed thinking about the next day. He thought... *I cannot believe tomorrow is June. I will be graduating in a few weeks. Pop told me he is very proud of me because I will be the first one in the family ever to graduate from high school. He wants to see if I could get a job in the steel plant. He says he knows a few of the foremen and I could probably get a few days a week working. I didn't tell him I would like to go to college because I don't know how he would react. Well, we'll see what happens. Maybe I don't have the marks to get into college so it won't matter."*

Ralph finally fell asleep. His dreams were not of college or the steel plant. They were dreams of Josephine, Mary, Johnny and him playing in the school yard, laughing, jumping and enjoying each other.

Chapter 75

It's finally here! Graduation day! Oh my God, I can't believe it. It's finally here ...thought Ralph.   He was standing in line in the cafeteria ready to go into the high school gymnasium where he would receive his diploma. Ahead of him in line was Coco. All through high school, because of their last names beginning in F and G, they were sitting either next to each other or only a couple of students apart. Coco gave Ralph the thumbs up. Both had their graduation cap and gown on.   Their high school teachers were yelling out different commands trying to get them quiet and in straight lines before they entered the gymnasium. This was the only place that could hold all the students and their families. Ralph didn't know for sure if his father would be able to come but knew his mother was going to be there with Mary and Johnny.   They were given their last orders from the teachers before the music began and they entered the gymnasium.

The music of "Pomp and Circumstance" was resonating throughout the high school.   It brought elated feelings to the prospective graduates and many tears to the parents and families. As the seniors walked in, everyone rose, family and friends, to give them a standing ovation. Every one of them felt shivers down their spines. As Ralph and Coco looked around in the bleachers to see if their families were there, Coco gestured to Ralph to look four rows up to the left side. Ralph turned and saw Horatio, Crystal, his mother, Mary and Johnny but not his father. A little feeling of disappointment came over him but he knew his father would have been there if he could. As he turned to go into the row where he was assigned to sit, he almost stopped dead in his steps. There was his father standing next to a man with a camera. He was speaking and pointing to Ralph as the man nodded and started to take pictures. Ralph thought... *He's here. He came.* Ralph's eyes started to water as he was watching his father. His father was excitedly pointing his finger at him while pulling on the photographer's arm. He was shaking the man so excitedly that the man looked like he was a puppet on a string.

The dignitaries got up to speak to the students and audience. Each speaker gave a short message to the seniors. The time finally came when the principal and the assistant principal approached the microphone and said that they were ready to distribute the diplomas to these deserving graduates. They started to call each student up by name to come to the podium to receive their diploma and be confirmed as graduates of Lackawanna High School. As the names were read, Ralph and Coco were only a few students apart standing in line. They looked at each other and smiled. Ralph mouthed the word congratulations to Coco. Coco smiled, winked and mouthed the word back. The time came when Ralph's name was announced and he walked up to receive his diploma. As he received his diploma, he raised his right hand in a fist, looked toward the area where he knew his parents were and smiled. He could not see it but his mother was crying and for the first time in many, many years, there were tears in his father's eyes. His father thought... *My son, my son, I am so proud. I can never ask for a better son than you.*

After the ceremony, everyone met in front of the Lackawanna High School. Students hugging students, parents hugging students; it seemed like everyone was hugging everyone, even the janitor was hugging someone. All the students wished each other good luck and waved to each other as they left with their parents to go back home or to parties that were set up for them. At the GAA clubhouse, the members organized a party for Ralph, Coco and the rest of the members who graduated. Pop Galanti provided the refreshments, soda, beer and his homemade wine. Many of the mothers of the graduates provided the food. The clubhouse was loaded with people. When Ralph entered the room, he was stunned as he saw his sister Josephine and Elizabeth waiting for him. He couldn't believe that she could make it and ran up to her and gave her a kiss on the cheek. He tried to be gentle but in his exuberance was a little forceful and she winced when he hugged her. Quickly, he stepped back and started to apologize. Josephine responded by saying, "Ralph, that was the best hug I have ever had." Ralph smiled and then turned to Elizabeth and gave her a kiss on the cheek and whispered in her ear, "Thank you, thank you so much." Elizabeth smiled.

The party in the clubhouse lasted until three o'clock in the morning. Of course, Josephine and Elizabeth excused themselves earlier in the evening. Josephine had to go back to the hospital because the doctors were going to do a full examination of her the next morning. If they found everything to be to their satisfaction, maybe Josephine could be living at home permanently by the middle of summer.

After everyone cleared the clubhouse, Coco told Mr. Galanti that they would all be there the next day to clean up. Coco told him not to worry, that everyone agreed to be there by ten o'clock in the morning. Coco and Ralph exchanged a big hug and said they would see each other tomorrow morning.

The clubhouse was empty and Ralph and his father started locking up the store. Philomena and the children went upstairs to go to bed. Ralph and his father stayed in the kitchen and had a glass of wine. His father said, "Nowa, Rafael, whata you going to do? I cana get you a job maybe in the steel plant. It willa be a start." Ralph responded, "Pop, I'll do anything you want me to do."

"It'sa not whata I want, it'sa what you want. I am very proud ofa you." "Thank you and I am proud that you are my father. What I really want to do, Pop, is go to college, maybe Canisius College. If I do not get accepted, I will work in the steel plant or anywhere I can get a job."

"Thatsa it. Then a college you go." He then took his son's face in his big hands, gave him a kiss on the cheeks. "Youa go to bed now. Youa got a lot of cleaning up to do tomorrow."

Chapter 76

It was a few days after graduation and the cleanup of the clubhouse. Ralph got up early in the morning as his father was leaving to go to the steel plant for work. His mother was up getting ready to open the store. Mary and Johnny were still sleeping soundly in their beds. In a few more weeks, Josephine would be there with them.

Ralph bid his father goodbye and started to help his mother get ready to open the store. She told him that she didn't need him until later that afternoon, so he had the morning free to do whatever he wanted to do. He told his mother he would be next door in the schoolyard. It was unusually warm that morning so he just wanted to relax under the old oak tree in the front schoolyard.

School was ended so no one was around except the janitors.

He laid on the grass under the oak tree, his hands behind his head looking up at the white, billowy clouds that were floating by in the beautiful sky. He felt like he was in a peaceful trance with no worries in the world. He started to reminisce about the whole school year from last summer until graduation. He thought it was a hell of a year with everything that was happening in Lackawanna, the country and the world. He thought of the bad times: his sister's accident; the horrible deaths of Angelo, Junior and Salvatore Lenti; the lingering Depression and the uncertainty of what was happening in Europe with Nazi Germany.

As he watched a large white cloud float overhead, it looked like a ship that was floating on the water heading nowhere in particular. He started to think...*Is that boat going to be me, floating with nowhere to go, no plans for the future, just continuing on wherever life takes me? No, I have to make decisions. Either I am going to go to college or try to find a job somewhere. Whatever happens, I am going to make my parents proud of me.*

As he continued to look up at the sky, he kept thinking... *This is my home, these are my family and friends, this is my life... I want to stay here in Lackawanna... My Lackawanna!*

His daydreaming was interrupted as he heard, "Hey dimwit, I can't believe you graduated from high school. I thought it would take you another four years, but I guess I was wrong. Congratulations," said Gracie with a smile.

Oh my God. I pray for the poor bastard who marries her... thought Ralph.

Acknowledgements

It is with my deepest gratitude that I thank the following people for all their knowledge, information, input and encouragement to write this novel. I interviewed the following people to gather information about that era and some of their stories helped to made this book a reality. My profound gratitude goes to Josephine Fistola, Neal and Adeline Marrano, Carmen Moretti, Carl and Sally Covino, Lou Marrano, Pat Bonitatibus, Florindo (Gene) Covelli, Aldina (Manna) Wichrowski, Eileen, Paul and Rae Petti, Geno Covelli and Frances Hetey.

I would like to thank the following people for their help with our research on the history of the Bethlehem Steel Plant, Our Lady of Victory Basilica and the city of Lackawanna. They are Mike Malyak (history of Bethlehem Steel), the staff at the Lackawanna Library (history of Lackawanna) and the staff at Our Lady of Victory Museum and Store for their insight on Father Baker and the Basilica. My sincerest gratitude to John Andreozzi (author of The Italians of Lackawanna, NY.... Steel Workers, Merchants and Gardeners) for all his help, insight and encouragement.

A special thank you to Mark Radominski for allowing me to go back home to my grandparents' store that brought back so many fond memories. I would also like to thank Vickie Twarog for the idea for the title of the book; Diane (Bonitatibus) Bond for designing the front and back covers and inside of the book; Greg Connors and Joe Kirchmyer for the editing; my wife Diane Galanti and "my right-hand girl," Joanna Nervo, who helped me with the research, writing of the book and putting up with my quirks!

I would like to acknowledge those who are no longer with us. My parents, Ralph and Grace Galanti, who gave me a wonderful life with so many great memories and the motivation to write. To the Charter Members of the Galanti Athletic Association, whose stories were related to me through the years (whether true, exaggerated or fictional) and made me believe that this was truly "The Greatest Generation."

Finally, I would like to acknowledge the legacy of a man I truly believe is a saint and a "Man of all Seasons," Father Nelson Baker, Padre of the Poor. He is the epitome of what I believe is goodness, kindness and truth.

About the Authors

Ralph J. (Chico) Galanti, Jr. was born, raised and is still living in his beloved city, Lackawanna, New York. This is Ralph's first venture into the writing of a novel. His professional career was in athletics. He was the athletic director at Erie Community College in Buffalo, New York for 36 years. Ralph started the ECC men's hockey team and coached it for 25 years. He also coached various sports throughout his college career; cross country, track and field, women's softball and men's soccer. He received numerous awards during his athletic career including the prestigious State University of New York Chancellor's Award for Excellence in Professional Services in 1998. He was inducted into the Greater Buffalo Sports Hall of Fame in 2004.

Ralph has been writing a column in his hometown weekly newspaper, the Lackawanna Front Page for over 25 years. He always dreamed of writing a book, not about athletics, but about his city and the people who lived there. He has accomplished that dream with this book, City of Steel, Hearts of Gold, My Lackawanna.

Ralph is married to Diane Galanti and has three children and seven grandchildren.

Joanna B. Nervo began her career in the Erie County District Attorneys Office in Buffalo, New York. After several years, Joanna left the DA's office to eventually become the Administrative Assistant in the athletic department at Erie Community College. She worked there for over 25 years before her retirement. Joanna's main duties were athletic eligibility, preparation of the athletic budgets and fundraising events. She held several professional offices; Assistant Women's Region III Director for the National Junior College Athletic Association, assistant chairperson for the 2010 Empire State Games and an officer in the International Collegiate Hockey League. This is her first endeavor in the writing arena.

She lives in Depew, New York with her husband Marvin Nervo. She has three children and seven grandchildren.